Also by Nik James

CALEB MARLOWE SERIES
High Country Justice
Bullets and Silver
Silver Trail Christmas

SILVER TRAIL CHRISTMAS

NIK JAMES

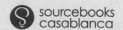

sourcebooks
casablanca

Published by Sourcebooks Casablanca, an imprint of Sourcebooks
P.O. Box 4410, Naperville, Illinois 60567-4410
(630) 961-3900
sourcebooks.com

Printed and bound in Canada.
MBP 10 9 8 7 6 5 4 3 2 1

For Ammara,
the joy of our lives.

CHAPTER ONE

Elkhorn, Colorado,
September 1878

THE HACKLES ROSE ON CALEB MARLOWE'S NECK, AND A chill prickled his scalp. In his fist, the hammer hung poised, ready to strike the nail home. He rolled his broad shoulders and raised his eyes from the barn roof he was about a day from finishing.

This was the way with him. Caleb sensed trouble before it barreled through the door. The instinct had kept him alive more times than he could count.

Near the edge of the rise where the ranch buildings were taking shape, Bear was on his feet and looking to the southeast. The large, yellow dog had smelled something on the crisp, midmorning breeze.

The speck of a distant rider appeared at the crest of a far-off hill and then disappeared. A moment later, he came into view again. He was coming hard.

Caleb knew instantly who it was. He'd know Henry Jordan in a dust storm a mile away. His partner had gone off this morning to round up two stray steers that wandered downriver. And the only time he'd ever seen Henry push a horse this hard, the fellow had a Cheyenne war party pounding along behind him.

Caleb stared out beyond the approaching rider, but he could see no one on his tail.

Henry was one of those people trouble trailed after like a hungry wolf. He didn't have to go out looking for it. He'd just turn around, and there it was. Once that happened, Henry's fierce temper blazed to the surface, and his customary good nature went up in smoke as quick as dry prairie grass in a lightning storm. He was strong and fast and deadly as a rattler once he got started. All kinds of mayhem generally broke out then.

Surprisingly, nobody died in the fight he'd won in a Denver saloon this past winter, but the damn thing had cost him six months in jail. And Caleb had to deal with the devil himself to get Henry out.

Caleb glanced over at the bucket holding his gun belt and twin Colt Frontiers. After laying down his hammer, Caleb worked his way over. Keeping his eyes on the far end of the valley—as far as he could see, anyway—he strapped on his guns and started for the ladder. Whatever was bringing Henry back without those steers, he had a good idea the roof was going to have to wait.

He picked up his Winchester '73 from against the barn wall and stalked over toward the corral. As he reached the gate, Henry roared in like an Express rider bringing bad news from the battlefield.

"We got trouble, partner," he shouted breathlessly as he reined in. Henry pointed at the line of forested bluffs that formed the eastern border of their property. "Up there near the waterfall."

"What kind of trouble?"

"There's fellas up there working our land." He pulled his black, wide-brimmed hat off and ran a hand through the long, brown hair that hung nearly to his shoulders. "At least, I think it's our land."

"This side of the ridge?"

Henry nodded.

"It's our land." Caleb peered at the black cattle grazing along the river in the valley below them. "You think they're after the herd?"

"They're prospecting."

Even after months of trying to carve a ranch out of this valley, Caleb had not quite settled into the idea that owning a piece of God's country meant you had to protect it. But he was learning. A while back, when six rustlers decided that they could just take his cattle, he'd suggested otherwise. That little incident didn't turn out quite the way those boys reckoned. They were now residing on Elkhorn's Boot Hill.

"On our land?"

"How many times I got to say it, Marlowe?"

As Caleb considered it, he knew that the last thing they wanted was to have prospectors find anything out here. When they discovered gold on Sutter's land in California, the poor bastard lost everything. Trying to keep 49ers off his land was like trying to keep fleas off an old dog.

"How many?"

"Four that I saw."

"Recognize any of 'em?"

"Nope."

"Talk to 'em?"

Henry shook his head. "I was thinking about running 'em off. But then I recalled what you been saying about me staying clear of law problems. So I came back for you."

"Well, that was damn thoughtful, partner." Caleb pulled his saddle off the fence and swung it up onto Pirate's back. The buckskin had been watching and listening, and Caleb was certain he already knew they were heading out. "Glad you were able to keep in mind that this ranch will require the both of us."

———

Caleb and Henry rode south across the grass-covered valley for over an hour, then turned east and moved up into forested foothills. Ahead of them, the long, rugged ridge rose above the tall pines, forming the boundary between the ranch and land belonging to Frank Stubbs, their neighbor.

Beyond the ridgeline, the Stubbs claim consisted of large areas of forest and open range, but their neighbor was only interested in the precious minerals that could be carved from the earth. Caleb had already had a few brushes with Frank Stubbs and knew him to be a tough, grasping, miserable bastard—a hard drinker with a penchant for bullying anyone he saw as somehow beneath him. The property border was clear, however, and good ridgelines made good neighbors. More or less.

When the two partners reached a ravine that led roughly southwest, they followed a creek that twisted and tumbled toward the valley lowland.

Caleb's plan was to approach the trespassers from above.

He knew the terrain. He'd been hunting here since he'd picked up the papers at the land office in Elkhorn back in January. He knew where the groves of cottonwood and aspen had fought to establish their space amongst the pines and other evergreens. He knew every ravine and wash and gulley, every mountain spring and creek. The ponds and small lakes formed by the lay of the land and the industry of beavers. The rocky bluffs and ledges where cougars and bears found shelter. The grassy meadows dotted with wildflowers in spring, now yellow as autumn encroached. Soon, it would all be covered by the deep snows of the long mountain winter.

"We're getting close," Henry told him when they reined in at the edge of the creek. The stream here was wide and shallow, with round, gleaming stones protruding from the surface of the rippling water. "I saw 'em where the gulley broadens out by the pond just before it drops over the waterfall."

Caleb nodded. Sure as hell, these fellas had to be panning for gold. Not three miles north of their ranch, miners were busily digging silver out of the hills that ringed Elkhorn, but he'd heard some talk of gold occasionally showing up as well.

He looked back at the ridge and then gestured downward at the muddy edge of the creek. Hoofprints.

"Guess those would be our boys," Henry said.

"Yep. From the looks of things, these fellas came down onto our land from the ridge."

"From Frank Stubbs's land."

"They are fortunate men. If Stubbs spotted these knotheads on his side, he'd already have their carcasses nailed to his barn door."

Henry grinned. "If'n you ever finish that barn, we'd have a door to nail 'em up on."

Giving him a look, Caleb nudged his buckskin forward. But they hadn't even crossed the stream when two gunshots rang out.

Immediately, Henry had his rifle out of its scabbard and looked around.

"A revolver. A quarter mile that way," Caleb said.

"Maybe our trespassers decided to shoot one another. That'd save us some work."

"Too much to hope for."

The two men dismounted on the other side of the creek, tied their animals, and approached on foot.

The forest floor was a carpet of pine needles, and they moved through the forest silently. The land began to drop off, and it wasn't long before the sound of voices reached them, along with the smells of a dying campfire and burnt coffee.

When they reached a ridge at the top of the wide gulley, Caleb signaled to his partner. They moved past a grove of cottonwood trees until they reached a small rise that afforded them a good view. They were eighty yards from the edge of a pond below. In front of them, the terrain dropped off steeply. The sun was still high overhead. Between their vantage point and the water, the grassy hillside was dotted with boulders and brush.

Lying on their bellies, they peered down into the gulley.

Below them, in a clearing on the near side of the wide creek, a slovenly camp had been thrown together. A few tarps had been hung over lines stretched between yellow-leafed cottonwood trees. Saddles and bedrolls lay beneath them. Smoke from a smoldering fire hung like a cloud over the camp.

Henry nudged him and held up four fingers. Caleb nodded.

Three tough-looking fellows were working with pans in the shallows. Shovels were stuck into the gravel at the edge of the pond. The fourth, stripped down to his breeches but wearing a pair of Remington six-shooters strapped to his hips, was busily butchering one of Caleb and Henry's stray steers by the edge of the camp, grunting as he cut into the belly hide. It must have been the steer that took the two slugs they heard being fired.

"Not too neighborly," Caleb said under his breath.

Saddlebags and gear lay in heaps by the fire, and Caleb spotted a pair of Winchester '73s, a Henry Yellow Boy, and a seven-shot Spencer carbine. Two more braces of Remingtons and a pair of short-barreled Colts lay in bundled coils close to the shoreline. In a wide, grassy spot just to the south of the camp, four horses grazed contentedly by as many saddles. Good horses, from the look of them.

Caleb only needed a glance to know these fellas were not typical prospectors. The pans and shovels they were using were still shiny, undented, and new. These chuckleheads weren't greenhorns, though. In fact, from the shooting irons they were packing, he'd bet his last dollar they were road agents laying low and hoping to strike it rich while they were doing it. Their one mistake was trying to do it on his and Henry's land.

One of them, big and burly and filthy as a hog, stood up, stretched his back, and threw his pan on the bank with disgust, cursing and eying his partners with disdain.

"Damn me but if that one ain't trouble," Henry whispered.

"They all are."

The big man's wide-brimmed hat was battered and had an ornate, beaded band at the base of the crown. He took it off and squinted at the sun. In spite of the cool bite to the air, sweat glistened off his not-so-recently shaved scalp. Stomping out of the shallows, he threw himself down in the gravel next to the Colts, propping himself up on one elbow.

The other two in the water noticed him and straightened up.

"You lazy shit, Dog," one of them scoffed. He was the shortest of the bunch, stocky and grizzled, with a ratty wisp of beard. "Not even one full day we been at this, and you're already quitting."

"Weren't this *your* idea?" the other huffed. He was tall and lanky, and his moustache drooped over this mouth, rendering his lips practically invisible.

"That's right," Rat Beard groused. "If you ain't kilt that lawman up north, we wouldn't even be here in Colorado."

Henry and Caleb exchanged a look.

Dog drew one of the short-barreled Colts from its holster and sat up, cocking the hammer and pointing it first at one of his partners and then at the other. The two men stiffened, edging backward into deeper water, and Caleb saw the fellow butchering the steer had moved one hand cautiously to the grip of his Remington revolver.

Dog's Colt barked twice, and water splashed up between the men, who dove to the side, away from the line of fire. The gunhawk guffawed and slid the Colt back into its holster.

The men came to their feet, soaked through, cursing under their breaths and sending evil looks at the shooter.

"Whad'ja do that fer?" Moustache shouted angrily, wiping water from his long, thin face.

"Reckoned you needed a bath," Dog sneered.

"You had no call fer drawing on us."

Dog stood, strapping on his gun belt, silencing the men. "Who's the chief of this here outfit, Humboldt?"

The gaunt-faced man stared a moment, then averted his eyes. "You, Mad Dog."

"That's right." Dog swiveled his gaze to the stocky little man. "Unless you think you're boss man, Rivers."

Henry had edged away to his right, where a tuft of grass made a good rest for the muzzle of his rifle. He knew how to position himself for a fight. The cottonwoods and pine and a jumbled stack of boulders behind them offered added protection.

Rivers shook his head.

"That's right," Dog crowed. "Then, do you no-account shit-for-brains got anything else you wanna say?"

The men stood still as rocks, and Caleb could practically see their frustrated anger—and fear—rippling across the surface of the water.

After a moment, the one called Rivers found his tongue, grumbling, "Just meant that this'll be easier once we get a long-tom set up, so's we can sluice this gravel."

"If you know so damn much about prospecting, you little shit, how come you ain't rich already?"

"Knowing how to do it ain't the same as being lucky."

"Well, you better hope your luck overall ain't running out."

Rivers scowled but said nothing. As he retrieved his pan from the shallows, Caleb saw him glance up at his gun belt a few feet away.

If that fella's fool enough to go for his gun, Caleb thought, he's a dead man.

Mad Dog saw the look too. "Two things, John Rivers. One, anytime you think you can take me, you'd best remember I can outdraw you any day of the week. And two, I got eyes in the back of my head, so if you think you can plug me in the back, think again."

The names suddenly rang a bell. Caleb knew them. John Rivers. Gustav Humboldt. And Mad Dog McCord. That would make the fellow butchering his steer either Lenny Smith or Slim Basher.

He'd heard of them when he was wearing a tin star up north. That was over two years ago. He'd found himself roped into serving as a lawman in Greeley after making a name for himself scouting and hunting with Old Jake Bell and leading folks across the western frontier from the Bighorn Mountains to the Calabasas. This gang never ventured into his town, though. And after the army conscripted him to work for them as a scout for a year, he didn't figure he'd ever cross gun barrels with the likes of Mad Dog and Rivers.

They were tough hombres. They'd made a name for themselves hitting rail depots, Wells Fargo stagecoaches, and the occasional solitary homesteader wagon making its way through the Black Hills of Wyoming. Stone-cold killers, every one of them.

Caleb nudged his partner, whispering, "Stay here. Watch the butcher in particular."

Henry nodded, eased back the hammer on his Winchester, and swiveled the barrel of the rifle in that direction. Caleb saw he'd have a clear shot.

Below them, closer to the creek, a pair of cottonwoods cast their shade over the trunk of a fallen tree. Caleb decided that was as good a place as any to call out to these blackguards. He could use the fallen trunk for cover if he needed it.

Getting there unseen would take some doing, though. The steep, grassy slope was mostly wide open, though it was dotted with boulders and clumps of scrub pine. In addition to the cottonwoods, several groves of aspen had established themselves on the hillside farther from the creek.

Leaving Henry, Caleb backtracked along the ridge. When he reached one of the aspen groves, he moved stealthily down the hill to the cottonwoods.

When he tossed that tin badge on the table in Greeley, Caleb told himself he was done with it. Never again did he want to spend his time gunning down outlaws in the streets of a town where the exploits of low-down vermin like these fellas made them heroes to schoolboys and merchants alike. It was true that he could find an albino mountain goat in a winter storm and track a water moccasin across a rushing river, but he had no interest in going after lawbreakers for the bounty money either. A man might as well shoot rats in a slaughterhouse for a living.

Right now, Caleb was not looking to shed blood. He just wanted these villains off his land.

As he reached the fallen cottonwood, he scanned the scene below him. The butcher had gone back to his work, and the two working the shallows had come up by the shore to shovel more gravel into their pans.

The sun was slightly behind Caleb, and he took his position in the shade beneath the spreading branches of the cottonwoods. The outlaws were in full sun, a good forty yards from him. Only the butcher had any chance of getting to the cover of the trees, but Henry would take care of him. Considering they'd only have their pistols, these boys would need to get off a good shot even to wing him. They'd never come close. Not with him and Henry raining lead down from the hill.

Caleb unhooked the thongs over the hammers of his Colts. Cocking his Winchester, he raised the rifle nearly to his shoulder.

"Listen up, fellas," he called out sharply. "And keep your paws clear of them irons."

Four surprised sets of eyes swung toward him.

"No need to get riled. But you're gonna pack your things and clear out. Got me?"

Mad Dog's hand drifted toward a short-barreled Colt, and the movement was not lost on Caleb. His Winchester barked, and the slug buried itself in the gravel two feet in front of McCord, spraying stones and sand at the big man, who flinched and raised his hands. The sound of the shot echoed off the woods and along the valley, louder and more authoritative than the pistol shots that had alerted Caleb and Henry earlier.

Caleb swiveled his rifle toward the butcher, who stood with his hands raised, a bloody knife in one of them. There appeared to be no interest in getting into it from that quarter. He swung the barrel back to the others.

"What do you want?" Mad Dog growled. "We ain't making no trouble here."

"That depends on what you call trouble. You're prospecting on my land and fixing to eat one of my steers. That sounds like trouble to me."

"That all?" The outlaw visibly relaxed, lowering his hands a little. "Well, hell, we're sure sorry about that. Ain't we, boys?"

"We sure are, mister," John Rivers agreed, jerking his bearded chin toward the butcher, who was nodding adamantly. "We found that steer a-wandering. It's an honest mistake, friend."

Mistake. Caleb eyed them coolly. He knew these four would happily put a bullet or two in him, mistake or no.

"Well, then, you can just leave that critter where he lies, put your gear on them horses, and get moving. Now."

"That ain't too Christian, fella," Mad Dog said, lowering his hands a little more. "We only reckoned we'd—"

"Don't test me, pilgrim," Caleb replied. "Or you'll be explaining to your Maker how Christian a fella *you* been. Now get moving."

The two outlaws behind him were edging closer to their gun belts. Caleb felt his hackles rising again. Some boys absolutely didn't know when to fold their hand and walk away.

"How about if'n we pay you for that meat?" Mad Dog suggested with all the charm of a fat mealy worm. "And the use of your creek here for a few days? A week or so, at most. We ain't fixing to be bad neighbors."

He shook his head. "No deal. You got nothing I want. Now, get moving, or the wolves will be dining on your mangy carcasses tonight."

Mad Dog's eyes narrowed, and his face darkened. Caleb could see he was calculating whether he could muster enough accuracy with those short-barreled Colts to drop him at this distance.

Before the killer could decide whether to throw down or live to fight another day, the bark on the cottonwood trunk exploded next to Caleb's head, showering him with splintered wood.

CHAPTER TWO

CALEB SPUN AND CROUCHED DOWN, PEERING UP THE hill into the deep shadows of the trees. He spotted the puff of smoke in the golden-leafed aspens he'd passed as another crack of a rifle shot came with a brush of air against his ear and the *thup* sound that told him it was another near miss.

"There you are," he muttered. He chided himself for letting this knothead get the drop on him. Five of them rode together two years ago. He should have guessed there'd be one more in the area.

The sonovabitch was standing in the aspens about seventy yards up the hill, his rifle propped in the crook of a tree. From where the outlaw had positioned himself, Caleb figured he couldn't see Henry.

Another shot whizzed by Caleb's head—this time from the creek behind him. The butcher got off only one more before Henry's bullet took off half his face, leaving him to sag and drop across the carcass of the dead steer.

The other three were not standing idle either. Humboldt and Rivers had both reached their guns, and Mad Dog was running for the horses. The big man snatched up a saddlebag as he ran and continued to fire wildly up the hill.

A bullet cut a groove across the shoulder of Caleb's leather vest, three inches from his throat. Humboldt. The gaunt-faced outlaw was moving straight at him, his Remingtons spitting fire.

Caleb knew if he swiveled his Winchester around, the gunman on the hill would plug him for sure. After all, he presented a sizeable target at a few inches over six feet.

Drawing his Colt from its holster, Caleb made a half turn of his body and fired over his shoulder.

Humboldt stopped as he took the bullet square in the chest. He looked down at the wound in surprise, his mouth dropping open beneath the drooping mustache. As the blood began to pump out and the red circle widened on his shirt, he shifted his gaze up toward Caleb and raised a pistol again. Before the killer could fire, Caleb shot him between the eyes, and a cloud of red mist exploded in the air behind his head. Humboldt dropped lifeless to the ground.

The sound of hoofbeats reached him. Glancing toward the south end of the clearing, Caleb caught a glimpse of Mad Dog McCord bareback on one of the horses and hightailing it, leaving his partners to fend for themselves. So much for honor amongst thieves.

"Guess that don't apply to killers," he muttered wryly.

Two left. One in the aspens above him. Twenty yards to the left of Humboldt's body, Rivers was going after Henry, weaving his way across the open ground, his short legs pumping hard as he cut sharply back and forth.

Bullets were being traded, but Henry had yet to hit the

man. Rivers made it to the line of trees by the tarps and bedrolls, and another rifle blast from above ripped into the log beside Caleb.

Henry would have to deal with the little man down below. The bushwhacker banging away at him was a sorry shot, to be sure, but Caleb needed to take care of business before the varmint got lucky with one.

He peered back up the hill. The gunman was in a safe place and didn't appear to be in any hurry to move. "You reckon you're in the catbird seat. Time to push you out of there, I guess."

Pouching his six-gun, he spotted a boulder about fifteen yards to his left and up the hill some. A spray of brush sprouted above it. He'd have better cover there.

Firing twice at the bushwhacker above, Caleb bolted toward the boulder. A bullet tore into a clump of tall grass by his legs, and he dove and rolled the last few feet.

As he put his back to the rock, a bullet pinged off the top, and a stone chip flew past. Caleb cast an eye around him and reloaded his weapons. A few feet beyond the boulder, the spring thaws had long ago carved out a wash about eight feet wide and deep enough to hide a man. At present, it was dry as a bathtub on a Wednesday and angled up the hill. Brush and saplings grew in clumps along the top of either side, adding to the cover.

His plan was simple. Move up the wash until he was even with that grove of aspens or a little above. Try to circle around the bushwhacker and drop him.

Caleb leaned his rifle against the rock where the muzzle

would be visible to the shooter, tossed his wide-brimmed hat onto the ground next to the rock and edged off into the stony ditch.

The firefight was continuing to his right. Above him, the gunman had stopped, but Caleb still envisioned him up there, reloading, scanning the hillside, looking for a clear shot.

Caleb was not about to give him one. He did not take kindly to being shot in the back, which was exactly what that fella had been trying to do.

Branches, accumulated debris, stones, and sand caused his boots to slip as he moved upward, and yet he glided with the soundless stealth of a big cat.

Caleb paused where the ditch made a bend to the left. He knew he hadn't climbed far enough to get above the gunman. Drawing one of the twin Colts from its holster, he peered over the top.

To his left—up the hill toward the ridge—small stands of pine were scattered among aspen and cottonwood. Fifty yards away, he spotted the grove where the rifleman had positioned himself. From where he was, Caleb couldn't tell if the shooter was still there or not. He raked the hillside with his gaze. Nothing. No sign of the bushwhacker.

He left the ditch and ran on an angle toward the aspens, staying low. The leaves gleamed like gold in the sunlight. A moment later, he was certain the shooter had moved. His foe had either retreated and made his escape—as Mad Dog McCord had done—or he was trying to get the drop on Henry.

Caleb reached the trees the outlaw had been using for cover. The bark in a crook of one was scraped raw and showed white wood where the bushwhacker had rested his rifle. Brushing aside the disturbed leaves at the base of the trunk, Caleb found boot prints in the soft earth and spent shells. He cocked his head, listening for any sound beyond the gunshots being exchanged between Henry and Rivers but heard nothing.

Quickly, he turned his trained eye to the ground. A few feet away, he found more prints. They were leading away from the camp, up the incline into the pine forest and the ridge. He was making a run for it.

Caleb lit out after him. The pine needles were made for silent running, but it was not difficult trailing his prey. Topping a rise, he heard the snort of a horse, and a moment later he spotted a mule, thirty yards away, tethered to a pine bough and loaded with a half dozen planks, a shallow, wooden trough, and other supplies. Just beyond him, the outlaw was mounting a lively dun mare. His rifle was already in its saddle holster.

The gunman saw him at the same time. The bandit was fast. Like lightning, he cleared leather. Ducking behind his horse's head, he fired. Not quite quick enough, though.

Caleb's Colt barked, catching the snake in the shoulder and sending him spinning to the ground behind the two animals. Caleb quickly closed in.

The bushwhacker had rolled toward the wide trunk of a tall pine, his upper body propped against the tree. The outlaw's shooting iron flashed in the dappled sunlight as Caleb came around the mule and horse, and his Colt Frontier blazed again, burying a slug in the center of the man's chest.

The mule was braying like the Apocalypse had come, and the dun pranced off a ways. Caleb strode to the man, kicked away the fallen pistol, and yanked a twin ivory-handled Remington from its holster.

The outlaw was still alive, staring at him. His face was twisted with pain, but his eyes still showed surprise.

How many times had Caleb looked into the face of some knothead like this one? The frontier was full of fellas like this. Men who believed they were unbeatable. They always thought they had the fastest draw, the steadiest hand, the best shot…until they ran into someone who was a hair quicker. They'd come at you with everything they had. Then, with a hole or two punched in them, they'd gaze at you, unable to comprehend what had happened.

Caleb picked up a new, green stovepipe hat that lay on its side in the pine needles. He dropped it in the dying man's lap.

"Damn," the outlaw gasped. "I reckon I ain't going to get as much wear outta this new suit as I thought."

"I reckon you're right."

Long, sandy-colored curls, newly barbered, hung down to his collar. He wore a mustache with upturned points and the trim patch of beard like Custer or Buffalo Bill. A dark-colored duster lay open like bats' wings around him, displaying a green coat and pants that matched the hat.

A silver brocade vest and fancy, hand-tooled boots completed the outfit.

Quite the dandy, Caleb thought.

"Cold here in the shade, ain't it?"

"The next place will be warmer."

A grin pulled at the killer's lips, but it disappeared as a shudder of pain wracked his body. He coughed and bloody spittle flecked his lip and chin beard.

"You Slim Basher?" Caleb asked.

The man's eyes brightened slightly. "You know me?"

"Only by reputation. And your friends down there." He gestured with his head toward the creek.

The outlaw nodded slightly. "Why'd you ask?"

"The folks in town'll want to know what to put on your death certificate."

"That's mighty considerate." His words were getting weaker. "Never thought I'd…I'd…"

He never finished his thought. Not in this world, anyway.

Leaving him, Caleb moved back toward the creek.

The shooting had stopped. When he reached the aspens overlooking the clearing, he saw Henry working his way down the hill, his Winchester against his shoulder. He was approaching the tarps like he'd found a grizzly going through a supper he'd prepared.

There was no sign of the escaped Mad Dog. Caleb figured he was probably halfway to Santa Fe by now.

He descended the hill. As he picked up his rifle and hat, Henry caught sight of him. He waited where he was until Caleb reached him.

"Got him," Henry said proudly, gesturing toward the tarps.

"About damn time."

A groan of pain reached them.

"Got him?" Caleb asked.

"You know how I feel about the sanctity of life," Henry replied with a straight face. "When I said *got* him, I meant *winged* him."

"Uh-huh."

John Rivers lay squirming on the ground by a bedroll, clutching his side. His pistols lay just out of reach.

Caleb laid down his rifle, strode over to him, and yanked a knife from the little man's boot. He tossed it over toward Henry, who'd picked up Rivers's six-gun. The killer moaned something fearful as Caleb rolled him onto his side. The bullet had ripped a hole straight through the meat just above the hip bone.

"You'll live, Rivers," he said, drawing a surprised look from the man. "Till they get a rope around your neck."

"Don't know nobody named Rivers," the outlaw managed to get out between panting breaths. "You got the wrong fella."

Caleb ignored him and turned to Henry. "You know, if you could shoot worth a damn, we coulda saved ourselves a ride into Elkhorn."

"It ain't too late," his partner replied. "I'm sure I can hit him from here."

The two men looked at the wide-eyed Rivers.

"Go ahead," the outlaw gasped. "Save us all a heap of trouble."

"Hell, I need to pick up a bag of nails for the barn, anyway." Caleb shook his head walking away. "Truss him up while I bring them horses over."

Before Henry could cut a length of rope from the lines holding the tarps, a rifle shot rang out, and Caleb spun around to see his friend's hat tumbling to the ground.

Caleb's Colt was in his hand in an instant, but before he even turned to look for the gunman, he knew it wasn't Mad Dog. He'd taken off with only his short-barreled revolvers, riding bareback. His rifle was sitting by the fire. But that didn't mean this outfit didn't have a sixth man riding with them.

Not far from the spot where Caleb had first talked to these outlaws, their neighbor to the east stood with his Yellow Boy rifle trained on Henry.

"Hold on there."

Stubbs lowered his rifle a little, but Caleb saw that Henry had cleared leather and was ready to drop their neighbor in his tracks. His partner's face was on fire.

Caleb took a step toward Henry. "Don't."

"The sonovabitch nearly took my head off."

He lowered his pistol, but he wasn't ready to pouch the iron. Caleb didn't blame him.

Stubbs came down the hill, eyeing them warily. "What are you doing, Marlowe, working men on my land?"

Caleb had only spoken to the man twice. The first time, he'd had to give Stubbs a sound thrashing, and the second time he'd needed to talk him down while looking into the barrel of that Yellow Boy. Caleb didn't particularly like fellas who pointed guns at him.

"This ain't your land, Stubbs. We've already covered this ground."

As he reached them, the man spat a stream of tobacco juice. "Who says."

Frank Stubbs had to be close to forty, but he was as hard and tough as an old oak root. If those silver mines of his were producing anything, you wouldn't know it to look at him. From beneath a battered, brown bowler, stringy hair hung nearly to his shoulders. A dusty work coat of dark-brown wool covered a black waistcoat. Brown pants, worn out at the knees, were stuffed into scarred boots. The only thing that hinted at prosperity of any kind was his rifle and a silver ribbon that was attached to a watch in his vest pocket.

The man was tall and lanky with a long, horse face that bulged on one side with a cheek full of chaw. A heavy, brown mustache drooped around his hard mouth and hung to the jawline. His nose was hooked and battered from more than a few fights. And above his dark, beady eyes, a scar split his left eyebrow, adding to the fierceness of his face.

Caleb's patience with this bonehead was running thin, but he slid his Colt into its holster. "That ridge a half mile behind you is the boundary between our properties."

"Don't matter. I seen these mangy dogs on the other side. You got them prospecting on my land. I followed this one down here just now." He pointed the rifle at Henry.

"You are one stupid sonovabitch," Henry growled. "You know I part own this ranch. You seen me at the Belle."

Stubbs's eyes narrowed. "Who you calling *stupid*? I've a mind to put a hole in—"

"Back off," Caleb barked.

Stubbs spat on the ground. "Matter of fact, I do remember you. We had words, you and me. You had my whore sitting on yer lap. You was playing cards with my woman cuddled up to you."

"*Your* woman? Mariah still got marks you gave her. She says she wants nothing to do with you."

"She's a cheap, lying whore. But she's *my* whore."

"She'd sooner sleep with a dying skunk than spend five minutes with you."

"I shoulda kicked in yer pretty face right then."

"I always wear this face right here in the open, where any stupid, *drunken* sonovabitch can take a crack at it...if he's got the balls to try."

"That right?"

"But as *I* recall, you went a-slinking out with your limp tail hanging between your quivering hind legs."

"I shoulda kilt you that night. Yer just lucky you had them boys to back you." Stubbs stopped and looked at Rivers and the two dead outlaws. "Matter of fact, these are the same mangy coyotes that was with you. I knowed it. They been working for you this whole time."

"You're a low-down, two-faced, lying piece of shit, Stubbs."

"One of us is. And I think maybe it's time we settled it, once and for all."

"I think maybe it is," Henry replied, his voice as cold as Wyoming winter wind.

Caleb had witnessed and taken part in enough gunfights to know if he let it happen, one of these fighters would die. The trash-talking was done, and the air crackled around them like a lightning storm was about to unleash its fury. But before he could step in, a gunshot from the edge of the clearing broke the tension, echoing off the distant ridge.

Zeke Vernon, looking for all the world like a gray boar in a stovepipe hat, sat astride his bay mare. Smoke curled from his Winchester '73. Elkhorn's burly sheriff was flanked by two deputies, and that made three rifles currently pointed at the combatants.

"Lay them irons down, boys," he growled. "I ain't shot nobody today, but it's still early."

CHAPTER THREE

"STUBBS, I DON'T CARE WHAT BRINGS YOU ONTO THESE fellas' property, but I got enough trouble on my hands," Zeke Vernon snapped. "I don't need no more. And from the looks of things, there's been enough killing for today."

The sheriff and his men nudged their horses across the clearing. Caleb watched Zeke slide his Winchester into its scabbard and dismount, a considerable drop for his diminutive person. The deputies stayed on their mounts, their rifles in hand.

"Just 'cuz the judge pinned a tin star on your sorry ass, that don't mean nothing to me," Frank Stubbs growled. "Me and this mangy coyote got something to settle."

Caleb felt Henry bristle beside him, but his partner was holding his tongue…for the moment.

Zeke's bushy eyebrows bunched up over his dark eyes, and his glare was deadly. "Whatever yer beef is, you'll have to settle it without any shooting. This here is 1878. This is the new minted state of Colorado. Ain't you heard? We ain't unlettered savages in Elkhorn no more. We're all civilized now."

Caleb took exception to the sheriff's rosy view of Colorado, but he kept his opinion to himself.

Zeke Vernon had taken the badge after the previous sheriff of Elkhorn—a no-good, murdering snake named Grat Horner—met his untimely demise at the wrong end of Caleb's smoking Colt. A veteran of the war between the North and South, Zeke had come to Colorado looking for riches and a place to forget the violence he'd left behind. So far, he'd found neither. But in Caleb's eyes, he was a good man and as solid as mountain ice in winter.

Their miserable neighbor wasn't giving up. "You can't civilize a coyote or an Injun. Don't matter none, though, 'cuz I can't decide which one Jordan is."

"Shut it, Stubbs," Caleb barked. He'd had more than enough of the man. "I've told you before, and this is the last time I tell you. You ain't welcome here. So, go find that nag of yours, and clear out."

Stubbs glared at him, spittle forming at one corner of his mouth. "I shoulda taken care of you the last time I saw you."

"Well, you missed your chance to put a bullet in my back. Now, dust."

The sheriff stepped between them, looking burly and fierce as a bulldog in a street fight. Zeke wore gray wool—jacket, waistcoat, and pants—and a pair of black boots so shiny, they would have made Custer's look dull. Built like a squared-off block of oak with legs, the former miner stared at Stubbs. His massive bush of beard, moustache, and eyebrows obscured most of his flushed face, but it was clear he meant business.

Zeke unhooked the thong over the Remington he'd taken to wearing cross holstered. "You heard him. Git."

Stubbs snorted, swung his ugly mug toward Caleb, and then settled on Henry. "This ain't over, Jordan."

"Anytime, neighbor," Henry replied coolly.

Without another word, Stubbs stomped up the hill.

Before the man had disappeared into the forest at the top, the sheriff turned to one of his deputies. "Follow him until he rides off a ways. I don't want him changing his mind and thinking he can pick us off from them trees."

"While you're up there," Caleb added, "you'll find a nice-looking horse, a mule, and a dandified fella with a couple of holes in him."

"Bring 'em back down here," Zeke ordered, turning to the other deputy. "You go with him. And don't let that sidewinder plug either of you."

As the deputies urged their mounts up the hill, the sheriff eyed the wounded outlaw, who was lying with his eyes half-closed, a grimace on his face.

"Getting pretty good at this, Zeke," Caleb said.

The sheriff frowned at him. "Three damn months I been stuck doing it, thanks to you."

"Seems like you're thriving, friend."

"Thriving?" Zeke yanked off his stovepipe hat. "Just look at that. My hair's falling out faster than it can turn gray. I can't hardly sleep. I can barely take a drink at the Belle without thinking some low-down varmint is sneaking up to shoot me in the back."

Henry handed Rivers's pistols to the sheriff. "They say that's why Wild Bill Hickock always drank with his back to the wall. So no dirty dog could get the drop on him."

"And you see what good that did him! Pushing up daisies in North Bumdingy." Zeke shoved the guns into his saddlebag and motioned to the trees Stubbs had disappeared into. "And now, thanks to you, I got another new *friend* to watch out for."

John Rivers moaned, drawing their attention.

"Always glad to see you, Zeke," Caleb said, turning away from the outlaw. "But how'd you happen to be near here?"

The burly little sheriff kept his eye on the wounded man. "Didn't *happen* to be. I come looking for you."

"All the way out here?" Henry asked.

"When we got to your cabin, we seen you two riding south, way off down the valley. We followed and lost you for a while, but then we heard the shooting. Reckoned you'd be at one end of that noise."

"You reckoned right. But that don't say why you came looking for us." Caleb gestured up the hill. "Looking pretty official, hauling two deputies along with you."

Zeke looked from Rivers to the two men lying dead in the clearing. "Come to ask if you seen a gang of outlaws. We got word that Mad Dog McCord and his outfit could be in the area. This wouldn't, by any chance, be them fellas?"

"This is why you were born to be a lawman, Zeke. You've got all the right instincts." Caleb pointed to the body draped over the partially butchered steer. "That there is Lenny Smith. That one over there is Gustav Humboldt. Your boys are up collecting the remains of the late Slim Basher. And this handsome fella is John Rivers."

"I don't know no John Rivers," the outlaw groaned.

"You knew who they were?" Henry cut in, wide-eyed, paying no attention to Rivers.

"I recognized 'em just before the shooting started."

Zeke gazed at each of the outlaws in turn then turned back to Caleb. "No sign of Mad Dog hisself?"

"Yep, he was here. Lit out and left his pals to face the music."

"I don't have no pal named Mad Dog."

"Shut up," the sheriff snapped. "Nice fella, that McCord. Which way was he headed?"

"He went on a direct line away from the shooting." Caleb gestured south. "But that don't mean he'll keep going that way."

"Reckon I'll have to send a couple of deputies after him…" Zeke paused. "Unless you and Henry'd be interested in a few extra dollars. I believe there's a bounty on Mad Dog. Dead or alive too."

They both shook their heads.

"We got a barn to finish before winter and a cabin for Henry and a—"

"What in tarnation?" Zeke asked, surprised. "A separate cabin?"

"Hell yeah," Henry replied. "This one lives like a damn monk. If one thing is outta place, he throws it out in the corral. Who wants to live like that?"

Zeke was about to reply, but Caleb kept going. "And we got a crew driving some cattle up from Texas for us. They could be coming in any day now. Thanks, but no, Sheriff. We got too much to do here."

"Well, have it yer way. I'll send a couple of fellas, but I ain't holding out much hope. These deputies I got now mostly couldn't find their asses with both hands."

Zeke tied John Rivers's hands as Henry went for the blackguards' horses. Caleb dragged the corpse of the butcher over to the gear by the fire, but before he could go for Humboldt, the sheriff stalked over to the fire and picked up one of the outlaws' saddlebags.

Just then, the deputies appeared at the top of the hill. One was leading the mule, and the other had the dead outlaw draped over the saddle of the handsome dun.

Zeke grinned at Caleb. "I'll take these carcasses and that sorry sonovabitch Rivers into town. You done made me look like a hero again, Marlowe."

Caleb recalled the first time he had Zeke go to town with the loot he'd collected from the Wells Fargo stage robbers. Telling tales in Elkhorn's saloons about Caleb's exploits gunning down road agents and killing giant cougars with his bare hands had cast Zeke in a shared glow of celebrity and earned him a bonanza of free drinks.

The sheriff watched his men descending the hill. "Judge Patterson will sure as hell bust a gut crowing to the governor how we're keeping our part of the state safe."

"Glad to help." Henry joined them, leading the horses up. "Be sure to tell him this Rivers fella is my personal gift to him…seeing as the judge got me sprung from the county jail up in Denver."

Caleb gestured toward the gear at their feet. "I'm

keeping one of them rifles, some of the ammunition, that mule, and the supplies. I can use 'em."

"Seems fair." Another thought occurred to the sheriff. "When we rode by your place, it looked like that barn was near built."

Caleb nodded. "Henry and me are figuring, if the snow holds off, we might try to throw up another outbuilding for grain as well."

"Ha!" Zeke slapped him on the arm. "So them rumors are true."

Caleb had a bad feeling about what was coming. "What rumors?"

"The rumors about the Christmas gala."

"What Christmas gala?"

Zeke tried unsuccessfully to look innocent. "Why, it ain't no secret that the Ladies' Event Planning Committee has already started meeting."

Caleb didn't go in search of news, but news from Elkhorn had a way of finding its way to him. He knew who'd been coaxed into being chairwoman of the Ladies' Event Planning Committee.

"A dress-up gala?" Henry looked entirely too enthused. "With dancing and all?"

"I hear tell they've already gone and started ordering decorations from Denver and St. Louie, even."

"Sounds like a real high-society affair," Henry responded brightly.

"With them shiny new boots and hat," Caleb said to Zeke, "it's a dead sure thing you'll get an invitation."

"Damn right." The sheriff was looking at him expectantly. "Maybe I'll find me a wife there too. It's high time, ain't it, for respectable fellas like us to be settled with a family?"

Ignoring him, Caleb pulled the two Winchesters from their saddle holsters and began to inspect the weapons. He was already sorry he'd let Zeke draw him this far.

"So she already talked to you?"

He knew exactly the *she* that the sheriff was referring to. But he pretended not to hear and focused on the rifles. Caleb's relationship with Sheila Burnett was no one's business. Choosing the rifle he wanted, he laid it aside with a few boxes of cartridges.

"Well?"

"Well what?" he asked sharply, feeling the heat rising up his neck.

"Has she asked you?"

Caleb was not a man who collected friends like a hound collected fleas. Aside from Henry, there were only a few people in Elkhorn he had no problem conversing with. Zeke was one, up to a certain point. Malachi Rogers, a former buffalo soldier who owned a livery stable at the east end of town, was another. Dr. John Burnett, however, was the first fella he'd struck up a friendship with after coming here.

Before Henry arrived, Caleb and Doc had taken to having dinner and playing chess at the physician's house weekly. He was a good man to drink with, and their chess games had become epic battles. They'd had to forgo their

Wednesday games this past month. Either Doc was too busy tending to Elkhorn's sick and injured, or Caleb couldn't get away from their building projects on the ranch. He missed going over there.

To be honest, though, it wasn't so much that he was missing Doc and their chess games. The truth of the matter was that Sheila Burnett was an itch Caleb couldn't scratch. When she'd first arrived in Elkhorn, he'd assumed she'd be the rich, spoiled product of her New York City grandparents. But she'd surprised him right off.

Sheila was as mouthy and bullheaded as she was brave and beautiful. And he was attracted to her. And that was a problem.

For his entire life, he had known his past had branded him with scars too ugly. Back in Indiana, after his father beat Caleb's mother to death, Caleb had thought he'd done the same to his father. Leaving Elijah Starr in a pool of blood, Caleb had gone west, sixteen years old, looking for a place to hide his shame. Unfortunately, shame was something a man carried with him. In the years that followed, he'd done plenty of things he wasn't proud of. Even if fellas like Zeke made them sound like the stuff of noble legends.

In the end, Caleb learned who and what he was at his very core. He was a gunslinger and a killer. No matter what he felt for her, Sheila Burnett deserved better than someone like him.

"Has she?" Zeke was like a dog with bone, and he wasn't giving it up.

"I don't know what she'd have to ask me. This gala shindy ain't got nothing to do with me."

"Miss Sheila is planning to ask you if them ladies can throw the gala out here, away from the miners and other riffraff in town. There's talk of a giant tent, like the circus has, a wood dance floor, an orchestra from somewheres, even a dang Christmas tree."

"Hell no!" Caleb replied.

"Hell *yes!*" Henry countered.

Caleb glowered at him. This was the difference between them. Henry loved music, festivities, drinking, and women. If the Ladies' Event Planning Committee could work up some cards and gambling tables, he'd be as happy as a bumblebee in a berry patch.

The memory of every holiday from his childhood, including Christmas, still haunted Caleb's nightmares. His mother, bloody and bruised and crying in the dark. His father's face, red from thrashing his cane across Caleb's back. Elijah's favorite saying still echoed in his head. *No sinners in heaven; no forgiveness in hell.*

"What do you say?" Henry asked. "We can make it a tradition for the Elkhorn ladies to have their Christmas gala on our ranch *every* year."

The only holiday traditions Caleb could recall involved pain and scars. He shook his head.

"Don't be a wet blanket." Henry slapped him on the back and turned to Zeke. "I'm a bona fide partner on this here ranch. You just have Miss Burnett talk to me. My answer is—"

"Our answer is *no*," Caleb cut in. "Have you lost your mind? We're talking about December. There'll probably be a blizzard, and we'll be stuck with these folks till the Fourth of July."

Henry snorted. Caleb had the distinct impression even that possibility appealed to his partner.

As they continued to talk about what the sheriff had heard, Caleb stalked off to help the deputies load the dead outlaws onto the horses.

He dismissed the thought of such an event ever happening. The last time he'd seen Sheila was a month ago, and that was at her father's house. She'd said nothing about it.

Sheila Burnett would never ask such a favor of him. Not for a happy occasion. Not in the place where—the last time she was here—so many bodies had lain in the dirt, men's blood staining the Colorado soil. Some of that blood had nearly been hers.

How could she think of this ranch as anything except a place of death? Caleb's father had brought violence to his door, and he'd met it with equal force. And more.

CHAPTER FOUR

HENRY CAME OUT THE DOOR OF THE BELLE AND PULLED his coat closed as the chill dawn air hit him. As he stood at the top of the steps leading down to Main Street, he glanced at the silver gleam of the sun easing up over the eastern peaks. Above him, the sky ran from graveyard black to slate gray. He breathed in the smell of snow in the crisp air and closed his eyes for a moment, allowing his senses to revel in the magnificence of being free.

A man didn't know what he was missing in life until he was thrown into a hellhole like the Arapahoe County Jail. No freedom to breathe fresh air. No scents of pine and flowers and the mountains and women. No warming taste of whiskey on his tongue. For six months, Henry's companions had been only stinking, angry men. His life had consisted of dusty, backbreaking work, darkness, and the cold, inescapable chafing of leg irons on his ankles.

Now, he treasured the good smells and the laughter and the warm body of a woman next to him. Unlike those long, lonely months, he felt alive again.

Henry patted the pocket that held his poker winnings. He'd been losing early last night, and he'd been wise enough to ease up on his drinking, a decision that others at the table had not made. As a result, he'd won back what he lost and then some.

The sound of a glass breaking inside the saloon caused him to cast a quick, cautious look back at the door. He descended the steps. He didn't want anyone sneaking up on him with the idea of getting back his money.

Elkhorn was quiet; the crunching of his boots was the only sound. As he crossed, he kept a wary eye on a pair of miners huddled together against a storefront between two barrels. Their hats were pulled down over their faces, their knees drawn up, and they had a horse blanket covering the two of them. He'd seen them inside a few hours earlier, both losing heavily at the faro tables.

They never stirred, but Henry's mind was drawn to two other fellas he'd run into in a fancy, new saloon on the east side of Cherry Creek in Denver last winter. Those sons of bitches hadn't even been playing cards at his table, but that hadn't stopped them from jawing at him.

They were locals; Henry was an outsider. They were losing; Henry was winning. The liquor went down steadily; the pestering got louder.

Henry should have folded his hand, collected his winnings, and left when he had a chance. He knew nobody in that saloon and didn't have a single person to watch his back. But the cards were falling his way, and he thought his luck was good.

When both men got up and decided to jostle him as they passed, he kept his composure. But when they came back from the bar, trouble came with them. One intentionally spilled his drink on Henry while the other told everybody at the table what Henry was holding in his hand. That was it. He'd had enough.

All it took was him standing up, and the fight they were hunting for began.

Two on one, the battle was fast and ferocious. The saloon had a policy of collecting guns as patrons walked in, so fists were what they had to work with. Both men were large and tough and younger than Henry, but they hit the floor one after the other. He could hear the circle of bystanders shouting encouragement to the pair. Quickly, they were on their feet and at him again, but Henry's fists put them back down.

Then, before the saloon management could get to them through the crowd, someone decided to escalate the excitement. Henry barely saw the glint of the knife in time as a third one came at him. Spinning, he arced a fist that landed like a hammer on the man's ear, sending him flying. Even with the noise, Henry heard the crack of his head on the edge of a table. When he went down, his face bounced a couple of times on the floor.

That was the end. The saloon bouncer and a few more latched on to him.

When the law arrived, the two bastards swore Henry had started it, and their friends backed them. The third man lived, but six months was a hell of a price to pay for a fight he hadn't started.

But that was all behind him now. He was in Elkhorn. Going past the jail and down the side street toward

Malachi Rogers's livery stable, Henry forced the dark thoughts from his mind. He had money in his pocket, women he could find comfort with, and a ranch to call his own. For a long time, trouble had been haunting his footsteps, but his fortunes were turning. Maybe.

Henry was close to the livery when he sensed a movement behind him. He spun around, his hand on his pistol grip. In the dim light, he stared at the animal crossing the road not thirty feet away. It was a good-sized coyote with a rat the size of small pony dangling from his jaws. The predator cast a sidelong glance at him and hurried into an alley across the way. Headed for the wooded hills to enjoy his breakfast, apparently.

"Don't offer me none," he murmured. "Couldn't eat a bite."

Keeping his eye peeled for any other varmints—two-legged or four—who might be lurking in the shadows, he accidentally banged into a stack of crates leaning into the lane, sending the top one crashing to the ground.

Before he could take another step, a small form materialized in front of him.

"Hey, Henry."

The boy wasn't wearing his usual battered hat with the bullet hole in the crown, and his red hair—looking darker in the dim dawn light—was standing up on end.

"Hey, Paddy."

Paddy Byrne had been a twelve-year-old orphan, drifting west with a no-good brother and heading to hell in a hurry when he crossed paths with Marlowe this past

May. The young fella had gone looking for Caleb, who'd gunned down the brother during a rustling attempt at the ranch.

Wiry and tough and smart as a street dog, the boy had been living with the livery owner's family and working for his keep ever since.

Henry never met the brother, but he was certain this urchin was cut from entirely different cloth. Paddy had a sharp tongue that he wasn't shy about using, but he was a good lad. He and Gabe Rogers came out to the ranch quite often, and Henry saw him nearly every time he came into town for a night at the Belle. One thing he knew: the boy's time with the Rogers family was definitely improving him, even if it wasn't doing much to curb the smart-assed remarks he regularly directed Henry's way.

"I'll go get your horse."

Something in Paddy's greeting told Henry something was wrong. The words didn't carry that chipper note they usually did.

"Wait a minute. How come you're minding the store this early? Where's Gabe and his pa?"

"They're getting something to eat before taking a couple of wagons up to the logging camp."

"They trust you to handle things here. You're learning."

"I guess." Paddy shrugged and kept his eyes down. "Want your horse or not?"

"Matter of fact, I do, young fella."

"I'll saddle him up and bring him out for you."

Henry watched Paddy go, his steps dragging. He

wondered what was wrong. Twelve years of age had its challenges for a boy. The recollections of his own childhood stirred in him. Back in Wyoming, the buffalo was on the move this time of the year. A busy time for everyone.

He felt like he barely had time to blink before the boy was back, leading the bay gelding out, all saddled and ready.

"Here you go," Paddy said.

Henry couldn't let that dog lie. "What's wrong?"

"Nothing. Why you asking?"

"'Cuz you ain't flapping your tongue this morning like you always do. Asking a hundred questions."

The boy shrugged. "How's things out at the ranch?"

"Marlowe's gonna have me building the Hanging Gardens of Babylon before we're done, but it's going fine." He took a breath and forced himself to look hard at the young fella. "What's the long puss for, Paddy? You look like you just lost your pet rat. 'Cuz if you do, I know where he went."

"I ain't got no pet rat, Henry."

"Come on. Out with it. Ain't we friends?"

The shrug again. "I guess."

Henry put a hand on Paddy's shoulder. "Come on. What is it?"

"Nothing."

Henry didn't believe it. "If it's something I can help with, you know I will."

Damned if a tear didn't run down the boy's cheek, but he dashed it away like it was a thirteen-legged spider.

"Paddy?"

"I heard something that I wasn't supposed to be hearing."

"What did you hear?"

"Don't think I oughta repeat it."

There was no guessing what Paddy was hiding. Between working in the livery and running around Elkhorn with Gabe, he could have overheard plenty of conversations.

"Do you think you'll get in trouble if you tell me about it?"

Paddy shook his head. "Not trouble."

"Then out with it."

The boy kicked the dirt couple of more times before starting to talk. "Gabe's two cousins are coming out from Memphis. Their folks died from some big fever, so there's no other place for 'em."

Henry had heard all about the yellow fever epidemic when he was in jail in Denver. New Orleans had been hit so hard, they called out the army to keep folks from traveling anywhere. But it still spread up and down the Mississippi. Memphis had thousands of people die of it.

"What's that got to do with you?"

"I can count. With two more in the family, there ain't no room for me."

"Did Mr. or Miz Rogers say something?"

"No. They don't have to." Paddy scuffed a boot in the dirt. "Besides, they was only s'posed to be keeping me for a while."

The way Henry heard the story, Caleb felt responsible for the boy. And there was some talk at the start that maybe someday Paddy would move out to the ranch. But nothing was set in stone.

"Maybe I oughta talk to Marlowe about it."

"You can't." Anguish crept into the boy's voice. "The Rogers been good to me. I don't want Mr. Marlowe blaming them for nothing. Also, I earn my keep. I don't want no charity from you or Mr. Marlowe or anyone."

Henry tried to think what the right thing was to say. Malachi Rogers and his wife were good people, and he had no doubt they wouldn't put Paddy out on the street. At the same time, he understood why the twelve-year-old would be worried about what might become of him.

"Then *you* talk to Marlowe," he suggested. "We're almost done with the barn. We got room for you."

"Maybe. But I need to sort out how to ask." There was a glint in Paddy's eyes as he looked up. "You're good for something, Henry."

He punched Paddy lightly on the arm. "When are they coming? The cousins, I mean."

"Next couple of months, I guess."

"Well, that gives you some time to sort things out."

"Promise me that you won't say nothing to Mr. Marlowe."

Henry nodded slowly. "I won't say nothing for now."

"You promise?"

"Hell, Paddy, after the brandy I drank last night, I'll be lucky if I can find my way out to the ranch, never mind remember this conversation."

CHAPTER FIVE

October 1878. Two weeks later.

THE BARN WAS ALL BUT FINISHED, AND CALEB WAS feeling damn good about it. The building consisted of two separate stables large enough for six stalls in each and space for tack and assorted gear. The two sides were connected by a roofed, fifteen-foot-wide workspace, open to the front and back. Having that, Caleb had decided, would allow them to pull a wagon straight through with hay or feed or whatever. The only thing left to do on it now was to hang the two stable doors, and they'd been holding off until their helpers could come out from town and lend a hand with the chore.

"It ain't straight." Gabe Rogers, the livery man's son, shook his head as he eyed the work Henry and Paddy were doing.

"Looks good to me," the younger boy said.

"Lift your side higher," Henry ordered.

Caleb hid his smile as Paddy threw his battered hat on the ground and ran a hand through his wild, ginger-colored hair. "It's too dang heavy, Henry. You lift it up, I'll jam the wedges in."

Before Henry was released from jail, the fourteen-year-old Gabe and the twelve-year-old Paddy had been a good help to Caleb, keeping an eye on Bear and the cattle when he'd needed to chase down road agents…and worse. Gabe's father had fashioned the iron pintle and gudgeon hinges that would hold the barn doors with their upper and lower sections, and the boys had brought them out this morning.

Gabriel Rogers had his father's dark skin and the developing strength that came with muscling horses at the stable. But he also had the amber eyes of his mother and a softness to his face that would probably be gone in a year or so. The young fella was solid and dependable.

Paddy wasn't lazy, but he was a kid. He was happier playing with Bear than he was doing chores. From what Caleb could see, drifting with his no-account brother hadn't helped him none either. He had spunk, though. The first time he saw Paddy, the boy was aiming an ancient Colt Dragoon directly at Caleb's heart. It was revenge he was after that day. Paddy's brother had been one of the fellas killed when they came looking to rustle Caleb's cattle.

Luckily, the boy had been more upset than vengeful. He had no one left and nowhere to go. After they talked it over, the old Dragoon had disappeared, and Paddy had ended up staying with Gabe's family and working at Malachi Rogers's livery stable. He was a good boy, and he and Gabe had become good friends.

"I'll give you wedges, lollygagger. You don't lift that side, you'll be wearing the damn wedges outta both ears," Henry warned.

"You just go ahead and try. I'll have Bear chewing off your right arm for his supper."

At the mention of his name, the dog appeared in the doorway and sat himself next to Gabe, all the while eyeing Henry and Paddy.

"See?" Paddy crowed. "All it'll take is one dang word."

"That right?"

"Bear does look a mite hungry, Henry," Gabe added.

"It'll be Bear and me and Gabe. So whaddya think about that?"

Henry glanced from one to the next and then looked at Caleb and laughed. "They're ganging up on us, Marlowe."

"Don't go dragging me into it. I ain't the one talking like old King Herod."

Listening to the banter continue between the three of them, Caleb recalled when he was twelve. His father ran a training school for Indian kids in Indiana. The Shawnee and Kickapoo students were more abused than he was. There was no kidding one another, no friendships allowed by Elijah Starr. Only hard work. Fear and gloom hung over everything, reinforced by his father's hickory stick.

Caleb glanced off to the south, hearing his cattle lowing in the distance. There was still no sign of the herd coming up from Texas. And that worried him a little.

If he and Henry were to make a real and ongoing success of the ranch—supplying beef to Elkhorn and the surrounding area—they needed a larger herd of cattle. Months ago, he'd sent a message and money south to a cowpuncher he knew from his travels. Duke Ortiz owned a spread about a day's ride west of Fort Concho. And he had all the cattle they needed.

But here it was, the first week of October. Duke and that thousand head of longhorns still hadn't arrived. Caleb shook off his concern. He just had to be patient. Never his strong suit, to be sure.

The sound of an explosion from some mining operation echoed along the bluffs and ridges bordering the valley. Three miles north of the ranch, Elkhorn was pretty much run by Judge Patterson. Being a prime spot to view the eclipse that occurred at the end of July, the town had grown fast. Hotels, saloons, boardinghouses, and restaurants. This all played into the plans of the judge, who was building himself a kingdom here in the mountains of Colorado.

What interested Caleb was the demand for beef, which was strong. Elkhorn was a boomtown with big plans for a big future. Might just make it too, so long as the silver held out.

If anyone could keep Elkhorn on the map, it was the judge. Horace D. Patterson was a force. A man of lofty ambition with a killer's instinct. Caleb recalled, the first time he met him, the judge struck him as a man always willing to stomp a fella into the ground if it put one more dollar in his own pocket. And if his business required that he kill you before breakfast, Judge Patterson wouldn't remember you at all come suppertime.

At the same time, he was a master dealmaker. Twice he'd used Henry's release from jail to convince Caleb to work for him.

"You two ain't getting any closer to hanging that door," Gabe was saying. He'd sat himself down with his back to the door he and Caleb had finished hanging a half hour earlier.

Henry cocked his head toward an open end of the barn. "Ain't that your old man calling you? Yep, I hear him. 'Gabe, come here. Your mother needs you to put some laundry out on the line.'"

"You can't hear nobody from Elkhorn way out here." Paddy scoffed.

"That ain't true," Gabe corrected with a side look at Caleb. "I'm thinking Henry hears Miss Mariah calling him from the Belle Saloon pretty clear out here."

Henry huffed, but Gabe was right. Caleb's partner had been riding into town every other night or so to play cards at the Belle and "look at prettier faces than yours and that dog." Bear was only mildly offended by the comment. Caleb ignored it.

The ginger-haired boy stepped back from the door, a look of disgust on his face. "Shoot, Henry, you ain't sweet on Miss Mariah, are you? Why, she's so mean! She's always shooing me and the other boys away from the door of the Belle."

"I ain't sweet on nobody, street rat," Henry said. "And Miss Mariah's right in shooing you away. You're twelve years old. You got no call sticking your nose in at the Belle."

Paddy planted his fists on his hips. "Why? I been in plenty of saloons. Bigger ones than that one too."

"Be that as it may, you might be handling horses for customers outside that place, but I'm thinking Malachi Rogers would tan your hide if he knew you were doing any more than that."

Gabe was smiling at the exchange. "My pa ain't one for tanning nobody's hide, Henry. But tell him, Paddy."

"Tell him what?"

The livery man's son shook his head. "Paddy likes hearing the music when that piano fella gets going in there. Ain't that right?"

"Well, who don't?" the younger boy groused. "I sure don't have any hankering to mix with Miss Mariah nor none of them other women."

Gabe turned to Caleb. "The only woman Paddy will give the time of day to—except for my ma—is Miss Sheila."

"That right?" Henry asked in a teasing tone.

Paddy's face flushed crimson from his ragged shirt collar to the roots of his spiky, red hair. His eyes flashed. "That's right. There ain't nobody like her in that old town. She's always nice to us. Ain't she, Gabe?"

"That's a fact."

Henry laughed. "I don't blame you none for that, young fella. Miss Sheila's as fine a woman as you'll find anywhere."

Caleb eyed his partner closely, trying to decide if he should get angry at him or not. Henry did enjoy needling him about her.

Henry reached out and squeezed Paddy's shoulder. "I'm just joshing ya, fella."

"Well, all right." The boy smiled, clearly thinking he'd won a major battle. "But let's get this dang door up. I'm getting hungry, and Bear is a dog that needs to be rassled with."

Caleb and Gabe exchanged a look. They were both itching to get in there and do Henry and Paddy's door.

"If you two fellas need a hand—" Caleb started.

"No!" they both barked at once.

Henry shot a look at him. "Why don't you two go work on something else, since you got nothing to do here? Ain't you always grousing about that half-dug well and that chicken coop you want?"

Despite Henry's regular trips to town, they'd been making good progress on their projects during the day. They had to. There'd been almost no rain in the past couple of months, but it was getting colder. Caleb knew snow couldn't be far off. For the past week, the two men had been busy putting up the walls of Henry's cabin. It would be identical to Caleb's to start with, but he knew once his partner moved into it, the place would look like the back lot of a laundry in no time.

Caleb shook his head. "I'm afraid the minute we leave you alone, that door is gonna fall on you, and Gabe and I'll have two dead bodies to bury."

Gabe snorted and then looked away to hide his laugh.

"If you don't let us get on with it, there'll be two dead bodies, but it won't be me and my young partner here."

"That's right!" Paddy added.

Camaraderie like this had no place in Caleb's history.

He had no brother. No sister. No family. His mother was killed when he was sixteen. And his father was in jail in Elkhorn. Hearing these three made Caleb feel wistful about something he'd never known. He shook off the feeling.

"You know, if you boys' tender feelings will allow it, how about if Gabe and me hold the door in place? Then you two can do the brain work securing them hinges."

Henry and Paddy looked at each other, then grudgingly accepted the help. Twenty minutes later, the doors were hung square.

They all stood back and admired their work. Caleb swung the top half of each door open.

"Good for a hundred years," Henry said.

Gabe gestured toward the horses in the corral. "Pirate will be nice and snug in here when winter comes, Mr. Marlowe."

The buckskin's ears pricked up, and he watched them with interest.

Caleb nodded and walked over to the fenced enclosure. Near the corral, Bear was on his back, rolling on a clump of grass, getting a good scratch, but the dog hopped up and shook out his golden fur before trotting over to greet them. Caleb scratched him behind his ears, and the animal turned his attention to the boys, who had a stick that they started tossing back and forth, getting the big dog running for it. Pirate came over to the fence to nuzzle his master.

Henry stood beside him, one foot up on a rail. "One

more thing to cross off that damn list." He looked up at the clear sky. "Crazy that we ain't seen them Texans. Where do you reckon our cattle got to?"

Caleb frowned. "Who knows? Maybe they got a late start. Maybe they hit bad weather. Maybe they run into one of them bands of Comanche renegades that ain't ready to give up."

Henry looked off to the south for a while. It was one of his rare moments of quiet.

"Can't really blame them Comanches," he said finally. "They've had as raw a deal as any of 'em."

Henry was a unique fella. It was fairly common among white men to lump the tribes together as "red Injuns," as if there were no difference between them. Not Henry. He had a profound respect for some of the tribes they'd fought while serving in the army and pure disdain for others. It came from knowing them.

Caleb figured it was his upbringing. The two men rarely talked about their past, which was probably one of the things that drew them together as friends. Caleb's past had caught up to him recently, but Henry still kept part of his life locked away. Caleb only knew his partner's father had been a horse dealer who traded with a number of tribes out in Wyoming and Montana. Henry traveled with him from a very young age, and he knew horses. But Caleb's friend never mentioned his mother or any siblings.

Caleb didn't ask either.

Paddy suddenly appeared next to Caleb, climbing up onto the fence. "Mr. Marlowe?"

"Yep."

"I got something to ask you." He turned and looked at Gabe, who nodded encouragingly.

Paddy obviously had something to say, and he was restless as a tomcat under a full moon. Caleb waited for the boy to find the words.

"Say what you need to say, Paddy," Henry prodded, "before you fall off this here fence."

Another restless tomcat heard from, Caleb figured.

The boy pulled off his old, wide-brimmed hat and twisted it in his hands. His reddish hair was sticking up, making him look like a nervous Irish porcupine.

"Well, it's like this, Mr. Marlowe. I was thinking maybe I could move out to the ranch. Now that you got the barn up, maybe I could put some boards across the rafters and bunk in there."

Caleb kept his eye on the boy. "What makes you ask, Paddy? I can't imagine Mr. Rogers or Mrs. Rogers been treating you poorly."

"That ain't it," he blurted out. "They're treating me real fine. Good as Gabe. Miz Rogers even started learning me reading and ciphering."

"Then what is it?"

"Well, I like working with the horses and mules and all, but I could be learning as much out here. I wanna be a cowboy, not a blacksmith. There's a lot you could teach me about that and about hunting and tracking and such too."

"I don't know, Paddy. That book learning you're getting is gonna be real valuable as you get older."

"I can still do that, Mr. Marlowe. But I'd rather be out here. I can be a good help to you. I'm getting bigger and stronger all the time. I can even go and keep an eye on Henry when he goes into town and can't find his way home for being brandy sick."

Henry straightened up. "You still harping on that, you little pissant? I'll show you brandy sick."

Caleb forced back a laugh as his partner dragged the boy off the fence and playfully roughed him up.

The two were soon rolling on the ground, with Gabe joining in. It wasn't long before Henry allowed them to pin him to the ground, with Bear barking and nipping at the "defeated" man's pants and boots.

When they were all done wrestling, Paddy and Gabe climbed in triumph back onto the fence, and the dog settled down again.

The younger boy looked hopefully at Caleb. "That mean yes?"

"I ain't said one way or the other."

From beyond the two boys, Henry was dusting himself off. He shrugged with a look that said *why not*, but Caleb wasn't convinced it was a good idea. Having Paddy out here was a responsibility he wasn't sure he was ready to take on.

His own father had certainly not showed him the right way to bring up a boy. At this very moment, Elijah Starr was waiting for his dance with the hangman. The devil certainly deserved it. But for reasons known only to Judge Patterson, they hadn't even held a trial yet.

"Hell, Caleb," Henry put in. "Think of all the work we'll have on our hands once them steers arrive from Texas."

Surprised, Caleb frowned at him. Henry and Paddy certainly got along fine, but having a kid here all the time would be different. It would be like having a family.

"I'll think about it, Paddy. Fair enough?"

The ginger-haired boy nodded, trying not to show his excitement. "Miss Sheila said you'd say that."

"She did, huh?"

"Yep."

"When did she say that?"

"Yesterday. Saw her when Imala came into town. They was going to deliver a cart full of spuds to the general store."

"And a whole satchel full of those beaded tobacco pouches Imala makes," Gabe added. "She's making good money selling them, my pa says."

Caleb was glad that the friendship between Imala and Sheila had continued to develop. He first met the Arapaho woman in late spring while he was chasing down the gang of road agents who'd murdered her husband, a miner named Smith. They had a place about ten miles east of Elkhorn, and she'd decided to keep it after learning of Smith's death. She was a fine woman with tremendous courage, and she and Sheila had hit it off immediately. Kindred spirits in a lot of ways, despite the difference in their ages and their backgrounds.

"Miss Sheila needed our help last week too," Paddy said, smiling proudly. "She was scouting for a tree to cut down in a couple of months for her big Christmas party."

"For the gala, eh?" Henry shot Caleb a quick grin. "You find one?"

"Yep. Gabe knew just where to look."

Gabe nodded modestly. "Found one that was just the right size and shape, Miss Sheila said. Not far from the road between here and town."

"Well, that'll be convenient," Henry said innocently.

Caleb said nothing. Since the shoot-out with Mad Dog McCord's gang, he'd only seen Sheila the two times he went to Doc's house for dinner and a chess game, but she'd said nothing about the gala. He was starting to wonder if he might just be off the hook.

"I heard the whole town'll be coming out for the thing," Paddy said. "It'll be like the eclipse all over again but without all the strangers."

Henry turned to Gabe. "Maybe I'll stop by and talk to your pa about getting a team of horses to put up a tent out here. That barn ain't near big enough."

Caleb straightened up next to the fence and faced Henry. "You and me need to have a serious conversation about this."

"A serious conversation?" Henry grinned and jerked a thumb across the valley. "Not with me, partner. But maybe with her."

Caleb glanced out beyond the rise. A rider was coming across the pale-golden meadow. And from the dark duster she was wearing and the wide-brimmed hat on her head, there was no doubt that Miss Burnett had come to call.

CHAPTER SIX

THE FOOL DOG WAS OFF ACROSS THE FIELD LIKE A SHOT, barking and prancing and escorting her in like she was the Empress of Russia. It didn't matter a lick that Bear was *his* dog. The animal only had eyes for her, as if Sheila were his long-traveling owner come home.

Caleb started to walk over to help her down from her horse, but Henry stepped in front of him and got to her first.

That fella had no idea how close he came to taking a beating.

Sheila, as always, had a mind of her own, and she tossed Henry the reins. Then, graceful as a hawk in flight, she swung her leg over and slid off the saddle in one fluid motion. Her boots hit the ground before anyone could help her.

"A very good day to you, Miss Sheila," Henry said, sounding like some Wyoming Don Juan.

The boys added to the general enthusiasm of the welcome. It was as if they hadn't seen her for months, never mind yesterday. Bear was not to be outdone, however, affectionately butting her backward with his head before jumping up and placing his giant paws on her shoulders, nearly knocking her down.

"Down, you beast," Caleb barked, stepping between Henry and Sheila. "You too, Bear."

The dog paid no attention to him, and he doubted Henry would either.

Sheila laughed, and it occurred to him that it had been too long since he heard that sound from her. She took hold of the ruff around Bear's neck, greeting him before pushing him down.

She tipped her hat back and glanced up at Caleb. "I'm happy to see him too. It's been so long since I've been out here and seen this big old pup."

Far too long, he thought. Her smiling eyes were a brighter blue than the Colorado sky above them, and he felt a tightening in his chest and a knot form in his throat. Thinking of her pretty face and golden-brown hair was a regular pastime for him.

The dog bumped her hard, rubbing his body against her legs, determined to push her over.

"Sit." Caleb's sharp command got Bear's attention. The animal sat and leaned against her, mooning up at her with his tongue hanging idiotically out the side of his mouth.

Caleb hoped he didn't have the same look on his face. At least he knew his damn tongue was still in his head. Unlike Henry.

He nodded to her. "Sheila."

"Marlowe."

Their personal relationship had advanced far beyond the need for formalities. They'd shared too many dangerous adventures. Caleb knew that she liked him. And it would be a fat lie for him to deny to himself that he felt the same way.

But that didn't mean he was going to do anything about it.

So much had happened over the past five months. For the first time in his life—because of her—he'd found himself dreaming and planning. He'd begun to see a future that was decent and good. The wanderlust and the wildness of his past faded and disappeared like wisps of morning mist on a mountain lake. The routine of dinner with Sheila and Doc gave him a glimpse of family life that could include him. It was a life that he'd never had, never known. And suddenly, he was thinking it was possible.

All because of her.

Without a doubt, Sheila Burnett had charms. Beauty and brains and character. Her father was his friend. The attraction and convenience were tempting. More than tempting.

His whole life seemed to be falling into place like the chess games he played at the Burnett house. Caleb found himself in a strange, new position. He had land and a deed with his name on it. He had cattle that needed tending and a ranch that needed building. He was in a good place. A place where he could put down roots permanently. His life was so good, he barely recognized it.

But in the back of his mind—like a worm in an apple— was that nagging thought that wouldn't go away. He never thought twice about taking a life when the situation called for it. To survive on the frontier, one couldn't dwell on

the sanctity of life, as Henry put it. A man had to act…
and the difference between living and dying often meant
the faster draw and the deadlier aim. On the other hand,
Sheila Burnett was her father's daughter. Doc would save
a life regardless of how despicable the crime his patient
committed.

Caleb and Sheila were cut from different cloth. They
were different people. They had a different outlook on life.

And when it came right down to it, he could never be
good enough for her.

He did his best to ignore that dark thought, though,
to push it back and bury it beneath the hard work and the
recollection of the fine meals and the talk and the image
of Sheila's bright face. A man could dream…

But how quick the fantasy he was living this summer
went up in smoke when he found out his father was alive.
All the fanciful notions he had were gone in the blink of
an eye. The killer inside of him rose like a prairie fire in
August, ready to consume everything in its path.

The killing was in his blood. And he'd be forever
tainted with it.

Still, all thoughts of trouble disappeared the instant
Sheila whisked the hat off her head and wisps of burnished
gold freed from the long, thick braid framed her face.

"Miss Sheila, welcome. You're like the sunshine, dis-
pelling the rain and gloom of our dull and ordinary lives."
Henry "the Love Poet" Jordan had also removed his hat
and quickly smoothed down his long curls. Buffalo Bill
himself could not have started a show with more flare.

Henry had a way with words. Caleb didn't.

He ran a hand down his face to clear his head. Every time he saw Sheila, he had to start all over again and remind himself where he stood with her. Remind himself that he had no claim on her or on her affections. It didn't matter a damn what Henry said or did.

She turned her attention to the boys. "Have you two been busy out here?"

"We didn't know you was planning to come this way, Miss Sheila," Paddy replied. "We coulda rode out together."

Gabe punched Paddy on the arm. "So she could've helped you hang the barn door?"

Paddy scowled at his friend but said nothing in response. He was clearly on his best behavior.

She shot a quick glance at Caleb before answering, "I didn't know I was coming until a couple of hours ago."

He studied her profile. Damn, but he liked seeing her back out here at the ranch.

The first time they'd met was here. Sheila came looking for Caleb's help finding her father. He hadn't believed Doc was in any trouble then. But that was the last time he'd doubted her.

Caleb decided her instincts told her to stay away after the shoot-out back in July. Looking at her now, he wondered if she recalled everything that happened that day. The danger. The gunfire. The blood and the bodies. The words that passed between him and Elijah Starr.

"When I went to get my horse from your father," she said to Gabe, "he told me you two were out here."

Her gaze met Caleb's again for a moment before those blue eyes shifted away. Something was on her mind. He could tell.

"I'd be honored to serve as your humble escort, Miss Sheila, whenever or wherever the need arises," Henry offered, bowing like some damn knight of the Round Table. Even his language improved. "With the blackguards roaming these mountains, you shouldn't ride alone, ma'am."

"I frequently ride alone, Mr. Jordan. I need no escort. I am quite capable of protecting myself."

Henry didn't know her as Caleb did. Her pretty looks and polished East Coast manners hid a tough and capable woman. And she was one quick thinker. Sheila had grit and spunk from the first time Caleb met her, but she was also a far different person today than the woman who arrived in Colorado five months ago.

Gone were the frills and the bows, the silly hats and the formfitting New York dresses. In their place were woolen vests and practical skirts, a wide-brimmed hat, and a duster. The fancy umbrella and silk purses had given way to a shotgun and the Colt Gunfighter he'd given her. The fact that she could bust a plate with it at forty yards was only due in part to a couple of lessons he'd given her in town right after the eclipse.

That duster was still buttoned up, but he had no doubt she was wearing the short-barreled pistol with the rosewood grips in a holster on her hip right now. Doc told him that since the bloodshed at the ranch, she'd started wearing it every time she rode out of town.

Regardless of his confidence in Sheila's ability to take care of herself, Caleb still worried. Henry wasn't wrong. They lived in wild and lawless country. Mad Dog McCord's gang was only the most recent example of the danger, and Zeke's men hadn't been able to catch the rogue. Caleb didn't want to think what could happen if a band of outlaws came upon her on the road. But it didn't matter what he or her father had said to her numerous times. She had a stubborn streak, and in some matters, she wouldn't listen to anyone.

Caleb enjoyed watching Henry stumbling over his words. "I meant no offence, ma'am."

"None taken, Mr. Jordan." Her eyes drifted toward the barn.

"It's finally finished, Miss Sheila," Gabe jumped in. "The roof and the doors, stalls and all."

"Wanna see it?" Paddy asked.

She sent Caleb another look. He gestured to Gabe and Paddy to lead the way.

The three went ahead, the boys on either side of her and the dog circling them excitedly, happy to have his pack together.

"I'm with Paddy, you know," Henry muttered in Caleb's direction as they followed behind. "Of all the women I've known, ain't none like her. She's something else."

"Good thing to remember. 'Cuz she ain't your type."

"And exactly what is my type?"

"The type whose affection you can buy at places like the Belle."

Henry sent him a cross look. "I might be interested in the teacher type."

"You think she's the teacher type?" Caleb snorted. She had her arms draped over the boys' shoulders. "Whatever that means, she ain't it."

His partner hitched up his pants and tossed back his curls. "She is a fine-looking woman, that's for damn sure."

"Don't matter. You keep your distance and your sweet-talking to yourself."

"Why? She's available, ain't she? Do you know one other man that's courting her?"

The question didn't deserve an answer. Henry was quite open about his interests. Poker. Whiskey. And women. With the emphasis on women. And not *one* woman.

Caleb realized Henry was trying hard not to grin. The sonovabitch was running his mouth just to get a rise out of him. Nothing else.

He and Henry and Bear stood outside the barn as Sheila got the grand tour. If it wasn't Gabe talking, it was Paddy. And the younger boy had such pride in his voice, a person would think he'd notched every beam and hammered home every nail.

Caleb thought about what the twelve-year-old had asked about moving out there, and his eyes rested on Sheila as she listened to Paddy with rapt attention. The boy had mostly just seen the hard side of life. He needed a mother. Someone to love him and teach him kindness.

Caleb kicked himself inwardly. Here he was, doing it again. Dreaming about things beyond his reach.

Henry broke into his thoughts. "So, if she brings up her Ladies' Event Planning Committee and the Christmas gala, my answer is *yes*."

Caleb didn't know why she was here, but he doubted it was about any party. As blunt and straightforward as she normally was, Sheila still had that New York breeding. She wouldn't ask straight out and put him on the spot. She'd more likely approach her father to ask. If that didn't work, then she would send a letter from the committee. If those two approaches failed, then she *might* talk to him face-to-face and try steering him into offering. But she wouldn't be doing that here. She'd be on her own turf at Doc's house, probably while feeding him dinner.

Sheila stood by one of the barn doors, pretending to be interested in the not-so-complicated workings of the iron hinges. She wasn't looking in his direction, but he could feel her attention was on him. He'd come to know her. He recognized when she was feeling jovial or snappish. He could tell when she wanted something. Right now, she was none of those things.

"Remember, Caleb. No turning her down."

"She ain't here about that."

"No?" Henry cocked an eyebrow at him. "Then what's she here for?"

Sheila came out of the barn ahead of the boys and was greeted by the dog again. Giving Bear a pat on the head, she walked directly toward where the two men stood.

Her eyes were on Caleb, and there was trouble in them. For a brief second, the crazy notion ran through him that maybe she'd finally decided to run back to New York and the comfort of her grandparents' wealth. There once was a time when he thought that might be the right thing for her to do. A grand idea, in fact. After all, Elkhorn was no place for a woman with her East Coast upbringing and accomplishments.

But no more. Doc Burnett had confided in him that Sheila left New York to escape a marriage arranged for her by her grandfather. It was, apparently, an effort to secure the family fortunes. Sheila was not about to let herself be traded away in a business arrangement to an older man. Doc told him then that his strong-willed daughter had no plans of going back East.

But was she here to tell him to his face that she'd changed her mind?

"Can I speak with you, Marlowe?"

Surprised, Henry looked from one to the other, tipped his hat, and walked away, taking the boys with him.

Caleb saw it in the tightening of the skin around her mouth, in the ripple of emotions darkening her blue eyes. Something had happened, and she was bearing bad tidings.

She was going. He was certain of it.

"What is it?"

"Can we walk?"

Without waiting, she headed toward the corral. He followed, wondering if there was anything he could say or would say that'd change her mind about going.

She walked past the enclosure and out into the meadow

until she reached a large boulder jutting up from the soil. She stopped and leaned against it.

"Has Zeke been here today?"

"Zeke? What does he have to do with anything?"

Her eyebrows rose. "He's the sheriff."

Caleb took a breath, a feeling of relief pouring through him. Zeke would certainly have nothing to do with Sheila returning to New York. He'd guessed wrong about why she was here.

"Nope. Ain't seen him."

"Did he send one of his deputies then?"

"What for? They chasing after somebody?"

"They should be." She frowned and hugged her middle. "I would have expected more from him."

"Why?"

Sheila huffed, her eyes flashing. "Well, he does claim to be your friend."

Whatever trouble was brewing with the sheriff, Caleb could settle it. He couldn't fathom why she was getting involved. "What's happened?"

She kicked the heel of her boot into the dirt, digging a hole. "Zeke's a coward."

Caleb couldn't help defending the man. "Zeke's just Zeke. He ain't really a lawman. He only got drug into the job 'cuz I pushed him into it."

Judge Patterson had wanted Caleb to wear the tin star permanently, but he had no interest in doing that again. He'd served as sheriff up north. That was enough. His refusals didn't stop the judge from continuing to pressure him, however.

"That doesn't matter." Her face was flushed. She was getting angrier. "As the town sheriff, he should show backbone. Integrity."

"What's he done?"

She paused, and Caleb waited. Finally, he brushed his fingers on her sleeve.

"What's wrong, Sheila? What's this all about?"

She still hesitated for a moment before she raised her eyes to his. "It's about Elijah Starr. Your father."

The hairs on Caleb's neck rose. It was too much to hope that Zeke had shot the miserable bastard in his cell. Or that he let a mob drag him out and string him up.

Sheila was the only person in Elkhorn who knew the truth of their relationship. The only one who knew that Elijah Starr was Caleb's father. She'd stood and witnessed the first time they'd met after years of estrangement. In Caleb's cabin they'd argued and fought, and he would have killed Starr if not for her. She stepped in and somehow made Caleb believe that he was better than his father. They were *not* the same. He didn't have to kill Starr to avenge his mother's death. There'd already been too many killings.

Somehow, she got through to him that day. He'd decided to let the law handle it.

Now, however, more than three months had passed, and no trial had been forthcoming. More than once, Caleb had wondered if he made a mistake.

"What about him? Did the judge set a date for the trial?"

"No trial."

Caleb shook his head at her. "You can't tell me the judge would hang him without it. Having Elkhorn look civilized is too important to him."

Even as he said it, though, it occurred to him that his father sent gunslingers after Patterson to take him down in the street. Elijah Starr kidnapped the judge and even used torture to try and force him to transfer land his boss wanted for putting the railroad through Elkhorn. There was definitely bad blood between them. Maybe the judge had had enough.

"There will be no hanging. I saw Starr a couple of hours ago. He was walking down Main Street like he owed the town. He even tipped his hat to me, smiling and smug as the Cheshire cat."

Caleb shook his head, not believing it. "You made a mistake. It had to be someone else."

The judge had a damn knife driven through his hand when Starr pinned the man to a table. He wouldn't just let him go.

"Do you really think I could forget that man's face?" Sheila held his gaze. "I walked directly to the jail and talked to one of deputies lazing drunkenly in a chair outside the door. The one named Beau or Billy or Bub...or whatever."

"I know the one. Useless as a tin jackass."

"He told me Zeke wasn't there, but he let me look inside. The cells were empty. He said the outlaw you captured—Rivers, I think his name was—had been sent off to Denver under armed guard a few days ago."

Zeke had mentioned a bounty on Mad Dog McCord's head. It figured there would be one on John Rivers as well.

"The deputy said Zeke came in this morning, unlocked the cell door, and let Elijah Starr walk free. Everything was a misunderstanding, they're saying."

Blood was roaring in Caleb's head. Zeke wouldn't turn Starr loose without the judge ordering him to. But how could Patterson justify letting that man go? There had to be some reason, and it had to be a damn good one. Doing it had to benefit the judge in a big way.

Elijah Starr's boss, Eric Goulden, had to have something to do with it.

Back in the summer, Caleb had helped Patterson get the upper hand on the ruthless railroad tycoon, whose director of operations in Colorado turned out to be Elijah Starr. Goulden was trying to put his tracks through Elkhorn, and the judge wasn't about to let that happen... unless he was top dog in that business deal.

Bullets had stopped the magnate's quest—or at least slowed him down—but whether the judge could put the railroad through by himself was still a question.

Goulden was one of the most powerful moneymen in the country. He'd been buying up and building railroads all over the West since the end of the war. Many saw him not simply as a smart businessman but as he was...a ruthless robber baron who crushed anyone and anything that stood between him and his next dollar.

Over the past few years, the newspapers had been full of stories about him, and even the editors who were in awe of his success didn't like him much. He was a man to be feared.

Sheila broke into his thoughts. "I hurried home and asked my father what he knew. He'd only just heard that Starr had been freed, but he didn't know why."

Doc was unaware of any connection between Caleb and Starr. The man was his friend, but he didn't need to know.

She slipped her hand into Caleb's. "We've never talked any further about what happened in the cabin that horrible day. About what I heard pass between you two. But I felt it was my responsibility to come and let you know he's no longer incarcerated. I know what a dangerous man Starr is, and I know he'll come after you. He'll try to hurt you."

Starr wouldn't have to come after him. Caleb would take the fight to him.

Sheila was the only person who knew that he'd come close to killing his father twice. Once after the death of his mother. The second time, in that cabin. The third time would be the charm.

And no one would stop him.

CHAPTER SEVEN

PIRATE'S HOOVES FLEW OVER THE ROAD LEADING TO town, and Caleb's anger grew darker with every thundering step.

Sheila had agreed to ride back to Elkhorn later with Gabe and Paddy, but she'd still tried to reason with him as he saddled up his horse and strapped on his twin Colts. Starr was probably long gone, she said.

Caleb's mother, Eliza, spent her young life trying to protect him from the unhinged violence of her monstrous husband. Something inside of her had died long before Caleb found Starr finishing her off in their house. For the thirteen years that followed, Caleb thought he'd killed his father. But this summer, the reality had roared back. And with it, his burning hatred returned. The need to avenge his mother's death drove him.

It was driving him now.

Approaching Elkhorn from the south, Caleb never eased up pushing his steed, even after he reached the houses and buildings at the edge of town. He barely saw the passing faces of people afoot—miners, tradesmen, drifters, saddle slickers, men, women, dogs, and street urchins. There was only one face he wanted to see.

Sheila had been correct in saying that Starr might not have remained in Elkhorn. More than likely, he was heading to wherever his boss, Eric Goulden, was waiting for him. Back in June, the center of their railroad operations was in Bonedale, more than a day's ride west.

Still, Sheila had seen him this morning. He didn't have much of a head start. Caleb would track him down.

When Caleb steered Pirate onto Main Street, the traffic was heavier, and he weaved through wagons and horses too fast, drawing shouts of anger and alarm from those in his path. He ignored them, urging his horse on.

Judge Patterson must have caved to pressure from Goulden. When he turned Elijah Starr over to the law, Caleb had underestimated the robber baron's influence.

He reined in outside of the jail and vaulted from his saddle. Looping his horse's reins over the railing, he cast his eye up and down the street. In the back of his mind, Caleb was hoping he'd catch the blackguard out here in the open.

Across the way, on the front of a large, substantial building, an equally substantial sign boasted the office and courthouse of H. D. PATTERSON, JUSTICE OF THE PEACE. In smaller letters beneath, the sign read, LAND AND MINE SALES, SIDE DOOR. A line of men was visible right now, disappearing around the corner to that side door, where the judge's clerks waited to take their money in exchange for the hope of sudden wealth in the silver-rich hills around the town. Caleb knew that his father would not be there.

A few doors up from the judge's building, drunken miners stumbled in and out of the Belle Saloon, celebrating and spending the gleaming fruit of their labor or drinking just as heavily as they mourned their lack of success. He peered at the small crowd milling about and loitering on the raised wooden sidewalk, but he knew that too was a waste of time. Elijah Starr was too arrogant to ever condescend to mixing with such "riffraff."

Before Caleb could turn away, two cowboys were carried out the saloon's wide doors and tossed without ceremony onto the dusty street. The handful of miners doing the honors were backed by several of the Belle's ladies and the bouncer, a formidable bruiser made even more formidable by the short-barreled Greener cradled in his massive arms. Laughing off the indignity of the situation and the demeaning comments heaped on them from the sidewalk, the banished pair stumbled to their feet and began working their way down Main Street in search of other entertainments.

Caleb turned his gaze westward, scanning Elkhorn's primary thoroughfare. The bustling crowds that filled the street offered no glimpse of the man he came for. Simply covered wagons pulled by teams of horses or mules, hand-drawn carts, buckboards laden with supplies and materials for building, and everywhere, miners.

The wooden sidewalks were equally busy. Businessmen with their posh suits and canes—some of them sporting a shiny pistol on their hip—doffed their beaver-skin bowlers to well-dressed women. The colorfully dressed women—all bonnets, ruffles, and kid gloves—nodded and passed by them or ignored the men and focused their attention on the shop window displays.

The two cowpunchers stumbled by him, smelling of tobacco and brandy. One was about to speak to him, but one glance at Caleb's face and the hand resting on one of his twin Colts, and the two hurried on without a word.

An explosion silenced the crowd noises for only a moment. Glancing northward at the hills that ringed the town, Caleb saw a cloud of black smoke rising above the buildings lining Main Street. A logging camp and countless mining claims were being worked in the rugged landscape up there.

Caleb turned his eye on the door of the jailhouse, and a short, boar-like fellow in gray wool shrank back into the building out of sight. There was no sign of the deputy Sheila had seen before.

Caleb climbed onto the sidewalk and strode into the jail, the fire in his blood no cooler than when he left the ranch.

Zeke was alone in the sheriff's office, standing by his desk, his back hard against a rack of rifles and a line of hooks holding dusty Colt Dragoons. He was frowning nervously through his bushy whiskers and eyebrows and had his hands raised, far above the cross-holstered pistol on his gun belt. Caleb supposed it was intended to be a placating gesture.

"Afore you shoot me dead, Marlowe, let me just say I ain't had nothing to do with it."

Zeke might not have known about his relationship with Starr, but he, the judge, and everyone else knew there was bad blood between Caleb and the man. No one in Elkhorn was more eager than Caleb to sit in the courthouse for that trial. And though he wasn't partial to hangings, he'd decided long ago this was one he'd attend.

"You let him go."

"I ain't nothing more than the sheriff. You know that. You know me. I just follow orders. It was the judge's decision."

Caleb glared at him. "Did Goulden's men come to town? Is that it?"

"Not that I know of."

Zeke glanced in the direction of the front door as if to make sure. Either that or he was hoping for reinforcements.

"Then how? Why? There was enough against Starr to hang him a dozen times over. The judge himself was a victim. How could he let that miserable bastard go?"

"I don't know!" Zeke pleaded. "All I know is that the two of them been sending messages back and forth for a couple of weeks. Starr started it. He asked for paper and a pencil, and next thing I know, he's sent a note to the judge. Then Patterson is sending a message back. And on it goes. Nobody never told me nothing about what was being said between them."

Elijah Starr was a snake who regularly shed his skin. From soldier to headmaster at a training school in Indiana to eliminating obstacles in the way of Goulden's railroad construction, it never mattered what skin he was wearing.

His venom was the same. Caleb grew up listening to him twist the passages of scripture to serve himself and his own vile desires. In the Good Book, Satan was the Great Deceiver. And Starr was the devil incarnate.

"So, yesterday, Judge Patterson sent two fellas over to get Starr and bring him to his office. He was gone for a couple of hours before they brought him back."

"Why didn't you go with him?"

"They said no." Zeke shook his head. "Personal business between Starr and the judge, they said. And them new fellas Patterson hired to work for him ain't to be trifled with."

Frissy Fredericks, Patterson's former bodyguard, had sold out to Starr. The pig-faced giant had been gunned down at Caleb's ranch the day hell broke loose, and that betrayal had nearly cost the judge his life. Since then, there'd been no single bodyguard. Patterson's back was watched by men who were watched by other men. And, according to Zeke, they were being regularly replaced.

"What happened this morning?"

"Patterson called me into his office and made me stand at his desk like a schoolboy. He said, as of now, Starr is a free man. Any charge against him was dropped. No trial. No hanging. Free."

"Just like that?"

"Just like that." Zeke squirmed and lowered his hands. "And that ain't the worst of it."

"Starr is staying in Elkhorn."

The sheriff's eyes widened. "How'd you figure that?"

Caleb shook his head, disgusted. "The judge told you Eric Goulden is running his railroad through town. And Starr is going to stay here and build it for him?"

"You're half right." Zeke ran a hand down his face. "Starr's gonna manage the construction of the rails. But he's doing it for Judge Patterson. Not Goulden."

Caleb felt the ground opening beneath him. "So this snake will be working for the man he tried to kill not even three months ago."

The sheriff nodded grimly. "And the worst of the worst. The judge told me if Starr told me to shit or cut bait, I'd best be shitting and cutting."

CHAPTER EIGHT

ELKHORN'S JUDGE MIGHT BE ITS LEADING CITIZEN. HE might be a man with grand aspirations for himself and for his town. But H. D. Patterson, Justice of the Peace, was also a swindler, an opportunist, and a damn rat.

Caleb had never trusted him, but he'd never taken him for a fool.

Somehow, Starr had proved his value enough to convince the judge—a man he'd injured and humiliated—to remove the noose from around his neck.

None of that mattered. What did matter was that Elijah Starr was free to walk the same streets that Caleb was walking. But not for long.

Zeke told him where Starr was staying, and Caleb walked down Main Street, barely noticing any of the faces he passed. The fancy new hotel, erected and open only a few weeks before the festivities surrounding the eclipse, was just beyond Lewis's hardware store and the bank, across the street from the Wells Fargo Overland office.

Caleb's bootheels pounded out a rhythm on the wooden sidewalk, and he recognized the tightening of his gut and the familiar stillness that came over his hands before a fight. But his mind was off on a track of its own, and his brain was filled with thoughts of what his life had been and what was at stake now.

So many hard miles separated Caleb from Indiana, the place of his birth. After his mother's death, he'd run, drifting farther and farther north and west for three years. The road he'd set off on was filled with more trouble than he'd ever expected. It was a road Caleb wasn't proud of. It was a path that required quick wits, a deadened conscience, and occasional savagery to survive. It was a journey that nearly killed him.

Then, one winter day over a decade ago, Jacob Bell— legendary mountain man, trapper, wilderness guide— found him on a snowy bank of the Keya Paha River up in the Dakota Territory. Beaten, robbed, and half-frozen, Caleb had been left for dead.

But he didn't die. The old man picked him up, thawed him out, and tucked him under his wing. In the six years that followed, Old Jake showed him how to take hold of the frayed edges of what was left of himself. He taught Caleb what it took to be a man. Together, they crossed the frontier from the wide valleys of the Missouri River Basin to the rugged gold fields of Montana, and from the cold shadows of Cloud Peak in the Bighorns to the scorching Plains of San Agustin. Jake was the father figure that he never had. The old frontiersman was the hero Caleb would try to be.

And one night, sitting around the campfire, he finally told Jake the truth about his past—of what he'd done. It had been the old man's suggestion that Caleb Starr become Caleb Marlowe.

Everything Caleb was today sprang from his time with

Old Jake. The legends that people spoke of were all due to what he'd learned from the aging scout.

Caleb had made a name for himself exploring and opening the frontier to homesteaders pushing ever westward. He'd blazed trails through Wyoming and Montana. Before long, even the army sought him out, conscripting him for his skills as a tracker. When he was through with that, he'd somehow found himself wearing a badge up in Greeley for a couple of years.

Caleb paid his dues, trying to make himself live every moment fully and not look back. His mother was dead. There was no changing that.

His murderous father was still alive, and so was Caleb's need for vengeance.

The code of the western frontier backed him. Where a man's honor or the honor of his family was concerned, he must fight. And no one had dishonored his family like Elijah Starr.

Caleb would call him out. And if the truth surfaced that they were kin, then so be it.

As he crossed the dusty street, he glared up through the early-afternoon sun at the new hotel. The place rose a full three stories above the street, and it had more windows than Caleb cared to count. The name, Silver Elk Hotel, was proclaimed proudly in six-foot-high, blue letters painted across its gleaming, whitewashed facade.

His mood darkened even more at the thought of his vile father living like a king in the finest hotel in town. In all of Colorado, maybe.

Caleb went around a covered wagon working its way slowly down the street. A small boy stared at him out the back, his face pinched and serious. A trio of ragged street urchins ran past, followed by a nimble, three-legged dog, and the boy's attention was diverted.

Caleb climbed the steps, crossed the sidewalk to the double doors, and went in. He stood just inside for a moment, letting his eyes adjust to the light.

The lobby of the hotel was as grand as anything he'd seen in Denver or anywhere else. A chandelier hung from a high ceiling. Beneath it, dominating the center of the room, a carved statue of an elk, painted silver, stood on a stone pedestal. To his left, the etched glass windows in a pair of doors identified the saloon. Beside the saloon doors, a clerk stood behind a counter, busying himself with a well-heeled traveler waiting impatiently for his room key.

Straight ahead, a wide stairway rose eight steps to a landing, where it split off in either direction to the upper floors. Dark, carved balustrades supported railings all the way up. To Caleb's right, many large, upholstered chairs had been provided, apparently for the use of the men presently occupying them with newspapers in hand. Blue smoke from fat cigars hung like a cloud over the loungers' heads.

Beyond them, four burly men wearing new, ill-fitting suits and shiny boots stood in front of two doors. Caleb recognized two of them. They worked for Judge Patterson. The etched glass bore the words DINING ROOM, and they were eyeing him with steely, guarded gazes. He had no doubt that the judge was in there.

By the door, a thin, nervous-looking fella stood behind a table. He was taking charge of hats and gun belts that hung on a row of pegs behind him.

Just to be sure, Caleb went to the saloon door and looked in. The place was full and buzzing with conversation. A few card games were taking place along a far wall. But there was no sign of Elijah Starr.

Going back into the lobby, he again drew the attention of the four by the dining room doors. Before he could reach them, two drew back their coats to reveal holstered revolvers. A third man—only slightly smaller than the others—stepped forward, raising his hand for Caleb to stop.

"Hold on, Marlowe," he said in a nasally voice. There was no hint of friendliness in the black, hawklike eyes or the tight gash of a mouth. A thin moustache lined the upper lip beneath a fist-flattened beak. "You got business here?"

"I got business, but it ain't with you." He started to push past, but the other three bruisers closed ranks, blocking the door. Caleb unfastened the thongs over the hammers on his Colts. His voice was low and cold. "Outta my way."

The lobby had gone deadly quiet, and Caleb waited for any one of them to make a move.

Hawk Eyes broke the tension. "We ain't making trouble for you, Marlowe, but we got a job to do."

"Is the judge alone?"

"Nope."

"Is Elijah Starr with him?"

The man said nothing, but one of the bodyguards behind nodded.

"I'm going in there."

"Look, Marlowe. The judge don't like having his dinner spoilt."

"Then you'd best get outta my way now."

Hawk Eyes shrugged. "Suit yourself. But hotel rules say nobody goes in without leaving their shooting irons outside. And that suits the judge. So this young fella here will be happy to hold 'em for you. Ain't that right, son?"

The clerk nodded uneasily. Caleb didn't like giving up his guns to anybody, especially since he knew his father was in there. But unless he wanted to shoot it out with these fellas, he wasn't going through those doors armed. And it wasn't their blood he came to spill. He assumed Starr was also unarmed.

Keeping his eyes on the judge's bodyguards, he unbuckled his gun belt and rolled it up. After tossing it to the clerk, he removed his hat and threw it on the table.

"You're gonna hafta leave that fancy knife of yours too."

Caleb pulled the long hunting knife that had once belonged to Old Jake and handed it to the clerk, who stared at it wide-eyed. It was as famous a weapon as any on the frontier. Some believed it originally belonged to Jim Bowie himself.

The bruisers, looking relieved despite themselves, made way for him, and Caleb went into the dining room.

His head pounded. His hands turned to fists at his side. Once again close to facing his father, every muscle in Caleb's body tensed in anticipation of what was to come.

He scanned the dining room looking for Starr. Only four tables were occupied, three of them with men suitably dressed for a place so stylish. Judge Patterson was seated alone at a table by a window halfway down. Four waiters of various ages stood by a door in the corner, wearing black pants and coats and white aprons that hung to below their knees.

But there was no sign of Elijah Starr.

The sun was streaming in through lace curtains. Patterson was holding a glass of something amber-colored and appeared to be lost in thought. A half-empty glass sat across the table from him.

Caleb looked around a second time.

The long, rectangular room was as fancy as the lobby but more brightly lit from the tall windows facing Main Street. Four tables across and eight rows of tables in length, two unlit fireplaces had been built into the wall on the left, and a set of stairs along the end wall led upstairs. Wood paneling about shoulder height ran around the outside walls with flowered paper above. The ceiling was covered with ornate tin sheeting.

Unlike most establishments in Elkhorn, there didn't appear to be any bullet holes in the walls. With its rule about firearms, the management was obviously planning to keep it that way.

The judge glanced up, spotting him standing by the

door. He looked startled at first then smiled and stood to greet Caleb as if he were expecting him all along.

The man was of medium height, at least half a head shorter than Caleb. He had a solid build and longish, graying hair that gave him a refined air of respectability. He was clean-shaven, but sported long, thick side whiskers. A watch chain draped from the pocket buttonhole on the silver-gray waistcoat he wore beneath his charcoal suit. Even standing still, the judge seemed to be about to burst with some tautly held energy. Caleb had seen the same thing in wild stallions out on the range.

Patterson motioned him over and gestured to a chair. "Marlowe, how well you look. Have you eaten?"

"I ain't eating."

"How is your partner?"

Reminding him of the favor he thought Caleb owed him. "Henry is fine."

"The ranch?"

"I ain't here to chitchat."

"Very well. Good to know. What brings you to town?"

Caleb held his gaze but didn't sit. "I got some business with a man I heard has become an employee of yours."

The judge laughed, a short exhalation of air, and motioned to a waiter to bring another drink for himself and one for Caleb.

"Sit, Marlowe. I can see we need to talk."

"Was he here?"

"He was. He's coming back." Patterson again motioned to the chair.

Caleb sat down, putting his back to the window. He wasn't about to let Elijah Starr get behind him.

"Why hire a man that tried to kill you?"

Patterson frowned and drummed his fingers on the tablecloth. On the back of his hand, a scar was plainly visible, jagged and red on the judge's pale skin. It was the mark where Starr's knife cut through his flesh and pinned him to a table on Caleb's porch.

"It took me a while to sort it out, but Starr is much more valuable to me alive than dead."

Zeke told Caleb about all the back and forth between Patterson and the prisoner. He was sure the letters his father had been sending the judge had something to do with this change of heart.

"It's a good thing, having him work for me. A very good thing."

Caleb gestured toward the hand. "I never figured you for a man to forget things."

"It's business." Patterson waved toward the window. "Our world is growing quickly. It's changing. A man like me can't hold on to slights from the past. I have to think of the future I want. And not just for me. For this town."

"You own this town. Everything in it. Every*one* in it."

"That's true, in many ways. I've staked my life and future on it. It's my town, and I don't plan to give it up to anyone, least of all someone like Eric Goulden."

The waiter returned with the drinks and placed them on the table. Neither man reached for his glass.

"I thought you settled that back in the summer when

all Goulden's hired killers were shot dead or hanged. You had Starr in jail, ready for trial and hanging."

"True. But I know Goulden will be coming at me again."

Patterson sat forward in his chair and smoothed the cloth with one hand. As he talked, he used his index finger to emphasize his points.

"Marlowe, no one knows how much silver is in those hills. Maybe we're sitting on another Comstock Lode, maybe we're not."

Caleb knew that the mines around Elkhorn were continuing to produce vast amounts of precious ore, but he also knew of men like Zeke, whose efforts to dig silver out of the mountain were showing less and less return.

"One way or another, the future of the West lies in its railroads. And the men who build and control them will be the titans of our time."

As the judge continued, Caleb kept his eyes on the stairway at one end of the room. He noticed that the lobby doors stood open a crack. No doubt Patterson's bodyguards were keeping a close eye on him.

He wasn't concerned about them. But he had no doubt his father would kill him without a blink of his one eye.

"There are great riches to be gained from gold and silver, I grant you. But what will happen to those men who fail to find it? Those men who left their farms and trades to chase the fevered dreams of gold?" Patterson spread his hand over the table. "I'll tell you what will become of them. They will look around them and say, 'This is land

I can farm. Land that's better than what I left behind.' They'll say, 'These are towns that need a cooper and a blacksmith and a cobbler and a tailor.' And they'll stay."

Patterson pounded his fist once on the table like a gavel.

"And what will provide the lifeblood for the thousand towns that will spring up?"

"Railroads."

"You're a smart man, Marlowe. You know the answer. Yes, railroads. Railroads are the future of the frontier. The future of the nation. And that's why I say Goulden will be back, unless I do something about it first. I'm getting into the rail business myself."

"You aim to be one of them titans."

The judge lowered his voice. "You're damn right. Think about the opportunity that we have if we're smart enough to grasp it." He took a deep breath. "You helped me beat Eric Goulden at his own game…but only for the moment. This is war. I outsmarted him on paper, but you outgunned him in the field. If we move now, we can run a rail line from Denver to Elkhorn. And we won't stop there. We'll extend that railroad south, past your ranch, all the way to Santa Fe. Think of it, Marlowe."

The judge looked out at the street again for a moment, and Caleb could see him envisioning an Elkhorn that would rival the great cities to the east. With himself presiding over it all.

"But to do this," Patterson concluded, "we need to act now. We need men who know rail construction. Men who aren't afraid to do what is necessary to complete this great enterprise."

"Men who are ruthless." Back in Bonedale, Caleb had spoken to a woman who'd been widowed and left with three young children. Starr had killed her husband in cold blood to take their farm. It stood in the path of his rail line. And no doubt there were hundreds like Widow Caswell.

"Yes. Whatever it takes. I don't need morality. I need commitment. And no one is more suited to the task than Elijah Starr. He's already proven himself to me."

As if he'd been conjured from some boiling cauldron, Caleb's father appeared on the stairs at the end of the dining room. He was holding some papers in his hand. He paused halfway down, stared at Caleb for a moment, and then continued his descent.

Caleb stood and crossed the room to meet him.

CHAPTER NINE

CLOSE YOUR EYES, CALEB. PRETEND YOU'RE ASLEEP. KEEP them closed no matter what happens.

Some memories stayed with him for his entire life.

No matter what you hear, Caleb, don't make a sound. Don't come out. Hear me?

Caleb's earliest memories became nightmares.

He's got his cane. Go out the window. Hide in the barn till I come for you. Go now.

For Caleb's entire childhood, the heavy tread of Elijah Starr's boots on the stairs was a sound that evoked fear.

Hearing it now brought out another emotion in him. Rage that he could barely contain. It flowed through him like fire.

Caleb never stopped trying to stand up for her, protect her. Always defiant. Always with his chin high. Always fighting to get between her and the monster. Always braced for the blows that would follow.

Regardless of what he did, regardless of how brave he thought himself to be, it was never enough to stop the beatings they both took. Fists. Boots. Cane. And always, the voice that haunted Caleb's childhood dreams and his waking hours.

His father stopped before reaching the bottom stair and lingered there. As Caleb fixed his killing gaze on the man, he felt the blood racing in his veins, but everything else in the dining room slowed. Light and shadow and color and sound became as sharp and crisp as an autumn dawn.

He didn't look like a man who'd spent three months in jail.

Starr's clothes were finely tailored, stylish enough that he could be mistaken for a banker or a lawyer. And they were new. No doubt bought at the judge's expense. His suit was blue, dark as the midnight sky, with subtle, gray stripes running vertically in the fine cloth. His double-breasted vest was silk brocade of a deep-maroon color, and his blue tie matched his coat and pants. A stick pin with a large stone, clear and sparkling, held the tie in place. He was clean-shaven, his dark hair slicked back.

Starr's free hand rose to his face, and his fingers ran just under the black eye patch before skimming over the scarred flesh that marked the left cheekbone all the way to the ear. The gesture was intended for Caleb, reminding him that Starr remembered who had marked him.

If only the sixteen-year-old Caleb had stayed back and made sure he finished the job.

Caleb focused on the eye patch. How many times as a child had he wondered if there was no flesh behind it, only a black hole? A glimpse into a devil's cauldron.

Judge Patterson appeared to Caleb's right, leaving some space between them. His voice cut through the sharp silence that had fallen over the room. "I recall what happened on my account at your ranch, Marlowe. I know there's ill will between you two because of it."

Starr, like the rest of them, was unarmed. He rolled the document he was carrying lengthwise and tucked it into his coat.

"It's time for you two to let the past go."

Caleb and his father were approximately the same height and size. But he knew he was stronger and faster. He'd bested his father in the cabin and would have killed the older man with his fists alone if Sheila hadn't stopped him.

"You and I outside. Now."

Starr didn't move from the step, resting one hand on the railing. The corner of his mouth lifted in a smirk of superiority. He was gloating. He was conveying to Caleb that he was in the victorious position.

"Neither of you two are going anywhere. I don't expect you to like each other. But you'll need to get along. I've hired you before, Marlowe, and I'll need you again."

Twice he'd worked for Patterson in recent months. Both times, it had been in Caleb's own best interests to do so. He kept his gaze on the tall man on the stairs. That wouldn't be happening again.

"Civility is all I ask," the judge continued. "For our enterprise to succeed, I need you to work together. You're now on the same side."

"Never," Caleb said under his breath. He called out to Starr. "You and I need to finish this."

"I'm done with you."

"Get your guns."

"I won't fight you, Caleb."

The sound of his given name on Elijah's tongue was like the twist of a blade in his gut.

"You've been looking for me. Here I am. You'll fight, or you'll die the coward that you really are."

Starr shook his head. "I spent three months in Elkhorn's jail. I had time to think, reading the Good Book, rediscovering the man I once was. Soldier, teacher, devoted husband, and father."

"You mean liar and murderer."

Elijah Starr's eyes narrowed, and then he scoffed.

The judge cut in. "You two knew each other before the ranch? Before the bloodshed?"

Patterson's words buzzed in Caleb's ear, but neither man responded.

"Your fate is between you and me, and we're going to settle it today," Caleb said.

"You are far too puffed up with your own importance, son. If a judgment is to be made about fate, I'm the one to do it. You are the one who has transgressed the laws of God and man. You are the one who savagely wronged both me and my wife."

"The wife you beat to death with your own hands?" Caleb took a step closer. He thought about dragging the man into the street right now.

"Lies again, Caleb? Don't forget, there are no sinners in heaven; no forgiveness in hell. Have you forgotten everything that I taught you, son?"

"What's this, Marlowe?" The judge's voice had an accusatory tone. "You never said anything about being Elijah Starr's son."

Starr's laugh was dry and mirthless. "Then I assume he's said nothing of his misspent youth as a violent troublemaker. Or that he ran away after setting fire to the home where I raised him, leaving his loving mother to die in that fire."

"You killed her."

In the blink of an eye, Caleb's hands were around Starr's throat. He slammed his father into the stairs and then dragged him down onto the floor.

All the burning hate of a lifetime come flooding back. Liquid fire scorched his brain and raced through his veins into every corner of his being as he dug his thumbs into the man's throat.

Elijah's lies about him meant nothing. Caleb wasn't interested in setting the record straight. He had only one thought. Kill this monster. Wipe this evil from the face of the earth.

Shouts rang out around him. Hands clutched at his arms and shoulders, yanking at his vest and collar. Still, he hung on.

His father's one eye bulged from its socket. The pale face went red and then blue around the scars he carried from burns and beatings.

Someone looped an arm around Caleb's neck as another managed to pry his fingers free.

The judge's bruisers were dragging him away, and

Caleb twisted his body in their clutches. Finding his footing, he turned and lashed out at the closest face, finding the point of a chin with his fist.

As the face disappeared, Caleb spun, firing a left hand at another attacker. Hawk Eyes, blood spraying from a mashed nose. The bushy face of Zeke appeared in the mix, only to disappear when Caleb caught him with an elbow to the side of the head.

Chairs and tables overturned. Silverware and glasses tumbled and crashed in every direction. He was fighting them all, still trying to get to his father, who was pulling himself up from the floor, coughing and waving off the judge's help.

"I won't tolerate this, Marlowe." Patterson's irate voice cut through the riot. "Hold him."

Suddenly, he was on the floor, fighting off the weight of a dozen men. Caleb caught a glimpse of Starr, looking down on him with the same infuriating smirk.

"Zeke, do your job," the judge shouted. "Lock him up. I'll deal with him after he cools off. He has a lot of explaining to do."

As they hauled Caleb upright, he managed to throw off two of them and land another punch.

The butt of a revolver thudded sharply on the back of his head, and the spinning world around him grew bright for an instant before the darkness closed in completely.

CHAPTER TEN

THE SHERIFF AND HIS GANG OF WORTHLESS DEPUTIES were carting the unconscious gunhawk out of the dining room, heading for the jail. As he watched the door of the dining room close behind them, the judge stared across the table at the untouched glass of whiskey.

The fact that Marlowe was Starr's son had come like a lightning bolt out of a clear blue sky. This was a problem he hadn't foreseen.

Damn Marlowe.

"...clear since he could walk, Caleb was heading for the fiery pit. His mother did nothing to help. I recall a time..." Starr hadn't stopped talking since he sat down.

Patterson raised his empty glass, motioning to the waiter to replenish his drink. Father and son. Together, they could have been great use to him.

Elijah Starr knew how to lay down the tracks of a rail line. He knew how to clear the way for the construction crews. He knew how to purchase and supply materials for the workers. He also knew Goulden's plans and secrets. He had real value.

"...and when I found her, the victim of my son's callous violence..." Starr continued to drone on.

Caleb Marlowe was as tough and indestructible as

ironwood root. He was cool and courageous enough to take on a dozen armed men and smart enough to whip them. He handled a gun with more speed and expertise than any gunslinger Patterson had ever seen. And he did not hesitate to kill a man when the situation warranted it. He too had real value.

"...I could have sent the law after him. He should have hanged..."

Starr was arrogant and self-righteous, and he was as indifferent to brutality as a Roman centurion. The judge frowned at the scar on the back of his hand. The place where Starr had driven his knife through his flesh still caused him pain whenever he tried to make a fist.

Marlowe was stubborn, and it was difficult to gain his allegiance. Despite their differences, however, the gunhawk had been smart enough to save Patterson's life. But he had his flaws. He had a sentimental weakness that drove him to protect the weak and helpless. A stray dog, an orphaned boy, a partner with too much baggage to be any good to him. How he'd ever thrived on the frontier was a testament to his toughness.

"Caleb is a dangerous man, Judge. There's no way your railway plans can proceed with him around. He'll interfere. Let me take care of—"

"Stop," Patterson snapped. Of the father and son, the younger man was the more trustworthy. But sometimes a man had to deal with the devil. The trick was knowing you're in league with Old Nick. "I'll handle Marlowe. I've told you what I want from you. Do it."

As the judge took a sip from his replenished whiskey glass, he hoped to hell he was banking on the right Starr.

CHAPTER ELEVEN

CALEB OPENED HIS EYES AND IMMEDIATELY CLOSED them. His stomach turned from the pain in his head.

He slowly pried his lids apart again, taking in his surroundings. He was lying on his side on a dirt floor that smelled of piss and puke.

He pushed himself upright and stayed there until the room stopped tilting and whirling around him. Late-afternoon shadows from the bars on the window played across the hard-packed floor.

Damn.

This wasn't the first time Caleb had spent time in Elkhorn's jail. Once, to settle an old score, Grat Horner, the last sheriff, locked him in here overnight just because he could.

And there were other towns. Other jails. As a very young man, before he got his head on straight, Caleb had done more than his share of drinking, fighting, and general carousing. Somewhere along the way, though, he'd come to realize it was more than looking for a good time that was steering him into the path of the law. He was trying to forget Elijah Starr. He was choosing the hard road, hoping to forget the brutality his mother had endured until it killed her. Guilt and anger create a thirst that can never be slaked with liquor, but that doesn't stop a man from trying.

He didn't know how long he'd been out cold. Maybe only an hour or two, if it was still the same day. The last thing he recalled was fighting the men trying to drag him away from Starr's throat.

Caleb touched the back of his head. His fingers came away bloody. Whoever had delivered the blow, they meant business. Voices came to him from beyond his cell door. He gingerly pushed himself to his feet and lurched toward it as footsteps approached.

The scruffy puss of a sheriff's deputy appeared. "Folks here to see ya."

Caleb had no interest in seeing anyone, but he had every intention of knocking the deputy on his scrawny tail as soon as he opened that door. Then he'd be back in that hotel if he had to shoot his way in.

That plan changed as soon as he saw Doc Burnett behind him, carrying his medical case. Sheila trailed them, looking pale and worried.

Damn.

He took a deep breath and stepped back from the door. He didn't like having her see him like this.

The deputy looked in and jingled the key. "Don't get no funny ideas, Marlowe, or…"

"Close your mouth and open that door," Doc snapped, interrupting Billy or Bub or Beau…or whatever his name was. "Now!"

Caleb saw the flash of anger cross the deputy's face as the man backed away. The look withered under Doc's hard glare.

"All right. Keep your shirt on."

"Never mind the smart mouth. Open it."

Doc was not a big man, but he had a bearing that made lesser men listen. Perhaps it was the dark eyes that could cut through a man as cleanly as his scalpel. Or his blunt directives that left little doubt of his command. Perhaps it was the result of generations of Burnett doctors who had been bred to convey confidence and control. He was the only doctor in Elkhorn, and he could be very intimidating when he chose to be.

Caleb knew from their conversations over chess that John Burnett had grown up in a well-to-do family of medical practitioners in New York. When the Southern states decided to secede, however, he'd joined the Union Army Medical Corps early on, giving up his practice in the city. That war had left in its wake a great many men bearing scars and missing limbs and broken spirits, and Doc's experience from the carnage changed him too.

By the time the smoke cleared and he returned to the city, his wife had passed away, and he could not go back to his old life treating the mostly imagined ailments of wealthy patients. He needed to find a greater purpose. Find himself. Leaving Sheila with his wife's rich parents, he'd traveled west, like so many others.

As far as Caleb could tell, Doc feared nothing. He never wore a sidearm but rode out at all hours to treat those who needed medical attention. At fifty years old, he was tough and sharp-witted. And Sheila had inherited many of his best qualities.

Caleb could see her standing impatiently beyond the two men. She too was scowling at the deputy. When she'd brought him news earlier that Elijah Starr had been set free, he was sure she hadn't expected Caleb to take his place in here.

"Only one can go in, Doc." Sulking, the deputy paused before turning the key. "Sheriff's orders."

Sheila nodded to her father. The scrawny bonehead kept one hand on the Remington holstered at his hip as he opened the cell door. As soon as Doc stepped across the threshold, the key turned again in the lock.

Doc turned and growled through the bars. "Go. Now."

The deputy glanced through nervously at the two men then at Sheila before going out grumbling into the front area of the jailhouse.

"How did you know I was here?"

"Everyone in Elkhorn knows. You caused quite a stir at the hotel earlier."

Caleb doubted he was that newsworthy, though the sight of him being hauled over here must have caused some gawking. He looked toward the small cell window. At least it was still the same day. He hadn't been knocked out that long.

Zeke, being a friend of Doc's, had probably gone to let him know. Or maybe Sheila had come looking for Caleb once she got back to town.

"When do I get out?"

"Sit down. Let me take a look at your head."

"Ain't nothing. My least vulnerable spot."

Doc harrumphed, opening his medical case. "I don't doubt it, but maybe you could use it to better effect."

Caleb knew how his friend worked, so he said nothing more. He wouldn't get an ounce more information out of him until the doctoring was done.

"Tip your head forward."

Caleb dropped his chin and immediately felt the room tilt. Holding his face in his hands, he made himself focus on the toe of his boot as Doc poked and prodded the wound.

"I should stitch that up."

"No need."

"Why, are you planning to have them bust it open again?"

"Maybe." Caleb wasn't going to give anyone the chance to get at him. He'd gotten angry. He should have attacked faster and with no remorse.

"Well, I'll clean it up then. Wouldn't want to waste good cat gut."

Doc uncorked a bottle of some bitter-smelling liquid. He soaked a cloth of white linen and began dabbing the wound. Caleb clenched his jaw, bearing the sharp pain. When the doctor was satisfied, he began gathering his things.

"So, Elijah Starr is your father?" he asked as he replaced the bottle carefully in the bag.

Caleb looked up, and his eyes met Sheila's. She was watching every move from the other side of the bars. Her arms were hugging her middle, and her shoulders looked stiff with tension. He wondered how much, if anything, she'd revealed to Doc.

"Starr is telling anyone who will listen that you're his son."

"It don't give me any pleasure to admit that."

"I understand your feelings. The man is a brute and a scoundrel. I see nothing of him in you, Caleb."

"Thanks, Doc."

"But for the moment, he has you in a tough spot."

"Looks like it. But soon as I'm out of here, him and me are gonna settle things."

Doc Burnett moved the case and sat heavily on the bench beside him. "Listen to me, my friend, and listen good. The way things stand now, that vile miscreant is sitting right on the judge's shoulder. And he's not whispering anything good about you in Patterson's ear."

Caleb nodded. "All the more reason for me to take care of business."

"I stopped and talked to the judge before coming here. As things stand, he has no intention of turning you loose. From the way he talked, I gathered that he'll keep you right in this cell until he pushes forward on some big plans of his. You and I both know he's the law around here."

"Then I'll find my own way out."

"How?" Doc ran a hand over his face. "Maybe Henry and Sheila and I can break you out."

Caleb scoffed. "I just can't see you three shooting your way in here, Doc. Sheila and Henry, maybe."

"You know we'll do it, if that's what you want. But then what? Will you run? Hide for the rest of your days?"

"I've done my share of running. No more."

"Then what?"

Caleb thought of the fear and the pain Elijah Starr inflicted on the students at his Indian training school. And on him. And on his own wife.

"He killed my mother." His voice was icy cold. "I will avenge her death."

Doc stood, glanced at Sheila, and moved to the barred window. The late-afternoon sun was throwing slanting rays against his troubled face. He finally turned and looked at Caleb.

"And how are you going to do that? Patterson has been building an army of gunmen, and Starr is as protected as the judge."

"Don't matter. I'll get to him."

"I have no doubt you can. It's known from here to Deadwood that there's no man with a quicker draw. But I know you, and you're not a cold-blooded killer. There are plenty of men in these parts who will stab another fellow in the back over a trifle, but you're not one of them."

Doc was partly right. Caleb wouldn't stab the man in the back. He'll be looking directly into his father's face when he killed him. He wanted the viper to know who was twisting the blade or holding the smoking gun.

A voice came from the other side of the bars. "You

could have killed him before, but you didn't. You are not him."

Those were the words she'd spoken to him that day at the cabin. She said them now as if she still believed them. Caleb lifted his gaze to Sheila's face. She hadn't moved. Anguish was etched in the corners of her eyes and mouth. He'd done that to her.

"I know you could have blasted your way into that hotel today, but you chose not to." Doc sat beside him again and put a hand on Caleb's shoulder. "Why? Because you want justice, but you want a fair fight."

"There ain't no fair fight in putting down a mad dog." Caleb stood. "And Elijah Starr is a mad dog."

"I don't doubt your word, my friend. But men like Eric Goulden don't see him that way. The judge doesn't see him that way. So you have to be smarter."

Doc was right. He had to use his head. A quick draw wasn't enough, not when Starr was hiding behind Patterson's wall of bodyguards. Not when Caleb was stuck inside this cell.

"You're a chess player. Right now, he's the most powerful piece on the board," Doc continued. "Take him down as you would my queen, because he's planning the same fate for you. He'll be moving his pieces into position. Waiting for you."

Caleb turned away. He knew what Doc said was the truth. Looking into his father's face in that dining room, he could see the old viciousness there. Starr would chip away at all of Caleb's defenses just to make him suffer. That was the way his father operated. Elijah Starr took immense satisfaction out of the pain he could inflict before striking the final blow.

"You need to be patient and vigilant, Caleb. I'll go and speak to Patterson again. For the moment, I have value to him because I'm the only doctor in Elkhorn. He has to listen to me. Perhaps if he thinks you've come to your senses, that you won't stand against him, I can get him to let you out."

"I ain't doing no groveling. And I ain't making peace."

"Fine. But you've already saved Patterson's hide enough times that there's no way he can forget that he owes you. Maybe that will be enough."

"Please, Marlowe." Sheila's plea reached him. "Let my father try to convince the judge to free you."

He looked at her and then at Doc. They were the only two people anywhere who treated him like family. Even if he didn't deserve it.

Caleb gave a curt nod. It was the smarter play. He'd lay low and wait to make his move.

It was a game of chess where checkmate meant death… for someone.

CHAPTER TWELVE

HENRY JORDAN SAT BACK IN HIS CHAIR AND STRETCHED as he glanced around the saloon. Now that Caleb was out of jail and back on the ranch, Henry was glad to have his old routine back. Tonight, he'd been playing poker for several hours, and his luck, so far, was holding.

The Belle Saloon was loud and busy, as it was every night. About as long and as wide as three railroad cars placed side by side, it was one of the most popular brandy holes in town. A sign on the wall claimed that it was the earliest of Elkhorn's permanent sporting and drinking establishments, and Henry had no reason to doubt it. The Belle was a few doors east of Judge Patterson's courthouse, and the town jail was conveniently located across Main Street.

The bar itself—a solid, gleaming mass of pine—ran lengthwise along the left side of the room. It could easily accommodate a score of men standing comfortably with a drink in hand and still have room to draw and shoot, should the need arise. Behind the barman's alley, four panels of looking glass lined the wall. The mirrors added to the saloon's feeling of spaciousness, but it also allowed the management to watch everyone and everything.

Considering the clientele, Henry thought, keeping an eye on things seemed a damn good idea.

The bartender—a tough, sharp-eyed Scotsman—shouted over the din at one of his assistants, who hurried toward a back room. Scarred and swarthy, the barman had tattoos visible from his throat to his collar and from his cuffs to his fingertips. He'd supposedly sailed the seven seas before landing in here and appeared to bear inked evidence of his travels.

Between Henry and the barman, a miner standing at the bar gestured to the mirror panel closest to the door, explaining a distinctive flaw in the upper corner of the panel to a young fella wearing the stiff new clothes of a greenhorn. A bullet hole and some resultant spider-webbing was the focus of their attention. Legend had it that Bat Masterson himself, stopping in for a drink and a card game on his way to or from Dodge City, had drunkenly wagered he could shoot the odd-numbered horn off a nine-point rack of elk antlers mounted beside the mirror. He'd missed and promptly been escorted out.

Along the right side of the room, a half dozen faro stations stood amidst another dozen tables arranged for poker and drinking. The place was abundantly illuminated by lamps hanging on the walls. A set of stairs broke up the space about a third of the way back from the front door. Four steps climbed to a pulpit-like landing before turning and continuing up to a handful of rooms provided for those seeking feminine companionship.

Off and on all night, a piano player had been plying

his trade on the tinny-sounding instrument at the foot of the stairs. This was the music man Paddy liked to come and listen to. He was a gray-bearded fellow with a wooden leg—a trophy from the Battle of Chancellorsville, Henry had heard. Right now, he was standing with the sheriff, Zeke Vernon, who was working his way through a bottle at the end of the bar.

The Belle had it all, and business tonight was brisk. There were fifty or sixty men in the place. The buzz of lively conversation filled the air, along with clouds of smoke and rough laughter. The card tables were nearly full, and the whiskey and brandy were flowing. Women were dealing faro or circulating flirtatiously, while two assistants to the barman were running back and forth delivering drinks. The burly bouncer sat attentively on a stool by the front door, his ever-present Greener coach gun leaning against the wall beside him.

Henry turned his attention back to the game. He was sitting with three fellas at a table about halfway down the saloon. A side door into an alley stood open, and he liked this table for that reason. Fresh air was a good thing, what with the smoke and the ripe smells of unwashed, hard-working men.

One of the players, a miner everyone knew as Fingers, was struggling to shuffle. The others were casting annoyed looks at him fumbling with the cards, but the difficulty was understandable, considering the fella had only half of a pointer finger and a thumb on his right hand. The impatience of the other players was to be expected, though.

They were looking to win back some of the money sitting in front of Henry.

The seat next to him had just been vacated by a player who decided to try his luck at faro. Henry winced as he caught the strong, familiar perfume of the woman who slid into the chair. He didn't have to look to know who was back.

"Hello again, Henry," she cooed.

He expelled a breath through puffed-out cheeks. "Mariah."

"Still doing good tonight, I see."

"I might be doing better if that seat was filled with some fella interested in playing poker."

She pouted and pushed back a red curl that hung by her ear. "Don't blame a girl for having a soft spot for you."

"We already talked this out." Henry didn't want to be mean to her, but he didn't like her hanging around him. Mariah was a working girl with a job to do, and they'd had their moment, but it was past.

The deal went around. Henry looked at his down card and immediately folded. Maybe his luck wasn't gonna hold.

The Belle wasn't a large saloon in comparison with other establishments in Elkhorn. There were a growing number of places for entertainment, showier and more pretentious than this place. Most of them offered the triple *w*'s—whiskey, whores, and wagering—but Henry liked the well-lit, friendly feel of the Belle. At least, that was the lie he kept telling himself.

Right then, the noise in the saloon suddenly dimmed, and the real reason he came here and nowhere else came gliding down the steps.

Gleaming curls of long, black hair were piled atop the woman's head and held in place by ivory and silver combs. Skin the color of summer prairie grass glowed in the lantern light. Ample curves of breasts teased above the silver drape of the dress that hugged every soft angle. The flare of hips needed no dresser's skill. Her face was a work of art. Large, black eyes and the delicate arch of her eyebrows dominated high, smooth cheekbones. But her full lips, the color of wild roses, knocked every thought from a man's head.

Belle Constant, owner and proprietor, stopped at the landing, one hand on the railing, the other on the shapely curve of her hip.

Damn, but she was a sight.

"You're gawking."

Henry ignored the voice in his ear.

From his first visit at her saloon, Henry had been smitten. He had a weakness for beautiful women. He'd be the first to admit it. But Belle was a goddess. And he wanted her.

"You oughta haul your tongue back in, Henry." Mariah wasn't giving up.

He'd come to realize the landing on the stairs was Belle's favorite spot. From there, she could survey her entire domain. She was the reason the saloon was so well run. A glance at the Scots barman got a slight nod in return. The same subtle exchange with the bouncer. All's well.

"Ante up, Jordan," one of the players said.

Belle absently pressed a finger against her lower lip, and Henry stared. He wanted to kiss those lips.

"I'm out this hand," he replied, not ready to take his eyes off her.

As far as Henry had seen, Belle didn't drink with customers, didn't sleep with them, didn't do any favors. She was the queen, and this saloon was her palace.

"You never stared at me that way," Mariah complained, beginning to sound peevish.

"Don't you have something to do? Some other fella to pester?"

Belle turned slightly on the landing, and her silver dress brushed against the railing. It was a sad day when Henry was jealous of a damn railing.

Mariah's hand moved onto Henry's lap. "I can give you whatever you're hankering for, cowboy."

He took her hand in his and gently pushed it away. "I'm fine eyeing that pretty one up there."

She scowled, and her chair scraped a few inches away but not far enough to suit Henry.

"Her Christian name ain't even Belle. It's Beulah."

"Shocking."

"And she's real plain without all the paint."

"Don't tell me."

Belle's watchful eyes paused at Henry's table, and he raised his glass to her as she held his gaze for a moment.

The sound of shouts erupted from a table of rowdy cowpunchers in the front corner of the place, ending the magical moment.

"Those boys ain't going to be here long, I'd wager," Mariah continued, turning her plump face toward the cowboys. "She don't like men. Especially the rowdy ones."

Henry let the comment pass. He'd seen fellas tossed out on their ears if it looked like they'd let their brandy or whiskey get the better of them. At the first sign of a ruckus, a mere raised eyebrow from her would send her bouncer into action. And there were always a few patrons who were happy to assist in ejecting the offender out into the street.

Henry looked back at Belle. Another woman went up the stairs, and the two put their heads together, whispering.

It was rumored Belle kept a pistol strapped to each calf. He wouldn't mind finding out the truth of it personally.

"You can try to catch her eye till the cows come home, hon. She'll never fall for your handsome looks. You ain't her type."

"Nobody's asking you."

"Whaddya say, Jordan?" the dealer groused. "You still playing?" The other men around the table were eyeing him and his winnings.

Newly dealt cards lay in front of him. He picked up his down card and glanced at it.

"Not this hand." He tossed the cards onto the center of the table.

Belle's attention turned to the piano man who was still jawing with the sheriff. Henry's eye traced her perfect profile. She shot another look at the barman and nodded toward the musician. The Scotsman rapped a knuckle on the pine surface, and the man quickly went to the instrument and struck up a lively tune.

Belle turned and moved smoothly up the stairs with her friend right behind her. Henry drank down his glass of whiskey and placed it on the table. Maybe it was time to call it a night. His luck had definitely changed. And what was stirring inside of him, there was nobody here to satisfy it.

No sooner had the thought of leaving crossed his mind than he heard over the music a drunken, gravelly voice that he recognized on the far side of the saloon.

"Move over, you."

Henry turned his head in time to see Frank Stubbs shove his way to the bar. A short, bowlegged miner glared and grumbled but made room. Stubbs just couldn't help making friends wherever he went.

"Brandy," he barked at the barman, rapping a stout walking stick on the pine. "Double."

"My man is here," Mariah murmured. "Last chance, Jordan."

Henry shook his head in disgust. Some people never smartened up. This was the same woman who'd complained loud and clear about Stubbs's rough treatment.

The mine owner leaned heavily on the bar and swung his gaunt horse face around, searching the saloon.

Henry had seen his neighbor a few times, notably when Stubbs nearly put a hole in his head up by the pond the day Henry and Caleb fought Mad Dog McCord's gang. But he never truly realized how ugly the sonovabitch was until now.

Above the raggedy, brown moustache trailing down both sides of his thin lips, his unshaved cheek bulged with tobacco. Small, black eyes—dull as cloth buttons—were bunched up against either side of a crooked nose. Henry couldn't help but think that more than a few men must have enjoyed knocking that beak around. And that scar up in Stubbs's eyebrow was itching for a match above the other eye.

As always, he was wearing a dark-brown coat and a black vest. His brown bowler was tipped forward on his forehead. The only addition to his attire that Henry could see was the Colt Peacemaker he was wearing strapped to his waist.

The dark eyes fixed on Henry for a long moment before flicking toward Mariah.

"He's coming," she said. "Now or never."

Stubbs downed his drink as soon as it arrived and ordered another.

Henry recalled a favorite saying of his father's. "Coals to Newcastle." Wherever that was.

The next hand was being dealt, and he looked at his down card. Not overly promising, but it had possibilities. Good for a street or maybe two. Maybe he'd hang around.

Mariah put her hand on top of his. Henry pushed it away again.

His next card dropped. As he got ready to fold, Stubbs lurched up to the table, reeking of old brandy, chewing tobacco, and sweat.

"Let's go, you," he growled to Mariah, his words slurring.

Without waiting for a response, Stubbs threw a five-dollar piece on the table in front of her and went out the side door.

"You had your chance, Jordan," she said lightly, rising to her feet.

Fingers spoke up. "That fella's a low-down dog, miss."

The others mumbled their agreement.

She shrugged. "I can handle him."

Henry shook his head. "Don't be a fool, Mariah."

"You're the fool, Henry," she scoffed, picking up Stubbs's money from the table.

With a flourish, she turned her back on him. A moment later, she'd disappeared out the door into the alley.

Henry stared at the table for a moment and then tried to shrug it off. Mariah was a grown woman in a rough profession, he told himself. She knew what she was getting into. The first time they'd met here, he'd stood up for her against Stubbs. But since then, he'd realized she had a destructive streak in the way she acted. Tonight was a good example of it.

"She went out there on her own two feet," Fingers told him, as if reading his mind. "If she gets herself into trouble with that mangy dog, well, she brung it on herself."

"Whose deal is it?" Henry barked.

"Yours," Fingers said.

"Then ante up, you no-account four-flushers."

Henry concentrated on shuffling the cards and was set to deal when the shriek came from the alley, loud enough to be heard over the piano music.

He was on his feet in the blink of an eye. Racing out into the passageway, he looked right and left. A burning lamp hung from a hook on the wall beside the door, casting light on the barrels and crates stacked against the walls of the Belle and the haberdashery next door. A wagon had been left toward the back of the alley, and he saw a movement by the right wheel, followed by the sound of wood on flesh and a cry of pain.

The stick rose to strike her again, but Henry was there before it could fall. Grabbing the cane, he dragged Stubbs backward and drove a fist into his lower back. The mine owner released the weapon, and it flew off into the darkness, clattering against the barrels.

As Stubbs staggered to right himself, Henry realized the man still had Mariah's wrist in his grasp. Henry stepped forward, planting his foot and pivoting his upper body sharply. His big fist arced through the air and caught his neighbor right below the left eye, flush on the cheekbone.

Stubbs released his grip on Mariah's wrist as his battered face snapped around and his hat flew off into the dark. He staggered backward, landing heavily against a broken crate.

The man shook his head and pulled himself upright,

spitting out a chaw of tobacco. He was blinking hard to clear his vision, but Henry judged the problem could be as much from drink as it was from the blow.

"Who the hell do you think you are?" Stubbs rasped. He had either blood or tobacco juice on his chin.

"I warned you before. You don't beat that woman."

"She come out here. Nobody dragged her out."

"Not for no beating." Henry felt his temper about to blow. "Nor for no killing, neither."

"I've had it with your do-gooder interfering, Jordan."

"And I've had it with you, Stubbs."

"You threatening me, shit bird? I paid for that whore. I'll do what I like."

"I'll kill you before you raise that cane again to her or any woman."

"Will you now?" Stubbs's hand was on the Peacemaker pouched at his hip.

"If you think this is our time, come on." Henry unhooked the thong over the hammer of his own six-gun. "'Cuz I owe you a bullet, and I'm ready to put you in the ground, once and for all."

The shotgun blast from the Greener sounded like cannon fire in the confines of the alley, and both Henry and Stubbs looked back at the door.

Zeke and the bouncer stood in front of a small crowd that had pushed out into the passageway.

"What in hellfire do I need to do to keep you two from killing each other?" the sheriff barked, pointing his bristly eyebrows at them.

Stubbs started to respond but stopped dead when the bouncer pointed the Greener directly at his chest.

"Stubbs," Zeke continued, "I'd say nobody wants to hear nothing you have to say."

Two women hurried by Henry and gathered up the injured Mariah. She was bleeding from her nose and holding her arm as they helped her back into the saloon.

Belle had arrived at the doorway, watching the spectacle. She came forward, and the crowd separated like the Red Sea. Silence fell over the alleyway. Her steps were measured, her eyes flashing. She walked past Henry and stood before Stubbs. Her voice was cold as death when she spoke.

"The next time you step foot in my place, my man will cut you in half with that shotgun before you even hear the blast."

Stubbs stared for a moment, then scooped up his hat. Not waiting to look for his cane, he jammed his bowler on his head and lurched off past the crowd and disappeared into the darkness of the alley.

Henry felt a hand on his sleeve and looked down into brown eyes so deep, a man could lose himself in them. He'd never before gotten close enough to see the flecks of gold at the edges.

"Mr. Jordan," Belle said in a voice like velvet, "there's a drink waiting for you inside."

She knew his name.

CHAPTER THIRTEEN

CALEB STOOD ON THE PORCH OF HIS CABIN AND studied the mountain peaks to the south and west of the valley. Snow in the summits gleamed like silver in the rays of the midmorning sun. Clouds clung to the deep ravines and passes between them, looking like gray-white blankets draped over the deep green of the conifers.

Winter was coming. The cold was settling in. His breaths formed miniature versions of those clouds before disappearing into thin air.

There was no doubting that the long, hard season lay just around the bend, and his gaze settled on the diminished herd grazing far down the valley. Caleb was beginning to wonder if the herd of longhorns coming up from Texas would need to winter over somewhere to the south. He and Henry had started supplying beef to the butchers and eating establishments in Elkhorn, but they'd need to replenish their herd soon.

Three weeks had passed since Caleb went for his father's throat in the Silver Elk Hotel. Doc's influence with the judge had secured his freedom, under certain conditions. He was to keep his distance from Elijah Starr. Any show of violence against the new top employee of Judge

Patterson, and Caleb would find himself back in the pokey and the key lost. Grudgingly, he accepted the deal.

Bear trotted up onto the porch and dropped a good-sized cock pheasant at his feet. Clearly proud of himself, he sat beside his master and leaned heavily against his leg to have his head patted. Caleb obliged.

"Good boy. Always work to do, ain't there?" The brilliant red, green, and blue markings of the bird's head and neck shimmered in the sunlight. "That's a big one."

He'd let Henry pluck and clean the bird for their supper.

Staying away from Elkhorn had shown results on the ranch. It appeared anger and frustration only made him work harder. He and Henry had finished digging the well, striking water last week, and the roof on the second cabin was done yesterday. His partner could finish whatever was left to do to make his new quarters livable. Logs he'd hauled down in the spring were sawn and ready to split for firewood. The grain storage building was next.

As it did ten times a day, the image of his father's smirking face edged into his mind's eye, and Caleb felt the churning feeling return in his gut.

He told himself for the hundredth time that the day would come for them to settle accounts. Doc had vouched for him, and Caleb couldn't let his friend down. He had to wait, but he wasn't too good at it.

In the meantime, Henry and Gabe and Paddy kept him up to date on Elijah Starr. A couple of weeks ago, Starr had taken some of Patterson's men and gone off to Denver, supposedly to work out whatever deals and arrangements needed to be made to facilitate bringing the rail line to Elkhorn.

As Caleb had finished up his chores this morning, he'd decided he was going to town. It wasn't just his restlessness that was finally getting to Caleb. Hunkering down on the ranch was grating on his nerves. Damned if he wasn't starting to feel like he was cowering out here like a rabbit in his burrow.

And Caleb, by nature, was no damn rabbit.

His Winchester was leaning against the porch post. He picked it up and headed toward the barn. He was going into Elkhorn to check on things himself.

Before he got ready, he'd told Henry he was going for flour and other supplies. That was enough reason to go, not that he needed any.

"I ain't too sure I trust you going into Elkhorn on your own," Henry called out as Caleb swung the saddle up onto Pirate's back.

In spite of the chill in the air, Henry was stripped to the waist, scraping the hide of an elk they shot yesterday. The meat would be good eating, and the skin was destined to be a winter coat for him.

"I reckon you'll have to get over that."

"What if Starr is back in town?"

"I'll deal with it."

"Don't make me school you on how this ranch needs the *two* of us."

"You. Schooling me about that." Caleb shook his head in amusement.

Henry hadn't asked a single question after the word got around that Elijah Starr was Caleb's father. If he was interested in why Caleb was set on spilling the man's blood, he'd never once even hinted at it. He and Henry were friends and partners, but neither pried into the other's past. Where a man came from and what he did before was his own business.

This conversation was about the closest they'd come to talking about it.

Henry watched as Caleb slid his rifle into its saddle holster. "You got the look of a man that needs reminding."

"We need supplies. I ain't going in looking for a shoot-out. Not today, anyway."

"Good to know." Henry picked up his sharpening stone. "While you're in town, you might wanna have a chat with Malachi."

"About what?"

"About what Paddy was asking you. About moving out here."

"I ain't made up my mind."

"Still, that boy is their family right now. They got a say about where he goes."

Caleb nodded. His partner was right. Before he got himself all worked up about whether Henry and him were ready to have a twelve-year-old boy move onto the ranch, he needed to talk to the Rogers family.

The yellow dog had carried his hunting trophy over to Henry.

"That's our supper," Caleb said. "Along with some of that elk."

His partner had something else on his mind. "That a clean shirt under that vest and coat?"

"What of it?"

"Hell, boy. You washed up and shaved too. What gives? As if I don't know."

"I ain't stopping at the Belle, if that's what you're asking."

A grin tugged at the corner of Henry's mouth. Damned if that dog wasn't wearing the same expression.

"I wouldn't be going to the Belle, neither, if I'd been invited in for sugar cookies with Doc's daughter."

Caleb shook his head. He should never have mentioned that Sheila occasionally baked sugar cookies for him and Doc on their chess nights.

"And I ain't planning on stopping at Doc's."

"'Course not," Henry scoffed. "But you cleaned up anyway, thinking you just *might*."

"I need to be getting along."

"I admit, three weeks of not seeing Miss Sheila's pretty face is a helluva long time."

Caleb checked the cinch on his saddle.

Henry addressed the dog. "Bear, don't you reckon it's a good idea if this miserable old cuss stops and sees the lady? Didn't you tell me yesterday that Caleb's been ornery as hell one minute and mooning like a schoolboy the next?"

Bear wagged his tail.

"That's it. I ain't gonna waste my day shooting the shit with you two. I'd say there's plenty of work waiting to be done."

Pirate pawed the dirt in agreement. Caleb climbed into the saddle.

"Give my regards to Miss Sheila," his pain-in-the-ass partner called as Caleb nudged the buckskin into motion. "And be sure to tell her we'd be honored to have her Christmas gala here at the ranch."

As Caleb started off across the meadow toward town, he could hear Henry still talking to Bear.

Caleb crossed the river at a shallow stretch, and he noted that the water was even lower than it had been. The lack of rain during the summer and fall was showing. He looked again at the dark-green slopes of spruce and pine, rising to gray cliffs in the west. Soon the snow would reach here too, the thaw eventually filling the lakes and streams for the coming year. For now, there was enough water for his cattle and the herd on the way. That's what mattered.

Caleb kept his eyes on the trail as he rode along, but his mind kept turning to Sheila. It was true. He *did* miss seeing her pretty face. The last time they'd seen each other, she was standing on the other side of the bars in Elkhorn's jail, staring at him with the weight of the world on her shoulders. He hated having done that to her.

The fact was that Caleb had taken on a life that brought cares and responsibilities he never had before. When he was off tracking and hunting and scouting with Old Jake and afterward, he'd pretty much had no one to worry about but himself. All he needed was his horse and his gun. The frontier provided the rest. And if he had something that needed to be done, he went out and did it. There was no waiting or hunkering down and very little worrying how his actions would affect someone else.

His life was all different now. He knew that his father walked free and his mother lay in her grave, unavenged. That needed to be taken care of. The work on the ranch tired his body and occupied his mind, but it was a distraction from what he needed to do. He had no control over whether to face the wind or put his back to it. For the first time since he was a boy, he had his doubts if he'd even survive the coming storm.

One thing he was sure of, he wanted Sheila far from the danger that was looming ahead. Starr knew she was important to Caleb. He'd used her once before to try to get at him. Caleb couldn't allow that to happen again.

He was still a mile from town, and the trail was following the river. Suddenly, Pirate's ears flicked forward, and Caleb felt his hackles rise. Reining in the gelding, he listened carefully but heard only the sound of the river flowing over the rocks. Just ahead, the river widened out into a marshy area.

Scanning the forest around him, he saw nothing unusual. A squirrel was busily gathering nuts for the coming winter. Some black-capped chickadees were flitting about, as well as a pair of gray jays. But if he was heading into an ambush, he saw no sign of it yet.

Caleb unfastened the thong on one of his Colts and drew it slowly from its holster. Urging Pirate ahead, he kept his eyes in motion, scanning the shadows and dappled light coming through the trees.

When he passed a sapling, he saw it. It stood in the water on the far side of the marshy area, less than forty yards away. Way too close.

The moose raised his massive head and stared at Caleb. His majestic antlers spread close to seven feet across, and marsh grass hung from his muzzle. He wasn't chewing. Just staring.

Caleb considered the chances of the beast charging. He knew from experience that there was no way of knowing how it would go.

Years ago, he and Old Jake had been leading a party up into the Montana gold fields. One night, they'd camped alongside the shallow end of a broad lake. The wise, old frontiersman had wanted to bed down for the night on a rise some distance from the water, telling his charges they'd be pestered by bloodthirsty insects of every variety. But the miners, exhausted from the trek, had simply thrown down their gear and set up camp close to the water. Jake and Caleb had retreated to the rise for the night.

Just before dawn, the two scouts arrived to gather the travelers, only to find a bull moose standing in the shallows. Some of the miners lay wide-eyed in their bedrolls. Others stood frozen with fear at the sight.

Even in the dim light, Caleb saw the eyes of the moose widen, showing the whites. His ears flattened back against his head, and the animal threw back his head like a horse. That should have been warning enough. When he charged, the closest men to the water couldn't get away quickly enough. One was tossed a good six feet into the air, scooped aloft by the wide antlers. A second was knocked down and kicked. Before the moose could do any more damage, Old Jake took the animal down with a single shot from his .45–110 Sharps, a rifle designed for far greater distance but certainly lethal at this distance.

Caleb holstered his Colt. He'd never stop this one with it, and he'd only make him angry.

Slowly, he pulled Pirate's head around and nudged him off the trail and into the trees. Working through the forest, he cut a wide arc around the marshy spot. When the man and horse finally returned to the trail, he saw from a safe distance that the moose had returned to his feeding.

Even though it was nearly midday when he rode into Elkhorn, Main Street showed far less activity than usual. A few wagons loaded with supplies and homesteaders still worked their way along, and the noon stage was loading up in preparation for the trip up the Denver road. A few urchins ran with dogs, drawing the ire of miners and shop-keepers. But the temperature was dropping, and a sharp wind whistled down from the hills. For the most part, folks on foot went about their business with purpose, coats and collars pulled snug, hats clung to tightly.

No one paid any attention to Caleb as he rode through town except for one of Zeke's deputies, who stood in the door of the jail with a heavy blanket around him. The lawman signaled to two guards standing on the sidewalk in front of the judge's courthouse and land office, but they shrugged, not caring.

Caleb figured Elijah Starr hadn't yet returned to town.

Turning the corner, Caleb dismounted under the sign MALACHI ROGERS LIVERY. HORSES BOUGHT, SOLD, AND BOARDED.

The greeting was far more cordial as Paddy ran out from the stable with a broad smile and took the reins from Caleb.

The livery establishment belonging to Gabe's father was one of two in Elkhorn. A large, wood-plank barn with a good-sized loft space for hay, the business had a wagon yard and a fenced corral. Inside the wide entry doors, the left side of the building consisted of a small office space with a cot where Paddy slept, and beyond that was a row of enclosures for storing oats. The back wall had stalls for horses, and on the right side, Malachi's forge and anvil sat under wide, overhanging eaves facing the corral.

"We didn't know you was coming to town, Mr. Marlowe. Gabe and I are planning to come to the ranch tomorrow. But everyone says we got snow coming, and Miz Rogers says we can't go if it's bad."

Malachi Rogers himself came out of the stable. "And you always listen to what Miz Rogers says. Don't you, Paddy?"

"Yes, sir." The ginger-haired boy hesitated and reddened. "Well, mostly."

Caleb figured there was more to this than they were saying. He knew the twelve-year-old had his moments. And from what he could recall, not always following directions and leaving jobs half-done was not so unusual for a fella that age.

"Take Mr. Marlowe's horse in and take care of him."

"Yessir," Paddy said, leading Pirate in.

"Trouble?" Caleb asked.

Malachi chuckled. "Nothing that a talking-to from Miz Rogers won't fix."

A former buffalo soldier, Rogers was clear-eyed, dark-skinned, and of medium height. He had the broad shoulders and massive arms of a man who'd put in his years muscling livestock and hammering hot iron into horseshoes and other necessities. He was wearing a well-brushed, black stovepipe hat and a gray wool coat over a black waistcoat and cotton shirt, buttoned at the neck. He was carrying the leather apron he wore when smithing.

The first time Caleb brought his horse in to be boarded, he spotted the blue cap of the Ninth Cavalry hanging from a peg on the wall of the tiny office. In the conversation that ensued, Malachi had been happy to talk about how he'd ended up settling with his family in Elkhorn.

Rogers had served as a corporal in a unit stationed at Fort Stockton. While he was there, he'd seen more action than he cared to. Luckily, his hitch was up around the time his regiment was sent to Fort Union in New Mexico in '75. It hadn't been a difficult decision. He'd hung up his spurs and made his way north to Colorado. At the time, Elkhorn was little more than a ragtag community of tents, log cabins, and mud. The son of a blacksmith himself, Malachi knew his trade, and the fledgling town needed him.

Caleb heard the boys' laughter from inside the livery and thought of what Henry suggested before he'd left.

"You and Miz Rogers done real good by Paddy since taking him in last spring."

Malachi looked over his shoulder and smiled. "Tough little varmint, but he's a good boy."

"I know I ain't in any position to be making a decision right now, but sometime in the future, how'd you feel about him moving out to the ranch?"

Rogers glanced inside the barn again. "The way my wife thinks, the more is always the merrier at our table. And that table will be stretching soon."

"Is the missus in a family way?"

"No." Malachi shook his head. "I got two nephews coming out from Memphis, so it'll be four of them running around here by spring."

"Won't things be a mite tight for you?"

"We'll make do. We always have," Malachi said. "But Paddy has a fondness for you. And although he and Gabe have become good friends, you ain't so far away."

"I still have a lot of sorting out to do."

"I understand. But whenever the time comes that you're ready for Paddy, we'll be good with it. And of course, he'll always be welcome here."

"All right," Caleb replied, looking into the barn. He had a few things to take care of right now, but it was good to know that Rogers would be fine with whatever decision was made.

"All this talk about the boys and I got distracted with telling you the news."

"What news?"

Malachi tossed the apron onto his shoulder. "Three fellas arrived at the livery around dawn. Two of them were shot, one pretty bad. I sent them up to Doc's house."

John Burnett's medical skills were sought after from here to Denver. The man's value on the Colorado frontier was without measure. And since Sheila's arrival in Elkhorn, she'd started helping her father at the house with his patients. This worried Caleb some. Not everyone that showed up at their door was bound to be an entirely upstanding citizen.

"One of them knew you."

Caleb felt a bad taste rise into his throat.

"A lean, tough Mexican cowboy. Stands about this high." Malachi held up a hand, indicating the man's height. "Talks like a Texan, and he's near as dark as me. Said his name's Ortiz."

Damn.

Duke Ortiz, the fella driving Caleb's thousand head of longhorns up from Texas.

CHAPTER FOURTEEN

CALEB CLIMBED THE STEPS TO DOC BURNETT'S PORCH and rapped on the door.

This was not good. He'd sent nearly every last dollar he and Henry had for the herd of longhorns Duke Ortiz was supposed to drive up from Texas. Now, from the looks of things, he had a couple of wounded cowpunchers and no cattle. He hoped the rest of Duke's men were off watching the herd somewhere close. Winter was about to roll in and bury them all.

Hearing no one coming to the door, he knocked again and then went and peered in the front parlor window. Through the glass, he saw Mrs. Lewis hurrying toward him from the back of the house. The woman always reminded Caleb of a prairie dog—small and wiry and quick, with a pinched face and a nervous way about her. She was the wife of the hardware store owner and had been helping keep house for Doc since before Sheila arrived.

Mrs. Lewis pulled open the door and ushered him in. "Come on through, Mr. Marlowe. It's fortunate that you've come. I heard the cowboys talking about you."

"They hurt, ma'am?"

"Two of them are. Doc is working on the one who's

hurt the worst. Miss Sheila is helping him. The other two are sitting outside the surgery door in the back hallway." She shook her head. "They refused to wait in the back parlor or the kitchen, even. Said they wouldn't muddy up the place with blood and trail dust."

Caleb went past her along the wide central hallway. An open stairway to the second floor was ahead of him and to the right. The steps turned at a landing and formed an arch over the downstairs hallway. Beyond the arch, at the end of the narrower passageway, he could see the trail boss and his companion sitting on kitchen chairs outside the closed door to the surgery.

The two men stood up as soon as they spotted Caleb and waited until Mrs. Lewis disappeared into the kitchen.

"Marlowe," Ortiz said grimly.

"Duke."

Ortiz hadn't changed much since Caleb last saw him. That was at Duke's Texas ranch, five years ago. A couple of inches under six feet, he was—as Malachi described him—lean and tough. His complexion was not as dark as his companion—a blend of a Mexican father and a Black mother—but his face had developed the deep lines of a man who'd spent a great deal of time in the sun and as much time worrying.

Caleb saw how bone-weary both men looked. They'd shed filthy trail coats that hung on the backs of their chairs. Their wide-brimmed, sweat-stained hats lay on the floor, and the man with Ortiz was wearing a bloody sling on his left arm.

Both men wore the clothing of their trade. Bandanas, heavy woolen shirts under leather vests, scarred cowhide chaps over the pants, and sturdy boots that showed the dirt and the wear of the trail. Duke had given up wearing the sash of the vaquero, but his bandana was still the traditional bright-red silk of his Mexican forebears.

"What happened to you? What are you doing here? Where's the herd?"

"We lost it," Ortiz said straight out.

"What do you mean you lost it? Lost it how? I trusted you, Duke."

"We was bushwhacked. They took the herd. Killed nine good men. These two are all I got left."

Caleb tried to take this in. A thousand head of cattle lost. Nine dead.

How was that possible? A hundred questions exploded in his head.

"This is bullshit, Duke." Caleb's temper boiled over. Everything he had, everything he'd put into their future was gone. "You've done this a hundred times. You never lost a damn herd in your life."

"Damn right." Duke was fired up, as well. "Don't think I just handed them critters over."

"You sure as hell don't have them *now*." Caleb slammed his hat on the floor. "Damn it. I thought you were good."

"I *am* good, *cabron*. Give me a damn minute to explain. I'm here, ain't I? I didn't hightail it back to Texas, did I?"

"Texas ain't big enough for you to hide from me."

"You know me, Marlowe. Say what you will, but I know you trust me. Just listen to me."

If he didn't know this man, if he didn't trust him, he'd be painting these walls with Texan blood. And when he was done, there wouldn't be enough of him left for Doc to piece together.

Caleb reminded himself that he was standing in Doc's house. Beyond the door, Sheila and Doc Burnett were trying to patch a man up.

"How?" he managed to get out through clenched teeth.

"We was ambushed. By rustlers."

"Rustlers." Caleb glared at him. "You ain't no greenhorn."

The trail boss's eyes darted fire. "No, I ain't no greenhorn, and neither were my men."

Mrs. Lewis poked her head out of the kitchen for the tenth time since the argument started. She was trying to catch Caleb's eye.

"I'm putting on coffee," she chirped as brightly as she could manage. "Would you fellows care for a cup?"

The cowboy standing behind Ortiz answered, "No, ma'am. But thankee."

Ortiz shook his head, and Caleb declined, as well.

Caleb waited until the woman went back into the kitchen before speaking again. "That thousand head cost me everything I got. This'll ruin me."

Duke shook his head. "You know better. Marlowe. I'll make good on this."

"How?"

"I'm going after the rustlers."

"And what if you can't find 'em? What if you can't get the cattle back?"

"I'll go down home to Texas and gather another herd. I'll drive them up here next spring. I'll start early and deliver by late summer. I'll eat half the cost. And you don't pay till I deliver."

Caleb considered the offer. The money had already changed hands. Any other rancher would just call it tough luck and move on. But Ortiz was trying to do the right thing.

"You are being decent."

Ortiz slapped Caleb on the shoulder. "Them dirty *pendejos* won't think so when I find them."

"We'll make 'em pay, boss."

Caleb looked at the wounded man standing behind Ortiz. He had a blood-soaked cloth wrapped around his upper arm.

"This here is Bass Dart, Marlowe." Duke gestured to the surgery door. "Tex Washington is in with the doc right now."

Caleb nodded to the cowboy. "Doc'll fix you up."

"First time being shot by rustlers, but I'll live."

Rustlers were a problem everywhere, but cattlemen had been driving longhorns up from Texas for over a decade. The three main cattle routes—the Shawnee Trail, the Chisholm Trail, and the Goodnight-Loving Trail— were well known to men like Duke Ortiz. When Caleb had been up in Greeley, he heard a fella say that he figured over a million head had already traveled those trails.

The westernmost route, the Goodnight-Loving Trail, was the only one that passed through Colorado. Starting near Fort Concho in Texas, it ran west until it picked up the Pecos River then north all the way to Denver. From there, Texas cattle often went as far as Cheyenne. All told, the drive north could cover two thousand miles. Duke wasn't going all the way to Wyoming this trip, but that route from Texas was the way he'd planned on coming.

A cattle drive was hard going, and it always had its dangers, but Ortiz knew what he was doing. Or should have.

"No one ever got the drop on you before, Duke. What happened?"

"Do you want the short version or long?"

"Start from the beginning."

"We left my ranch figuring, with a little luck, we'd make it up here before the snow shut us down. It was a good herd, Marlowe. 'Course, we hit a few snags along the way. We were still in Texas when a prairie fire burned out everything west of Horsehead Crossing for fifty miles. We had to go south to get around the charred grass. Then we lost two weeks rounding up the herd after a *pinche perra* of a hailstorm hit us south of Fort Sumner. Even so, I thought we'd beat the winter snows."

"Did you cross the Arkansas River west of Pueblo?" Caleb asked.

"We did. We left Goodnight there. Followed the river where we could. We'd driven the herd north around a place called Charlotte Falls. We had the mountains ahead of us, and we knew we were at the beginning of the difficult part of the drive."

Caleb knew that area very well. They would have been climbing pretty steadily, and the going would have been slower, but eventually the Arkansas would turn north. His ranch and Elkhorn were a straight shot from there.

"That's where the dirty *culeros* were waiting. We'd been funneled into a narrow pass. For a half mile, we had rocky bluffs above us on both sides." Duke's anger showed in his eyes. "A dozen or so rode right at us from the west, boxing us in. We had nowhere to go. They had the sun behind them, and they were firing their guns and shouting. The herd panicked and turned on itself."

Bass Dart glanced at his boss. "Tell him about the gunmen."

"They had riflemen above us. I don't know how many. There we was, hemmed in good and tight, the cattle in a damn frenzy, and the bastards shot down five of my men before we even knew where it was coming from. By then, the herd was stampeding. Even if I had a hundred men, there was no chance of stopping them. Three of my drag riders got stomped in the run."

Caleb had seen stampeding buffalo and cattle. He knew how deadly the hooves and long horns of these steers could be once the terror got hold of them.

"Here we was in a gunfight and the cattle running. I killed two of the gunners above us, and Bass here got the one that shot him, but then they was gone. And we had nothing but dust and blood and the dead." Duke shook his head. "I followed them for a few miles. But there was nothing I could do against all of them. I think they planned to run them critters till nightfall."

He stopped, staring fiercely at the wall across from him.

"So you went back for your men," Caleb prompted.

Ortiz nodded. "There was only three of us left. They even killed my cook in the mess wagon as they rode by him. A good old man who served my father before me. I knew him from the time I was knee-high to a jackrabbit."

Bass spoke up. "That old fella could cuss up a storm, but he wouldn't hurt nobody. And he could cook too."

The sound of a man's cry came through the surgery door, causing Ortiz to pause. The lines of his face deepened as he stared at the door.

"That fella in there. He's hurt pretty bad?" Caleb asked.

"Tex," Duke said. "He sure is."

"You said you were close to Charlotte Falls. Why didn't you get help there?"

Bass let out a short mirthless laugh, and his boss shot a look at him.

"We stopped there," Ortiz replied. "We couldn't get nobody to look at him. His skin didn't exactly make him too welcome."

Along the established cattle trails, there were plenty of dark-skinned cowboys. There'd always been a mix of colors among the ranch hands in Texas, even before slavery was abolished. After the war, freed men came west from the southern states. Ranchers were glad to hire them and put them to work. In the area around Duke's ranch near Fort Concho, maybe two out of three cowboys were white. The rest were Black and Mexican.

Once Duke left the Goodnight-Loving Trail, though, any chance of a hospitable reception went to hell in a hand basket.

"Elkhorn's a long way from there," Caleb said.

"Took us four days. And it weren't easy, neither. Tex was hurting bad, but he was making it the first day. After that, he got worse and worse. He started with a fever two days ago. He was out of his head. We had to tie that poor boy to his saddle the whole way."

"Where was he shot?"

"In the leg. About halfway down from the knee."

"When we started to take the boot off," Bass put in, "it looked like the foot would come off with it."

That didn't sound good. "Well, ain't no doctor anywhere better than this man."

"Kind of him to take care of us, Marlowe. That's a fact. But I also came here to get you. I'll need help getting your herd back. We both know there ain't nobody better at tracking or handling a gun. But I'll also need a place to leave Tex and Bass to mend."

"Wait," Bass said. "You ain't leaving me here. I'm coming too."

Caleb gestured to the wounded arm. "Doc ain't seen to that, yet. Maybe you oughta see what he says."

"I'm going. Them boys they killed was friends of mine. I owe them sons of bitches."

"If you're fit to ride, I ain't gonna stop you," Duke said, looking back at Caleb. "But Tex is gonna need..."

The discussion came to an abrupt halt and all three came to their feet when the door to the surgery opened and Sheila appeared. Her eyes immediately lit on Caleb, and a brief smile pulled at her lips.

"Good to see you back in town, Marlowe."

He nodded in greeting. Despite the grimness of the situation, he couldn't help but feel that her blue eyes and golden hair brightened the day. Duke's offer of settling their business one way or the other took some of the worry out of it. He could breathe again.

Caleb imagined Sheila and Doc must have been surprised when these men landed on their doorstep. From the looks of her, she'd been hard at work with her father. The apron she wore over her light-blue dress was blotted and streaked with blood. Her own handprints showed at the hips where she'd wiped them. Her sleeves were pushed up above the elbows. Her hair was pulled up and tied out of the way. Despite the circles under her eyes, she was still the most beautiful thing he'd ever seen.

"Your friend is sedated," she told Ortiz. "Doc will speak to you about his condition after he's done with Mr. Dart's arm."

She motioned to Bass, and the injured man followed Sheila through the door.

"Like I said," Caleb said to Duke, "John Burnett is a damn good doctor. He had plenty of practice doing surgery during the war. And he ain't no bogus, two-bit snake-oil man."

The muscles in the cattleman's jaws clenched. "That gunshot looked real bad, Marlowe. But Tex can't survive without his leg. Riding herd is all he knows. And he's damn good at it."

"Wait till you talk to Doc."

Ortiz ran a hand down his weary face. "You probably think I should have gone after the cattle. Track where them *pendejos* took them. But I couldn't let my last two men die."

He'd lost nine men. "I know how you felt about your ranch hands."

"I been lucky, Marlowe. My men are aces at what they do. Or did, I reckon I should say. And brave. They'd fight off a Comanche raiding party for a single dogie. I never rode with a truer gang of men than them that was bringing your steers north. And now they're about gone. They never had a chance with them bushwhackers."

"How long these two fellas been with you?"

"Bass been riding for me for more than four years. Tex been with me for seven. He was only twelve years old when he started rassling longhorns. You know I got no boys of my own. Tex ain't had no family for as long as he can recall, and he was like..." He stopped, fighting to keep his voice steady. "Well, this job is all he got."

"You did right coming here," Caleb said. "We'll find the killers who did this."

The rancher straightened up. "And find your cattle while we're at it."

Caleb certainly planned to. A thousand head of

longhorns left tracks. And there were very few trails the rustlers had to drive them over.

"Once we find them and repay that band of *culeros* for what they done, we'll need help driving them the rest of the way. I reckon we'll find enough saddle stiffs in Pueblo looking for work before winter."

He understood Ortiz's desire to make good on these things, but he was getting ahead of himself. One step at a time.

At least with Henry back, Caleb had the peace of mind that he could leave running of the ranch to his partner. Gabe and Paddy were available to help, but he couldn't rely on them once the snow started piling up.

The sound of a man calling out Duke's name could be heard from the surgery. Caleb and Ortiz pushed to their feet.

Sheila reappeared in the doorway. "The sedative isn't settling your ranch hand. He's asking for you."

Ortiz hurried into the room.

"Mind if I come in?" Caleb asked before Sheila followed. "Maybe I can help."

She thought a moment and nodded. "My father may want to move the patient off the table and onto the bed. Why don't you stay near the door? If you're needed, you'll be close."

He trailed her into the surgery and waited by the door. Doc Burnett lifted his head and acknowledged his presence with a nod.

Caleb had seen the inside of this room more than he

cared to. Immediately, the coppery smell of blood nearly overpowered the bitter odor of the liquids Doc used to clean wounds.

Bright light was streaming in the windows, illuminating the space that was used as a surgery and for consulting with patients. On one side of the room, Doc had a cluttered desk, a bookshelf, and a gun rack holding a rifle and a shotgun. Near it, a worktable had been cleared, and Bass Dart was lying on it. Closer to the door, several tall cabinets stood open, displaying medical instruments and supplies. A bed extended from a nearby wall, and in the center was a high table Doc usually used for operating.

Tex Washington lay on that table. He had a boyish face that was twisted with pain. He was agitated—half-asleep, half-awake—his arms jerking about with sudden spasms that ran through his entire body. Doc and Sheila had removed his leather chaps and cut away his boot and his pant leg to get to the wound, and the lower leg was now covered with a linen cloth from the knee to the ankle. Duke was standing beside the table, leaning over him and talking calmly.

Doc, carrying a bottle of something, crossed the room to Bass Dart. He had a scalpel and other instruments in a shallow pan that he handed to Sheila, who stood beside him at the worktable, assisting.

A moment later, restrained grunts of pain told Caleb that Doc was digging the bullet out of Bass's arm. The cowboy was a tough one. That was for sure.

It took a good fifteen minutes after two pieces of lead

dropped into the pan before Doc was satisfied with his work and another ten for him to stitch and bandage the wound. After helping Bass sit up, he put the arm in a sling and then washed his hands.

"So what do you think, Doc?" Ortiz asked, gesturing to both of his men.

"Bass looks good. He's fortunate that wound didn't fester. It's surprising, really, but we'll take all the good luck we can get." He glanced at the bandaged arm. "If all goes well and he doesn't use it for a week or so, he should heal up nicely."

"Thanks, Doc," Bass told him, glancing at Caleb with a weak grin. "Told you it weren't nothing."

"I wouldn't go that far," Doc said sternly.

"How about Tex?" Duke asked.

Doc frowned. "Not quite the same answer, I'm afraid. You can see he's burning up with fever. That's a bad sign. That alone might kill him. It's hard to tell. What we need to do is keep him on that table and immobile for now. The extra laudanum I gave him should settle him soon."

"What about his leg? Can you fix it?"

Before he could respond, the young cowboy's eyes fluttered open. "Duke…Duke…are ya…?" He was reaching out, and Ortiz took his hand.

"It's okay, Tex. I'm here, *hijo*."

The patient closed his eyes.

Caleb recalled Duke saying that Tex was twelve years old when he took him in. Twelve. Paddy's age.

"Can you save it?" Duke asked again, not lifting his gaze from the young man.

"I did what I could to see if it was possible to piece it together. The bullet sheared off the fibula and shattered the tibia."

Caleb's eyes moved to the wounded limb. The foot extended from the linen covering, kept upright by two rolls of cloth on either side. At least it was still attached. Doc was looking at him from across the room. The quick shake of his head was meant only for Caleb. It conveyed volumes.

Certainly, his friend had done everything in his power for the young man. But that only meant that the choice now lay between saving the life or losing the leg.

"Tell me what that means," Duke said grimly.

"I have to take it off at the knee. And even at that, there's no telling if Tex will survive. But he'll die for sure if I don't amputate now."

Ortiz looked away at the window, his face clenched tightly. Finally, he took a breath and nodded.

Doc told Bass to go out and wait in the kitchen. Sheila helped her father gather what he'd need for the operation.

Caleb steeled himself for what lay ahead.

Tex's eyes were open but unfocused. "Where are you, Duke?"

"Right here," Ortiz answered. "I'm right here."

Two callused hands—one old, one young—held tight to each other.

"I'm scared, Duke. Where are you?"

"I'm right here with you. You'll be fine, son."

CHAPTER FIFTEEN

OVER THE YEARS CALEB HAD BEEN RESPONSIBLE FOR the taking of more lives than he cared to recall.

Compared to the East, the frontier was a violent place, and he lived the only way he knew how. That was who he was. That was the world he lived in. To survive, he'd learned to use the guns that he carried. More often than not, it wasn't the fastest gunman who lived, it was the man more willing to pull the trigger. Many times, he'd killed in self-defense, though not always. Still, he'd always reasoned that the men he killed deserved to die. He'd been a lawman on occasion, and that had required the willingness to kill to protect others who counted on him.

More than those he'd killed, however, there were the men he'd wounded with his guns, his blades, and his hammerlike fists. He himself carried a half dozen scars of various sizes and origins. Knife wounds. Bullet holes. Even a nasty-looking thing on his chest from a hatchet.

The sight and smell of blood and the sound of pain in a man's throat were no strangers to Caleb. He often wondered how he'd become numb to them.

Still, helping in the surgery while Tex Washington's leg was amputated had been difficult for Caleb. Not so much for what the young cowboy would face, though that was a horror, to be sure. But for Ortiz. Watching and listening to Duke as he stayed by the nineteen-year-old, as he spoke to him, as he tried to soothe the boy—all the while hanging on to some shred of hope for the life Tex could have afterward—was as painful as it was inspiring.

It reminded Caleb once again the importance of responsibility.

That night, he rode back to the ranch and had a long talk with Henry about everything that had happened. About the loss of their herd. About his plan to search for them with Ortiz. About what he'd seen in that surgery and what he planned to do. About his talk with Malachi Rogers about Paddy.

He was back at Doc's house early the next morning. The mountain peaks to the west were invisible behind a gray shroud, and Caleb knew that snow was imminent. In spite of it, plans were made that he and Ortiz and Bass would leave the following day. Doc thought it was too early for Bass to be on the road, but Caleb could see that they'd have to tie the cowhand to keep him from coming.

Ortiz asked Caleb for help finding a place for Tex to stay while they were on the road. Caleb and Henry's ranch was too far away from town. Doc wanted his patient closer so he could check on him every day. His practice didn't have rooms for patients, but he would hold on to Tex for as long as it took for arrangements to be made.

Caleb knew there were plenty of new rooming houses operating in town, but he was also well aware that many people and business owners in Elkhorn weren't any better than Charlotte Falls when it came to their treatment of folks with darker skins. Still, he was sure he could find some place for Tex.

Before going off in search for accommodations, though, he needed to talk to Sheila about another matter. Mrs. Lewis went up to fetch her and returned, saying the doctor's daughter had been reading but that she'd be down shortly. He was to wait for her in the back parlor.

Yesterday, she'd assisted her father in the surgery, and Caleb was fairly certain that it had been the first time she'd ever witnessed an amputation. Still, he'd been impressed, as he always was, by her strength and courage in a grim situation. He doubted if anything in her East Coast education or experience could have prepared her for it.

Caleb immediately rose to his feet when she glided into the room. She looked pale to him, and furrows of strain creased her forehead. He wondered if she'd gotten any sleep at all. More alarming, it seemed to him that the spirit and optimism he'd come to associate with Sheila had deserted her, replaced by listlessness.

"Hello, Marlowe. You wanted to talk to me?"

The urge to gather her in his arms was almost overwhelming, but he forced back the desire. What he was considering was going to complicate his life enough. He didn't need to add anything more to it.

He motioned to an upholstered chair, and she sat down. He dragged a straight chair over and sat close to her. He also didn't want this conversation carrying all over the house.

"What would you think of me bringing Paddy out to live on the ranch after I get back from this trip with Ortiz?"

"Have you spoken with Mr. and Mrs. Rogers about it?"

"I talked to Malachi yesterday."

"He's fine with it?"

"Yep, he said Paddy can stay with them whenever he wants."

Her face lit up. "Then I think it's a marvelous idea."

"That right?"

"I do. I like thinking of you looking to the future, instead of…" She stopped and shook her head, obviously realizing that she didn't want to finish saying what was on her mind.

Caleb finished it for her. "Instead of hanging on to the past?"

She nodded.

"I won't let that go. My mother's murderer is out there, and it sits in my craw that I haven't avenged her death. When the time comes, I will right that wrong."

"But think about what you're saying. Elijah Starr is protected by armed men. What will happen to Paddy if something happens to you? He lost his brother. Is he going to lose you too?"

"I don't plan on dying."

"I've seen your father. I know the violence he's capable of. You're underestimating him if you think you're safe going after him."

"Starr has set his sights on killing me, regardless of what I do. I remind him too much of what he did to my mother." Caleb leaned toward her with his forearms on his knees. His voice sounded low and bitter even to himself, but he hoped she would understand. "For him, finding me here was like seeing her climb out of her grave, telling the world what he's done and what he is. One of us has to die, Sheila, but it won't be me. I want you to trust me on that."

Sheila's chin dropped an inch, and she studied the carpet at their feet for a few moments. He sensed that she was trying to decide if there was anything else she could say, if there was more she could add that might sway him. Caleb already knew the answer. There wasn't.

She finally rubbed her arms. The thought of what he planned to do obviously chilled her. When she looked up, sadness was etched in the corners of her eyes. But she pretended to sound enthused, at least.

"Paddy will be so happy. He already thinks of you as his family. What made you decide now?"

"Yesterday, watching Ortiz with Tex. They've known each other since that cowboy was twelve and went to work for him. Duke is the only family the young fella has. And he thinks of Tex as a son."

Fathers and sons. A sacred bond that had nothing to do with blood ties.

His natural father was a monster, but Caleb had been lucky. He'd been saved from death by an old frontiersman who'd guided him and taught him. Old Jake was a loner, always on the move, but he still had enough kindness in his heart to recognize something worth saving in the half-dead boy he'd found.

"Watching Duke reminded me of my own responsibility," Caleb explained. "When you know the right thing to do, only a coward or a villain ignores it."

"Have you talked to your partner?"

"Talked it out last night. Henry is fine with it. More than fine with it. He thinks it's a grand idea. He and Paddy get along like a pair of wolf pups. Hell, Paddy will probably be a good influence on Henry."

Her lips lifted in a welcome smile, and Caleb felt the warmth flow back into the room. "Then I'd say it sounds settled."

"Not entirely. You see, I need to know your feelings on a related matter."

Sheila's throat suddenly reddened, and as the blush climbed into her cheeks, Caleb looked away, immediately realizing his mistake. How easy it was to be misunderstood! He spoke quickly to clarify.

"Education."

"Education?"

"Yep. I need to get your opinion on schooling for Paddy," Caleb explained. "My father ran a training school in Indiana. Mostly that meant using Shawnee and Kickapoo children as work slaves and as targets for his cane. When it came to me, I was raised having reading, arithmetic, spelling, penmanship, and the rest of it beat into me. More of what I remember came from my mother than the schoolroom, but I still learned enough to help me later on."

Caleb paused, trying to shake off the horrors of child-hood and the memory of those battered children. It was impossible. Some things he'd carry to his grave.

"There's no way Henry and I can give him the book learning he needs. Now, I don't know what Paddy's already learnt. Or if he's ever gone a day to school."

"I don't believe Paddy has ever gone to school," she replied. "The little he's learning now, he's getting from sit-ting in on the lessons Mrs. Rogers is providing for Gabriel. But he's far behind. When she and I talked about it, she said that's part of the reason for the way he acts up and occasionally defies her."

Caleb was impressed that Sheila had already talked to Mrs. Rogers about Paddy. She cared. That was who she was.

The young boy was totally smitten with Sheila, but that was for other reasons. She paid attention to him, asked questions, and showed an interest in what he did. She *listened* to him. There was only one person that Caleb ever recalled listening to him when he was a child.

"I recall hearing that Elkhorn has a real schoolhouse and a teacher. Know anything about it?"

"Do I know anything about it?" She gave him a look of mild disbelief that he would ask such a question. "The schoolhouse is down at the west end of town, up from the creek. It's a one-room affair, and the town pays for a teacher to work with all the children. That's eight grades. I've visited the school a couple of times."

Of course she has, he thought. Being involved with the

ladies' committees in town, Sheila would naturally make it her business to know these things.

"Would that be good for Paddy?" Caleb asked. "Him being behind and all?"

"Well, the boy is spirited. As you know, he can be a handful," she reminded him. "And the schoolhouse is crowded. There are currently three to five students in each grade. When all thirty-five or forty of them show up, which isn't all that often, the conditions are quite cramped. Miss Polly Kaufman, the new schoolmarm, tells me she's sometimes ready to pull her hair out after a day like that."

"I wouldn't blame her."

"Me neither. Polly arrived in Elkhorn last fall, and I think she's already looking elsewhere. She's not happy, I can tell you that." Sheila stood and walked to the window. "And she has good reason for leaving. I don't know how she'd be able to stay with the pittance she receives to live on."

He didn't know how things worked now, but when he was younger, married women weren't permitted to teach. They had only themselves to rely on, unless they came with money.

"It's shockingly unfair. Did you know that the town paid the last teacher—who was a man—a yearly salary of seventy-five dollars but offered Miss Kaufman only fifty when she arrived from Ohio?"

"I didn't." He didn't know anything about it. He had no idea before how little teachers were paid. He imagined stacking wood at the lumber yard paid more than that.

A working cowhand got twenty-five to thirty dollars a month plus board. Hell, he gave Gabe a dollar a day to look after the ranch and his dog when he went away. Fifty dollars a year wasn't much to live on.

"And she was given no supplies to work with. No slates for the children, no charts or maps, no books. I don't know what the last teacher did, but Polly believes he took everything with him. She was simply ushered in the door and told to do her best."

Caleb realized Sheila had found another friend in Elkhorn. And it sounded like this Miss Kaufman could certainly use an ally.

"So one of your ladies' committees is doing something about it?"

She nodded. "Unfortunately, some people don't see it as a priority."

"So you don't think the Elkhorn school would be a good thing for Paddy?"

"Let me talk to Polly. She was considering dividing the classes so not all the children show up at the same time. Maybe having the lower grades come in for three weeks and then the upper grades come in three weeks and so on. If that's the case, Paddy could live out at the ranch and only come to Elkhorn for school when it's his time to be there."

Sheila had a head for solving problems. Caleb had done right in asking her.

Just then, the sun pushed through the clouds, and light poured in through the window. Her golden hair glowed like a halo. It was like a damn sign. For a wild moment, Caleb thought about what it would have been like if Sheila were also living out there on the ranch. As quickly as the idea formed, though, he pushed it away. He wasn't allowed to have such fanciful dreams.

"When are you going to tell him?"

"Not until after I get back with Ortiz. No reason to stir things up."

"You'll take care out there, won't you?"

"I got to. There's a twelve-year-old boy's future to think of."

She walked slowly toward him. "And is Paddy the only one you'll be thinking of?"

Caleb jumped to his feet, feeling his body come alert. She was playing with him. He recognized the expression on her face. They'd exchanged a few brief kisses in the past. Right now, though, he didn't think he could keep himself reined in if he let down his guard and kissed her properly.

"'Course not. There's Bear. In spite of how bad he smells when he's wet, I've come to be very fond of him. Then there's Henry. Come to think of it, he don't smell so good either. Then there's Doc, who still can't play chess worth a lick. And—"

Sheila pushed herself up on the tips of her toes and took hold of Caleb's chin. "Can't say it, can you? You'll miss me. I know you'll miss me."

They were close enough that he could have fallen directly into those blue eyes. He felt his guard slip a notch.

"Say it, Marlowe."

He took a deep breath. "I will miss you, Miss Burnett."

"Good. Because I'll miss you too." She pressed a kiss against his lips then started toward the door.

Caleb was still trying to think of something clever to say in parting so she wouldn't know how much her little flirtations affected him. He was about to give up, figuring something would come to him when he was halfway back to the ranch, when she stopped.

"I heard my father say you're looking for a room where Mr. Washington can convalesce."

"You heard right."

"I think I can help you with that."

"You can?"

"He can stay at Belle Constant's place."

The words caught Caleb by surprise. For a moment, he wondered if Sheila actually knew what kind of place the Belle was.

"I recently learned that Miss Constant has a small rooming house that she built for the flood of visitors that came to Elkhorn for the eclipse viewing last summer."

"That right?" Sheila's knowledge of this town was beginning to amaze him.

"It's located at the end of an alley that runs alongside her saloon. Since then, she's been using it to house some of her employees."

"I wonder if she'd object to renting it to Tex."

"I'll ask her. But I'm fairly certain she won't mind at all."

"You'll ask her? You *know* Belle Constant?" Every time

Caleb thought he knew everything there was to know about Sheila Burnett, she knocked him all akilter.

"Of course. She's a member of the Ladies' Event Planning Committee."

CHAPTER SIXTEEN

CALEB REINED IN HIS BIG BUCKSKIN ON THE ROCKY RISE and looked back at his two traveling companions. Their sturdy, Texas-bred horses were trudging through the snow, kicking up powder as they came.

Duke and Bass were tough fellas and used to hard travel, but they weren't accustomed to pushing along this fast in winter conditions. On the trail, driving their cattle, they were lucky to make ten or twelve miles a day. And if they happened to be caught north of the Arkansas River when the snows came, they just hunkered down and wintered with their herd until spring.

The three of them had been on the road for the past day and a half, and the Texans were doing a fair job of keeping up, but Caleb had hoped to be farther along than they were at present.

Back in Elkhorn, he'd been anxious to get on the trail as soon as possible. As it was, the rustlers already had a huge jump on them. Too many things seemed to conspire against him.

By late Thursday afternoon, the snow had begun to fall. Very soon, every alley and thoroughfare was covered. Riding back to the ranch after speaking with

Sheila, Caleb began to doubt that they'd be leaving the next day.

Friday morning, the snow was nearly a foot deep—not enough to stop them from going—but he'd arrived at Doc's house to find it was still a question as to whether Tex would survive. The fever had not eased its grip on the young cowboy, and Ortiz was hesitant to leave him until he had better news.

By noon, it didn't matter. A second onslaught of snow roared in from the west with winds that battered the walls of the Burnett house. Caleb could barely see ten feet in front of Pirate's nose as he struggled home through the near darkness of midafternoon. He had the directional sense of a hound dog, but he was still relieved to see the blurred shapes of the ranch buildings loom ahead. Over the years, Caleb had seen quite a few situations similar to this where men had become confused by the swirling snow and wind, only to be found frozen to death within yards of their cabin or destination.

By the next morning, the storm had blown itself out. The snow had eased and then tapered off to nothing during the night. Caleb rode into town through powder that the wind had, in some places, heaped up into drifts taller than he was, leaving wide swaths of almost bare earth in other spots. The sky was swept clear, a brilliant shade of blue. Without the wind, the cold didn't have the same bite, and good news greeted him at Doc's house. During the night, the cowboy's fever had broken.

In Elkhorn, at least, things were falling into place.

After his conversation with Sheila, she'd spoken to Belle Constant. The tough, enterprising saloon owner had no problem with renting rooms to paying customers, regardless of where they came from or the color of their skin. Duke and Bass had stayed in the boardinghouse for two nights already. And Tex would be moved over whenever Doc Burnett decided the young man was ready.

Caleb looked behind him. His companions were closing the distance.

Pirate tossed his head and shook snow off his dark-brown mane. He was eyeing the spring-fed pool just ahead. The pool was dark, the edges fringed white with ice, and the water spilled into a narrow ravine that dropped off to Caleb's right.

"That's why we stopped, fella. Go get yourself a drink."

Leaving Pirate by the pool, Caleb walked to the edge of the bluff.

Where normally he could have seen five miles in either direction along the river below him, today the sight was very different. Two separate snow squalls to the north and another to the south limited his view of the valley. The expanse of whiteness blanketing the normally grass-covered ground was broken sporadically by scrubby spruce standing alone or in clumps and frost-killed brush huddled along the edge of icy river. At the moment, between here and the western foothills that should have been directly across, dozens of tributary streams and small rivers formed a web of draws and gulches. Even as he looked at them, though, they floated in and out of sight, like ghostly veins on the back of an old man's hand.

They'd been following the eastern ridge to avoid that terrain. Caleb didn't mind getting wet fording the streams—even though it was getting steadily colder—but the steep embankments alongside many of them made for slow going. He was looking for the fastest route possible.

Heavier snow began to fall, and Caleb looked up at the sky. Steel-gray clouds covered the wide expanse. The peaks to the east and west had been completely snow-covered, and they were invisible now.

He figured they had another four or five hours of riding before the dark lid of night clamped down hard over them. With luck, they'd reach the point where the river swung hard to the east before then.

Once they made that turn, the wide valley would narrow, and the spruce-covered mountains would rise sharply on either side for a long, winding stretch. Depending on his companions, it would take them a day or two to reach the place where the rustlers bushwhacked Duke and his men.

The two cattlemen pulled up beside him. They'd used the days before leaving Elkhorn to clean up, rest their horses, and outfit themselves for the trip. Both men were sporting new woolen coats beneath their leather dusters, and Bass had needed a new shirt to replace his torn and bloodied one.

Upon leading their mounts to the water, they got down, knocked the snow off their hats, and came to stand beside Caleb.

"When we came along here with Tex," Duke said, gesturing down into the valley, "we didn't think of moving up and away from the river."

Bass frowned, tentatively stretching his injured arm. "Woulda been easier going."

"No way you woulda known," Caleb said.

In the distance, a low-hanging cloud thinned, and a herd of pronghorns came into view, their striped faces foraging in the snow for grass. Their snow-dusted brown backs, white bellies, and white rumps made them nearly invisible, but Caleb's eye had long ago been trained to spot game.

"We'll give the horses a few minutes to rest," he said, turning his attention back to the other men. "But then we got to keep moving."

Duke nodded and started to say something. But before a word left his mouth, a far-off sound stopped them.

Gunfire, muffled by the falling snow.

"Hear that?" Bass asked.

"Sounds like trouble," Duke added.

"We oughta find out," Caleb added. It was better to know who was on the warpath instead of getting caught unawares.

In a moment, they were on their horses and moving as quickly as they could along the ridge. The snow, heavy at times, cut their ability to see to just a few yards, but the sound of rifles, mixed with the sporadic bark of a pistol, led them on. By a pile of frost-whitened rock, the three men reined in and peered down into the valley.

Caleb breathed in the mingled smell of gun smoke and cooking fire. He had a bird's-eye view of the fight.

The river wound along like a great black snake below, and rocks showed above the surface of the wide bend closest to their vantage point. Almost directly below them, five horses were tied behind a grove of spruce. From the shelter of the trees, men were firing across the river at four wagons that had been pulled into a circle.

From the trampled snow and the smoky fires by each wagon, Caleb judged that the travelers must have been there for a while, waiting out the storm before continuing their journey. He counted seven men, five women, and a passel of young ones. Three of the women were huddled with the children on the far side of the encampment. Mules and a couple of sturdy-looking horses were tethered nearby.

The shooting was accompanied by threats and shouts from the travelers and taunts from the gang on this side.

"What do you think is going on?" Ortiz said in a low voice.

"Looks to me like these fellas over here found some homesteaders they thought would make for easy pickings."

Bass nodded. "If they run out of ammunition first, they probably will be exactly that."

Caleb kept telling himself that he didn't need to get involved in fights that didn't involve him, but there were children here. He was starting to think there was a soft side of him that would probably get him killed one day.

But maybe today wasn't that day.

He looked at his two companions. "What do you fellas say we lend them homesteaders a hand?"

CHAPTER SEVENTEEN

CALEB CONSIDERED THEIR SITUATION, TRYING TO decide on the best approach. If they drove these black-guards off to the south, they stood a good chance of running into them again since he and the Texans were going that way. That didn't seem too wise.

So that left him with two choices. Either they could try to send the coyotes skedaddling over the river and west across the valley, or they could kill them all right here.

Caleb decided to try going the first way. If that didn't work, they always had the second.

He turned to Duke and Bass and ran his plan by them.

A few minutes later, Bass took his Henry Yellow Boy and moved south along the top of the ridge for about a hundred yards. With his arm being what it was, climbing didn't seem to make much sense. Caleb and Duke would do that.

Caleb watched until Bass was in position. He nudged Ortiz, and the two men moved north along the ridge.

Before they got far, a cry of pain reached them, and Caleb looked down to see one of the homesteaders, now hatless, clutching the side of his head. He was sitting by one of the wagon wheels. Another man went to check on him. This one was wearing a fringed leather coat and a hat with a feather sticking up from the band. The guide for the party, Caleb figured.

The homesteader pushed him away, picked up his rifle, and got back in position, firing furiously.

"Let's go." They hurried through the snow.

Ortiz was carrying a Winchester '73 that appeared to be a twin of Caleb's rifle.

"That rifle of yours looks brand-new. You any good with this one?"

"I told you I killed two of them *pendejos* that took the herd. Why are you asking now?"

"Just don't want you shooting me by accident."

Duke snorted indignantly. "I can take needles off a cactus from five hundred feet, one needle at a time. Don't you worry about me."

"I ain't worried, my friend."

They stopped by a narrow cut in the ridge wall.

"And if I shoot you, Marlowe, it won't be no accident."

"You know how to make a fella feel all warm inside, Duke."

It felt good to be able to joke with Ortiz again. Caleb knew how capable he was with a rifle. The last time they'd been in a situation like this, the two of them were facing a bunch of drunken greenhorns hunting on Duke's land. The trespassers were shooting buffalo reserved by treaty for the Comanches. Ortiz took particular exception, however, to the fact that the hunters couldn't tell the difference between buffalo and his longhorns. It had been the two of them against a dozen, and they'd driven them off with their tails between their legs.

It had been hot as blazes down there beneath the Texas sun. The weather was a bit different today.

Snow and ice lay in the narrow gulley leading down to a jumble of large rocks about halfway down. Ortiz would have a partially obstructed view from there, but that was all they needed.

Caleb gestured for the cattleman to go. "I'll wait till you're in place down there."

Ortiz nodded, his expression serious again. "Good luck, amigo."

The rancher picked his way carefully down the cut. Caleb could see Duke slip on the larger icy rocks occasionally. Gravel and pebbles slid out from beneath his boots, tumbling downward.

One thing he and the two cattlemen had going for them was the advantage of surprise. He didn't want to give that up until they were ready to make their move. But there was no need to worry about alerting the outlaws of their presence. The bandits were continuing to shoot at the homesteaders and taunt them with shouts and calls to give up and throw out their weapons.

As soon as Duke waved to him, Caleb moved on and descended as quickly as he could. When he reached the lower slope just above the valley floor, he kept down and ran to a boulder twenty yards from the face of the ridge. The red rock, nearly flat on top, was about five feet high and eight feet across. It would do just fine, he decided.

Caleb peered over the top. In spite of the falling snow, he had a clear view of everything—the horses tied in the shelter of the trees, the five gunmen, the river, and the circled wagon train. Once he started shooting, the bandits would be taking fire from across the river and from him. They'd have to move or get cut down.

As he watched, one of the bushwhackers left the cover of the woods and ran on an angle toward the river. He took some fire from the wagons, but the shots went astray. In a moment he'd made it to a brush-covered hillock stretched along the bank of the river.

That complicated Caleb's plan.

From there, the gunman would have a clearer shot at the men firing from the wagons closest to the water. Instead, Caleb saw him take aim at the women and children huddled by the mules. Immediately, the sonovabitch fired and the shot struck a wheel a few inches from the head of a small boy, showering them with splinters and drawing cries from the youngsters.

"Damn me," Caleb muttered as the shooter chambered another cartridge.

The rogue raised his rifle to his shoulder again, but Caleb wasn't having it.

His Winchester spit fire, and the outlaw's head tipped forward as a spray of blood painted the snowy bank in front of him. The rifle dropped, and the gunman slumped to his side, twitching once before lying still.

The shooting on both sides stopped, and the loudest

sound in the valley was the water burbling over the rocks and the snow-filled breeze.

Caleb swiveled the barrel of his '73 toward the grove of spruce trees. Four men were staring wide-eyed at him, stunned by the entrance of another shooter.

"Time to go, boys," he murmured.

Aiming high, he fired. His bullet ripped into the trunk of a tree three inches above the head of one of the outlaws.

That was all it took to set them in motion.

They jumped back, trying to take cover, but the home-steaders now had clearer shots at them. Rifles and pistols barked from across the river, and the blackguards imme-diately retreated in the direction of the horses, firing in Caleb's direction as well as back across the river.

Just then, Duke began shooting from his vantage point, dropping one and drawing loud curses from the others. Caleb added a couple of shots, and the men really began to scramble. Getting pinned down from three sides had never been part of their plan in attacking the wagon train.

Leaping onto their horses, the three remaining gunmen wheeled and kicked their mounts into action. As they started off, moving south away from Caleb and Duke, shots rang out from the top of the ridge, where Bass was firing and shouting. The outlaws yanked the heads of their mounts to the southwest, and Caleb saw them splash across the water far downriver, out of range of both the homesteaders and Bass.

The bandits hadn't even disappeared behind the

curtain of falling snow when a cheer went up from the men inside the circled wagons.

———————

Near the place where Bass had been shooting, a wide ravine opened to the valley floor. Caleb gathered the weapons from the dead bandits while Duke went through their saddlebags to see if there was anything useful. The young man above grabbed the horses and worked his way down.

Caleb was picking up an old Spencer carbine from the grove of trees when the leather-clad guide mounted up bareback and rode across the river. It appeared the homesteaders were content to wait where they were and lick their wounds.

"Well, I'll be jiggered," the man said as he drew near. He spat a stream of tobacco and jumped down from his sturdy dun. "If it ain't Caleb Marlowe."

"Bill Clark. Finally escaped from army duty?"

The feather stuck in the band of his wide-brimmed hat bobbed as the scout spat again. "Not a minute too soon, neither. They was ready to send me out to help that lunatic General Howard fight the Shoshone. It was time to get out."

"So now you're leading farmers to the Promised Land?"

"Yup." Clark looked across the way. "I'll be happy to be rid of this bunch, though."

"That right?"

"Yup. Think they're God's chosen, sent to civilize the damn frontier." He shook his head. "Got their prayer books wedged so tight up their asses, you couldn't pull 'em out with a twenty-mule team and a barrel of axle grease."

Bass rode up, leading Pirate, with Ortiz approaching on foot as the snow began to fall more heavily. They shook hands all around, and Clark thanked them heartily for coming to their rescue. Then, at his invitation, the four men rode together across the river.

As they approached the circle of wagons, Caleb pulled on his bearskin coat, and Duke and Bass donned their leather dusters. They'd already lost valuable daylight, but he figured all of them could use a cup of coffee, a few minutes by a fire, or even a hot meal, if the grateful travelers offered.

Before they reached the wagons, a short, bull-necked farmer approached. The traveler stood in their path, fixing them with his pale blue stare. The farmer had a black beard that draped from his chin and jaw and left his wide, pale face as naked as a baby's ass.

"Stay right there, you fellas. Don't come no closer." The man waved a rifle at them.

He was wearing a churchman's black, flat-brimmed hat with a round crown, the likes of which Caleb hadn't seen since he was a boy. Right now, it was dusted with snow, as was the heavy, mud-colored wool coat. The coat was buttoned tight around the neck that appeared to be one piece with his block-shaped head. Black wool trousers were tucked into stove-top boots that came almost to the knees on his short, stocky legs.

"I want you to meet these men who saved our skins," Bill said. "This is—"

The farmer stopped him with a motion of his pudgy, callused hand. Gesturing with a jerk of his head for the scout to follow, he turned and stomped back toward the other travelers.

Caleb leaned forward and laid a hand on Pirate's warm neck as a sick feeling clutched at his gut. He knew what was going on.

With a frown, Bill dismounted and walked across the encampment to where the entire group was gathered by the far wagons. The children peeked around the adults, staring with eyes like saucers at the strangers still on horseback.

The guide's back was to Caleb, and he was talking with the same farmer, who appeared to be the leader of the group. From Bill Clark's stiff-legged stance and the quick gestures he was making with his hands, it was clear he was losing the argument.

Duke put a hand on Caleb's arm. "Seen this a hundred times, amigo. Bass and I ain't staying, even if he changes their minds."

"Some people don't deserve saving," Caleb said under his breath.

Shaking his head with obvious disgust, the frontiersman strode back to them.

"I'm sorry, Marlowe. These sons of bitches—"

"Don't say no more."

Without another word, Caleb, Duke, and Bass wheeled their horses and rode back across the river.

CHAPTER EIGHTEEN

THE THREE MEN RODE ABOUT A HALF MILE SOUTH ALONG the river. To their left, the rocky bluff quickly lost its height, and the snow-speckled ledge gave way to a slope of tall spruce trees that spilled down to the edge of the valley and extended upward into the foothills like a white-dusted blanket. Clouds obscured the higher elevations of the forest, but Caleb had seen those peaks before and had no interest in them today.

None of them talked about what just happened. There was no need to. Caleb was angry, though, for it was his nudge that got them involved in the first place.

Deciding that they'd had enough for the day, they set up camp at a good place near an icy creek. Leaving the horses to graze in the shelter of the conifer boughs, the men built a fire and unpacked their bedrolls.

Caleb hoped the snow would ease up before morning, but no matter what the Colorado winter held in store for them, they needed to press on.

Before they even had time to start their supper of beans and bacon and coffee, the sound of an approaching rider's voice had them all reaching for their guns.

"Don't shoot me, damn it." Bill Clark rode up to their camp and dismounted.

They all holstered their weapons, though no one extended a warm greeting.

"I know y'all are hot about what went on back there, but don't blame me." Clark looked at Caleb. "You know I don't hold with boneheads like that. I just got to take them through these mountains. Then I can wash my hands of 'em."

Caleb figured Bill Clark was about ten years older than him, and he was starting to show the wear of his years on the frontier. He'd seen him in passing over the years— trapping beaver up by the Canadian border, leading would-be prospectors out to Montana, even selling "hunting rifles" to a camp of Cheyenne up on the North Fork of the Platte in Wyoming. They'd only gotten to know each other well while both of them were scouting for the army in the Dakotas.

Caleb and Bill and Henry had shared a bottle or two, along with some adventures that nearly cost all three of them their hair.

But Caleb also knew the scout didn't cotton to the narrow-minded thinking of the homesteaders he was leading west.

Upon receiving a shrug from Duke, Caleb gestured for Bill to have a seat at the fire.

"Well, thankee, fellas," the scout said. Before joining them, he pulled a large package from his saddlebags. Something wrapped in a bloody cloth. Their eyes were all on him as he tossed it to Caleb.

"As a token of my esteem and gratitude to y'all, I brung

you a nice piece of elk that I shot day before yesterday. I can't stay and join you in eating it...I need to be getting back afore my employers think I lit out and left 'em. But I don't feel much like sharing this meat with 'em."

Caleb laid the package aside for their supper. "Where you headed with that bunch?"

"You know that river that runs into this here Arkansas about a half day's ride north of here? It comes in from the west."

"I know it. There's a deserted tumbledown cabin up on the northern bank."

"That's the one. I'm taking them up there."

Caleb thought about the route. "Some mountain passes up that way are tricky even in the summer months."

Bill shrugged. "Yup. And if we make it through, we got Ute territory for quite a stretch."

"You knew them Utes ain't particularly happy these days. The Great White Father in Washington just tricked them out of more of their land."

"Yup. If we get through there with our scalps, we got Mormon country next. And they ain't never overly happy, period."

"So why take 'em that way?" Caleb asked.

"That was their choice. They hired me in Pueblo, showed me their gold, and said that was the way they wanted to go. There wasn't no holding 'em over till spring, neither. Them boneheads think they got some divine angels or something keeping watch of them. Hell, they didn't even know you three was their angels when they saw you today."

Bass snorted. "Can't speak for Marlowe, but Duke and me ain't no angels, Bill."

Ortiz nodded. "But it sounds like you gonna need them where you're going."

Clark jerked a thumb at Caleb. "This fella here can tell you about some spots we been in. One or two of 'em was so tight, you couldn't fit even a little angel in there with us. And we got out. Didn't we, Marlowe?"

Caleb nodded.

"And speaking of the angels and such, how's that devil Henry Jordan doing? Ever hear from him?"

"Yep, we went partners in a ranch straight north of here near Elkhorn. He's doing fine. Same as always." Caleb didn't figure he needed to share anything about Henry's time in the Denver jail.

"Well, I'll be jiggered. Never saw neither of you fellas settling down to ranching."

"Something new for both of us."

The scout pulled off his feathered hat and scratched his head. "So what are y'all doing out in all this sunshine and butterflies?"

Caleb made a point of not looking at Duke and Bass. He didn't want Bill Clark attaching any blame to them. "Some rustlers took a herd belonging to me coming from Texas. Killed some men. We're out looking for 'em."

"How big a herd?"

"A thousand longhorns."

"Where'd it happen?"

"North of Charlotte Falls," Duke answered, clearly

interested in gathering whatever information the scout might have.

Bill pulled his hat back on. "I believe I can help you fellas out with that. One good turn for another. I seen a herd of longhorns a day or two after we come out of Pueblo. They was heading east—going the wrong way, seemed to me—but we didn't get close enough to find out no more."

"How long ago was that?" Ortiz asked.

The scout stared into the fire, thinking about it. "Mebbe ten days ago."

Damn. That herd was still more than a week ahead of them.

"Did you get close enough to see the fellas driving the herd?" Caleb asked. "Any idea how many?"

"I just said we didn't get too close." Bill scratched his chin. "But there was one other strange thing to the business. They had extra fellas back with the drag riders. Like they was keeping watch. And they looked like they meant business. Wherever they was headed, they was pushing them critters hard to get there."

For the first time, Caleb wondered if it was no accident that it was *his* herd that had been stolen. He thought of everyone in Elkhorn that knew he and Henry had the longhorns coming up from Texas. Practically everyone, from the judge on down. The town was counting on them to supply meat for the coming year.

Duke said the rustlers were waiting for them. This route was off the Goodnight-Loving trail. If they were gunning for *this* herd, for Caleb's cattle, they'd have an easy time of it, knowing where to attack.

Caleb looked out from beneath the boughs of the trees into the snowy gloom, impatient for the storm to die.

After Bill Clark went back to his wagon train, Duke and Caleb bedded the horses. Ortiz cut the meat into steaks and prepared the supper, roasting the elk over the fire to have with their beans and coffee.

Sitting around the fire later, Caleb thought about the road ahead, the snow, and the thankless reception they'd received from the travelers. The other two men had settled back against their saddles, coffee cups in hand, lost in their own ruminations.

Duke broke the silence. "Them steaks were mighty fine."

"Nothing better than the feeling of being full," Bass added.

"Almost nothing, amigo," Ortiz joked, drawing a laugh. He waved his cup at Caleb. "That friend of yours, he's okay. Wouldn't mind running into him again."

"But not the folks he's taking west," Caleb said.

Ortiz shrugged. "I see all kinds along the trail, and folks don't deal with you the same. Sometimes it's good, sometimes it gets real ugly. But Bass here come from Louisiana. I reckon what I seen over the years ain't nothing to what you been through."

"I seen changes. I can tell you that," Bass said. "I didn't come to Texas till I was fourteen. Come with my older brother."

Caleb hadn't spent any time in Louisiana or any other states around it, but he'd heard some stories from other freed men who left the former Confederate States and moved west after the war.

"My folks was both slaves on a plantation in Union Parish, Louisiana. That's where I was born and drug up. The place was famous for breeding horses. For racing and for farming, both. Till the war got bad." Bass turned his gaze into the flames. "The master lost three sons in the fighting, and it was almost like he blamed us for it. Things got much worse than before."

He poured himself more coffee and set the pot back by the fire.

"After the Union come in and General Butler captured New Orleans, everything went crazy. My older brother, Win, went off one night and joined the First Louisiana Native Guard. I was too young to sign up. Anyways, when old General Lee surrendered, Black folk was getting strung up all over the place. Win said that he didn't believe things would ever be put right, so we talked to our folks about it. The next day, we started walking west."

Caleb had walked away from everything he'd known too, but his situation—as bad as it was—was nothing compared to what this fella went through. "Must have been tough leaving them behind."

Bass nodded. "It was, but there was nothing we could do for them or ourselves there, and my folks was too old and set to go anywhere. Still had little ones to feed too."

"So you walked all the way to Texas."

"Yep. I was fourteen. When we got to Parker County, we both found work on a ranch that broke horses. We growed up with horses, and my brother had a special way with 'em. For the first time in our lives, things was looking up. We was never the same as the white cowboys on that ranch, but we had work and got paid decent wages. And when we was out on the range, we was all the same, no matter a man's color."

"Unless you was Mexican," Ortiz put in.

"I reckon that's right, Duke."

"Tell Marlowe how you come to work for me."

"And you said you and your brother was working together," Caleb said.

"Yup. Like I said, Win had a way with them horses, especially the wildest ones. He made a real name for his-self." Bass took a deep breath. "Till he got stomped by one."

Caleb glanced at Ortiz, who frowned and nodded. He must have known this.

"We was in Texas six years when he died, and I didn't want to work breaking horses no more. So I got me a job on a cattle ranch, but I found out there was better money driving them critters north. Life on the trail was mostly pretty good, if you can get used to the snow and the damn cold. And, as far as folks go, there's a few places way up at the northern end that I wouldn't mind never seeing again. Anyways, after a couple years on the trail, I signed on with Duke."

"And he never got treated so good or paid so fair, so

he stayed." Duke laughed and slapped Bass on the knee. "Ain't that the truth?"

"Sure is." Bass turned to Caleb. "Those homesteaders don't mean nothing to me. Not after all I seen. But if your friend gets fed up and decides to leave 'em up in one of them mountain passes, I ain't about to lose no sleep over it."

They all listened for a while to the crackle of the fire and the wind sighing in the trees until Duke broke the silence.

"And then, you got me. Folks come and go. Governments rise and fall. And, all the while, my family been on the same land for over two hundred years…and the so-called 'Texans' still treat us like dirt."

"You showed me that land grant your family got," Caleb put in. "All in Spanish with wax seals and stamps and ribbons and all."

"And we still had to fight to keep our ranch."

Caleb knew a few things about the Mexicans in Texas. The old landowners changed from being Spanish to Mexican to American in only about twenty years… and never had to move an inch. First they stopped being Spanish when Mexico declared its independence from Spain. Later, after Santa Ana gave up the war against the US and they all signed the Treaty of Hidalgo, that made them Americans. But afterward, regardless of what they owned, they were treated like defeated foes. A lot of them, rather than putting up with the abuse, just up and went to Mexico, leaving everything they owned behind. Duke Ortiz's family stayed.

"You're a good man, Duke, and you done good with what is yours."

Ortiz nodded and pulled at his red silk bandana. "I wear this to honor my heritage, but my father and his men were the last of the true vaqueros. It was from them that the white newcomers learned to handle the longhorns that roamed free across the land. Without the knowledge of the Mexican hacendados, there would be no cattle trails north. The Americans in the East would be eating only chickens and pigs."

He looked hard at Caleb.

"That's why I am here in the snow with you, Marlowe. It's a matter of my family's honor—and the honor of those men I lost—that I make good on our deal."

Caleb reached out and shook hands with Duke. "And at dawn tomorrow, my friend, we go after the low-down bushwhackers that took the herd."

CHAPTER NINETEEN

"YOU DIRTY, LOW-DOWN PIECE OF HORSE SHIT." HENRY shook his head in disbelief, looking down at the men panning for gold in the icy water of the pool. "Some mangy curs never learn."

He sat astride his bay gelding on the snowy ridge overlooking the same creek where he and Caleb found Mad Dog McCord and his gang. But it wasn't those outlaws this time.

Frank Stubbs stood near the edge of the creek, jawing away with another man standing by him. Two more men were working with pans in the shallows. They'd cleared snow off a stretch of shoreline, and their shovels lay on the glistening gravel. From the raggedy looks of the fellas doing the panning, they were hired laborers. And every other breath or so, Frank clearly felt the need to holler at the workers.

"You knew Caleb was off hunting for our cattle, so you thought you'd just slip right in here." The sonovabitch figured he'd see if Mad Dog was on to something in this creek.

The man standing with Stubbs took a bottle from his pocket and had a good, solid pull from it before passing it on to Frank. Wiping his black whiskers on his gray wool coat, he turned slightly and looked at the fire that they'd lit in the center of the clearing. He gestured with his head toward it, and Stubbs grudgingly followed him over.

Henry had been down checking on the cattle in the lower end of the valley when he saw the smoke from the fire.

"With all the brandy you drink, Frank," Henry muttered, "I wouldn't get too close to them flames."

Their neighbor took another drink and shouted a few more curses at the workers.

"On the other hand, go ahead and get *real* close."

Having seen the face of Stubbs's companion, Henry knew exactly who he was.

"You too, you mouthy sonovabitch."

Henry had seen the man in Elkhorn yesterday. He'd been standing on the back of a wagon on Main Street in front of the Belle, shouting at the top of his lungs and calling out the men going in and out of the saloon as "godless sinners" and "drunken reprobates" and other such nonsense.

The fellas on the street were entertained, and Miss Belle didn't seem to care much one way or another. But Zeke had taken exception to it when he showed up ready to do his own drinking.

That was when Henry found out the man's name was Amos Stubbs. He was Frank's brother. New in town, he was passing himself off as a parson.

Watching the preacher take another swig from that bottle, Henry shook his head.

"You are a self-righteous hypocrite, parson," Henry muttered with a frown. "And I ain't no expert. But the Good Book has something pretty clear to say about not stealing from your neighbor, I believe."

Henry drew his rifle from its scabbard and nudged his mount down the steep, snowy slope.

Frank spun around at the sound of the approaching horse and started to go for his pistol.

"Go ahead, you stupid sonovabitch," Henry called down, leveling his rifle at Stubbs's chest. "Give me one more reason to fill your gizzard with lead."

Frank stopped and moved his hand out away from his body, clear of the Colt Peacemaker at his hip.

"What's the meaning of this?" Amos Stubbs snapped before turning to his brother. "Frank, what's going on?"

Neither man answered him, and Henry spoke instead to the two workers standing ankle deep in water that had formed a lacework of ice on their boots. "Come out of there, boys. I hope Stubbs paid you in advance, 'cuz your workday is over. Go and warm your bones by that fire."

Henry considered telling Frank to unbuckle his gun belt but didn't bother. He almost hoped Stubbs would decide to throw down. The worm had overstayed his welcome on earth.

"How many times Marlowe and me got to tell you stay off our property?"

"Your property?" Amos Stubbs said. "You're mistaken. This land belongs to—"

"This ain't your property. The ridge is mine right down

the valley," Frank barked, interrupting his brother. He spat a stream of tobacco juice into the fire, raising a crackling hiss. "I don't care how many damn times you say so."

"We been through this, you no-account, stinking, dog-faced meathead. We own this land from that ridge down."

Frank's face looked like he had a lit charge of explosives about to go off in his ass.

Henry watched the two workers edge wide-eyed away from the Stubbs brothers. They surely never heard anyone talk to their boss like that before. And when the shooting started, they didn't want to be anywhere near it.

"Last time we did this, Stubbs—if you recall through your usual drunken stupor—even the sheriff told you to git."

Stubbs stuttered, tried to get some word out, but he couldn't quite manage it.

"Pack your gear, boys," Henry ordered.

The workers hurriedly picked up their equipment and were standing by their horses quicker than a prairie dog hits his hole at the smell of coyote.

"This is it, Stubbs. No more chances. I ain't going through it again," Henry said with a coolness that surprised even him. "You will get on your horse, ride up over that hill there, and keep going."

He raised the muzzle of his rifle until it was pointed right between Frank's hate-filled eyes.

"And hear this good," Henry said. "The next time I even see your shadow peeking over at our land, I'm gonna kill you. Understand?"

"We'll just see, Jordan," Frank finally spat out. "I know the damn law. We'll just see."

As the four men spurred their horses up the hill toward the Stubbs property, Henry thought about how well that went.

"Damn me," he murmured as he slid his rifle back into the scabbard. Marlowe would be pretty damn proud of how he handled that. "And not a drop of blood nowhere."

CHAPTER TWENTY

CALEB HADN'T BEEN THROUGH PUEBLO FOR A COUPLE of years, and as he and Duke and Bass rode in through two-foot-deep snow from the west, he wondered if he would have even recognized the place.

Beneath a lowering sky that showed no break in the dark shades of gray, a manufactory along the river was belching smoke. Duke informed him it was a smelter. "And they're building a damn steelworks too."

Orderly city blocks that were being laid out before were now nearly filled with wood-frame houses, and the main streets boasted large brick and wood homes, businesses, and even a school that rose two full stories to a high sloping roof and a bell tower.

Caleb decided this was a city that would surely make Judge Patterson shrivel with envy.

The Denver and Rio Grande Railroad had arrived in Pueblo six years ago, and they were itching to push farther south and west. Caleb read in a newspaper at Doc's house a while back that when a rival railroad came to town, the two companies had hired gunfighters out of Dodge City to protect their turf. A "Railroad War" the newspaper called it.

In spite of the frontier tradition of fighting out disputes, the city was being crowed about as a "beacon" and a "triumph." Somebody even said that Sharps rifles and revolvers had been replaced by plows and mowing machines. At least, this was the politicians' and newspapermen's version.

"The stockyards still south of the river?" he asked Ortiz, half in jest, and received an affirmative nod.

The men crossed the Arkansas on the wide bridge built by Charles Goodnight himself for his northbound cattle. Following the tracks to the stockyards, they quickly found out that no herds had arrived in the past week.

Caleb looked back toward the river and past the buildings of the growing city. "They had to take 'em north."

Ortiz agreed as they started back toward the Arkansas. "I know of a place where we can find out. Just a hole-in-the-wall, but a lot of cowpokes passing through Pueblo stop in there. And I know an old fella who *always* drinks there. Buck knows everything that goes on."

"How far is it?"

"Right up yonder. The Silver Dollar." He pointed at an alley up ahead.

A few minutes later, the three men entered the saloon. The Silver Dollar was a smoke-filled brandy hole that made the lowest, filthiest deadfall in Elkhorn look like a palace. Lit only by a few flickering lamps hanging from the ceiling, the dive boasted a bar consisting of several scarred and warped boards across three barrels. Behind it, two tough-looking barmen—one white and one with skin as dark as Bass—were pouring nose paint and brandy as fast as they could get the bottles open. Milling around the bar and sitting at six full card tables, cowpunchers of every color barely glanced at the newcomers.

One of the barmen nodded in recognition at Ortiz and Bass. As the man poured drinks for them, Duke asked if he'd seen Buck Sanders lately.

"'Course. Every damn day. Should be in any time now."

"Still working down at the stockyards?"

"Far as I know. Y'all know an old cow slick gets shaky if he can't be around them beasts."

They laughed and moved away from the bar to where they had a clear view of the door.

"Buck used to ride with us till he said his old bones couldn't take the long days in the saddle no more," Duke told Caleb. "He been living up here for a couple of years now. We see him when we come through."

Bass snorted. "Last time, I don't think any of us could see after drinking this rot gut all night."

The barman was true to his word. Twenty minutes later, a cowboy Caleb figured was about fifty years old shambled in.

Buck Sanders's trail-worn face lit up as soon as he saw the two Texans. "Damn me, but I knowed you boys was in here. Saw that nag out there with your fancy saddle on it, and I knowed it was you, Duke, you ornery sidewinder."

He had the bowed legs of a man who'd spent a lifetime in the saddle. His blue eyes were clear, though, and the moustache that trailed down the side of his thin-lipped mouth was streaked with gray. The brim of his sweat-stained hat was curled upward on both sides, and he was wearing a warm leather coat that he'd unbuttoned as soon as he entered. He wasn't wearing a gun but had a well-used knife sheathed at his belt.

Bass immediately appeared with a drink for the aging cowboy.

Sanders's grin showed a mouth that was missing half his teeth. "Thankee, Bass. Can't believe y'all are still riding for this skunk." He spat in the general direction of a brass spittoon. "Come into my office, boys."

After leading them to a corner where a small, smoke-covered window looked out onto the alley, he stared at Caleb for a moment, nodding slowly.

"It's Marlowe, ain't it? Don't think we ever met, official-like, but I recall seeing you down at this one's ranch." He flicked a gnarled thumb at Duke. "Heard plenty of stories about you, though. You used to ride with Old Jake Bell."

Caleb nodded. "I was just hearing about you from these fellas."

"Don't believe nothing they tell you. You ain't gonna find two lowlier varmints than these two this side of the Mississippi."

"Not that you ever seen the other side of the Mississippi, you scraggly old cactus," Duke replied with a laugh.

Buck drank down his brandy, smacking his lips with satisfaction, and laid the glass on the wide windowsill. "What brings you boys to town?" He paused and frowned. "And where's the rest of your outfit?"

"Dead," Duke said grimly.

"All but Tex Washington," Bass added.

The two men told the older man what had happened—the drive north, the ambush, the gunfight, and the ensuing journey to Elkhorn.

"Sons of bitches." Buck shook his head. "Young Tex gonna make it?"

"Looks like it," Ortiz said. "But not with his leg."

"That's a damn shame."

The aging cowboy's face grew somber. He stared out into the alley for a respectful moment. They all knew that Tex's days riding the range and the trail were over.

Buck shook himself and turned his attention back to the others. "So what are y'all doing here?"

"We aim to get them longhorns back," Bass said.

"We ran into a wagon train a few days west of here," Caleb told him. "The scout told us he seen the herd coming toward Pueblo."

"They didn't come to the stockyards," Buck said. He thought a moment. "But there was a fella who come down there some time back, looking to hire some hands for a job. Had a bunch of toughs with him."

"You hear what the job was?" Duke asked.

"No, I didn't," the old cowboy said. "I happened to be going by when he stuck up a sign on a board they got outside the entrance. I wasn't looking for nothing, so I didn't even stop to ask. Heard he was offering good money, though. And looking for experienced men. Not just cowpunchers. He wanted men good with guns.

Sounded awful strange to me. But I didn't think no more about it."

The words all rang a bell in Caleb's head. Not five months ago, he'd traveled to Bonedale, the center of operations for Eric Goulden's railroad construction in the region. There he'd found a sign posted on a wall in a local saloon. Every word was fresh in his mind:

MANY POSITIONS AVAILABLE

FOR EXPERIENCED MEN
Ex-Military. Ex-Pinkertons. Ex-Lawmen.
To aid in the PROTECTION of company property
and in the capture of TRAIN ROBBERS.
Inquire at Dry Bottom Saloon
Mr. Elijah Starr

This was exactly his father's way. Hire experienced men to do the job he needed done.

"Did you catch the name of the fella doing the hiring?" he asked.

Buck shook his head. "Never got that close to him."

"Anything else you can tell us," Caleb pressed.

"Not more than I already told you." The old cowhand started to shake his head and then hesitated. "You know, just the other day, I heard a couple of fellas talking in here about something they was part of. Now that I think about it, that coulda been the same job."

"What did they say?" Caleb asked.

"They was bragging about taking back a herd that some rustlers stole down near Trinidad. Said the scoundrels was driving the cattle west toward the mountains."

Duke bristled. "We ain't no rustlers. That was our herd. Whoever hired them clowns was a lying dog."

"They say what happened?"

Buck nodded. "They drove the critters up to a rail siding north of here, near a patch of dirt called Little Buttes. Had cattle cars waiting, they said."

Caleb thought about what he'd just heard. It all sounded exactly like something his father would do. Starr had his rail connections. He'd have the cars waiting.

Losing that herd wasn't a coincidence. And it wasn't just business. It was personal.

"This fella that was hiring. You saw him put up the job notice," Caleb asked. "What did he look like?"

"Only saw him the once. But I'd know him at the bottom of a box canyon on a moonless night."

Caleb knew what Buck was going to say next before the words even formed.

"He had one eye—wore a patch over the other—and had more scars on his face than a Comanche warrior."

CHAPTER TWENTY-ONE

CALEB HAD BEEN PUSHING HARD FOR TWO DAYS, BUT the wall of clouds eating up the peaks to the west told him that another storm was about to hit him like a herd of runaway buffalo.

"Damn."

Standing on a rocky ledge with the wind whistling around him, he glanced back at Pirate drinking contentedly from a mountain pool fifty yards away. Ice formed over the shallow stream where it crossed a worn channel from the pool to the ledge before tumbling off and disappearing to the base of the cliff far below. Fifty feet beneath him, Caleb could see the snow-covered tops of pines a hundred feet tall.

The mountain trail coming up here was barely wide enough for Pirate's sure feet, but it wasn't completely treacherous going. The ever-present wind had at least blown the snow from the rock surface. He'd considered taking a route that led along the thickly forested slopes below him, but he'd wanted to get a better look at the weather coming in from the west. Now that he had, Caleb wasn't all that happy.

He'd come far since leaving Duke and Bass, but the

miles he'd covered wouldn't matter if he got buried in another few feet of snow up here and lost a week.

After they left Pueblo, the three of them had ridden north, following the train tracks that ran mostly parallel to a winding stream that Buck called Fountain Creek. In the fading light, there was little to see on the flat, snowy plain except for the occasional farm building that looked cold and forlorn amid the unyielding emptiness. As they rode, Caleb saw plenty of evidence of a herd being driven north, but eventually they had to stop and camp when darkness descended over them like a shroud.

They reached the rail siding by midmorning, but as Caleb feared, there was nothing left of his herd or the men who'd taken it. Asking the lone watchman at the railroad site, he learned that a man resembling Elijah Starr, along with his band of henchmen and a thousand head of long-horns, had stopped through, but they were long gone.

Together, they'd decided that Duke and Bass would continue on with the dim hope of catching up to the cattle in the stockyards at Denver. They had little chance of recovering the herd at this point, but they might be able to confirm who was responsible. Caleb, however, decided to cross the mountains, staying south of Pike's Peak, and try to cut the time it would take to reach Elkhorn. He knew Elijah Starr would head that way eventually. And he wanted to be there waiting.

Snow had continued to fall off and on for the next two days, slowing him down as he traversed the rugged moun-tain range. On the second day, he reached the high, broad plateau he remembered. The wind howled mercilessly across the treeless expanse, but the snow cover was far more forgiving. He'd made good time across, but the deep gorges, rocky ridges, and plunging ravines that followed had taken their toll on Pirate and on Caleb.

Still, he figured he was only a full day away from the river valley that would lead him north to Elkhorn…and his father.

Studying the approaching storm, Caleb knew he and his horse needed to take shelter soon. In his days of scouting and leading travelers across the frontier, this was the moment when he'd tell his charges to prepare to camp for a week. But he didn't have a week. He couldn't afford to waste a day. He had to get back.

Caleb had no doubt that Elijah Starr was responsible for the stolen cattle. He would've known from his dealings with the judge that a herd of longhorns were coming for the ranch south of the town. There were no other ranches around Elkhorn raising cattle.

Starr had known how to stab him where it would hurt him financially, and Caleb hadn't seen the gleaming knife's edge. He'd only felt it once the point had been driven deep into his flesh.

Icy barbs stung his face now as he looked out across the mountains, but he barely noticed, lost in thought about the poisoned relationship he had with his father. Some relationships between father and son seemed doomed right from the start. Caleb knew that was true of his family.

Somehow, he'd been named by his mother. Strange,

considering how controlling Elijah was. However it came about, she'd called him Caleb. She told him she'd believed he would be—like his biblical namesake—brave, faithful, devoted. And Caleb *was* brave, faithful, and devoted...but only to her.

In his father's warped mind, Caleb had turned out to be a fraud, faithless and disloyal, because he sided with his mother against Elijah. Because he stood against the violence directed at her. Because he loathed and defied his father's brutality. One night, in a fit of twisted rage, Elijah told him he was no different than the Caleb trusted by Moses but who worked in stealth only to enrich himself.

And now that father and son had been thrown together on the Colorado frontier, each was filled with the inescapable need to destroy the other.

To reach his father, Caleb had scaled to heights ten thousand feet above the snowy plain. And though he knew that he would need to fight his way through drifts seven feet high and make his way along treacherous ledges, he still chose the most direct route to his nemesis.

But now the storm was about to hit.

Caleb's head snapped around at the sound of Pirate's sudden snorts. The buckskin had his head up and was nervously pawing at the icy rock at the edge of the pool. The horse backed away from the water, his nostrils flaring, and Caleb saw the cause of his panic.

Beyond Pirate, a wide, rocky meadow rose steadily for a half mile before forests again closed in around it. Only forty yards upstream, a young bear had lumbered out of the trees and now stood on his rear legs, eyeing the gelding.

That grizzly might be less than a year old, Caleb thought, but the danger he posed was lethal. And he was already moving in Pirate's direction.

There was no way Caleb was going to get to his horse before the young grizzly. The beast was fast, and on this terrain, the advantage of those huge feet and four-inch claws was insurmountable.

Caleb took a few steps forward, drawing his Colt as he shouted at Pirate to get moving. Firing his gun in the air, he startled his horse into action. The buckskin spun and bolted back the way they'd come.

Then everything got worse.

The mother bear came out of the woods with her head swinging from the cub to Caleb. The smell of gun smoke still hung in the air, but that didn't deter her one bit. She was not just looking at him as a threat to her young one. She was clearly thinking about how tasty a meal he'd make for the two of them.

She had to be five hundred pounds, Caleb reckoned, and when she stood up for a better look, he figured she stood seven feet tall. Her coat was light brown, and her head had to be close to three feet from ear to ear.

She stared at him. He stared back.

"You look full and happy," he called out to her. "I'm just traveling through. Ain't much meat on these bones."

He knew this bear had no fear of him. Hell, she'd probably never even seen a human before.

One thing he was sure of, she'd be impossible to kill with his revolver. He'd heard stories of hunters shooting one of these monsters with a Winchester '73 thirty times before it died. Even a Sharps with a .50–90 cartridge was no sure thing. That rifle could drop a buffalo at a thousand yards, but unless you got the grizzly in the eye or right behind the ear, you weren't going to kill it. That was how he'd gotten the one whose skin he was wearing right now. Old Jake was impressed, but Caleb felt that luck had been on his side.

He thought about the Colt in his hand. If he shot her with it, he'd only make her mad. Then she'd maul him a few times, toss him up and down to break a few more bones, bury him under a rock for a few days to make him good and tender, and come back when she was really hungry.

Right now, though, she already looked mad. As she took a few steps toward him, he instinctively backed away. He stopped at the edge of the cliff. It didn't matter that this beast could outrun him, Caleb had nowhere to go.

Sometimes the sudden movement of a strange object would frighten a wild animal. It occurred to him that the report of his pistol hadn't done anything but draw the attention and the ire of the mama bear, and it hadn't done anything but stop the advance of the cub for a moment.

Waving the pistol in the air, Caleb let out a wild whoop and then fired two rounds that raised sparks from the rocks between him and the grizzly.

The sight of her teeth told him that idea wasn't going to work here. She came at him with surprising speed.

Knowing he had no chance reasoning with her any further, he pouched his iron, turned, and leapt as far as he could off the ledge.

As the tops of the tall pines raced up to greet him, Caleb wondered if this is what a hawk felt like as it plummeted toward its prey in the forest or meadow. When he hit the first branch, however, he felt more like a rock tossed from the edge of a precipice into a canyon.

Then he didn't do any more thinking.

Branches tore at him, ripping at his hands and face and sending him tumbling end over end. His back hit something, knocking the wind out of him, but he was still falling. The next jarring blow glanced off his shoulder and head, bringing bright lights into his brain before quickly going out.

When Caleb opened his eyes, he was lying on his back on a soft, cold bed of pine needles. It was dark beneath the trees, and he couldn't move and could barely draw a breath. He heard falling water somewhere nearby. His head was pointed down a slope and he turned it to the side. His hat lay brim up a few feet away. Lucky.

He bent his knees slightly and heard a moan from somewhere nearby. When he moved an arm, he heard the groan again and realized the sound came from him. His left arm had no feeling in it, and he realized that his whole left side was numb.

Caleb decided he'd done enough today and closed his eyes to rest a while.

When awareness returned, snow was filtering down

through the pine boughs, coating his face. He blinked and reached up with his hand to wipe away the flakes. It took a moment to realize he'd used his left hand. He didn't know how long he'd been lying there, but if he didn't do something, some wolf or cougar...or bear...was going to have a frozen feast.

He forced a breath into his lungs. Better. He tried moving his limbs again. Shockingly, everything was working, more or less. Bracing himself against the pain, he rolled to his right and pulled his legs around until his head was pointed uphill.

He was short of breath, but he didn't want to stop now. Using his right arm, he pushed himself into a sitting position. His head spun for a moment, and he felt a lump on the side of his head the size of his fist.

"Well, Marlowe," he muttered. "At least you're alive."

Reaching for his hat was painful, as well, but he pulled it gingerly onto his head.

The lowest branches above him were twenty feet above the forest floor, a fact that filled him with sense of awe that he *was* alive.

Carefully, he reached for the trunk of the tree that had ushered him not so gently to the ground. Taking another deep breath, he used his right hand to pull himself to one knee and then to his feet. Then he just hung on until the world stopped going in circles.

When he was sure his legs would support his weight, he slowly started down the slope, moving from tree to tree and using each one for support. When he reached a break in the pines, he realized the snow was falling heavily, and the treetops far above seemed to be shuddering in the wind. A stream ran across one end of the opening, and he staggered toward it.

Following the running water, he moved back into the shelter of the tree limbs and continued his slow trek downward. After what seemed like a year of half walking, half dragging himself, he felt the terrain begin to level out. A few moments later, he emerged from the trees to find a large, partially frozen lake spread out in front of him. The snow was falling hard, whipping into swirling clouds across the surface.

Caleb raked his eyes along the shoreline and stopped suddenly. Drawing breath, he whistled as loudly as he could manage.

The buckskin raised his handsome face from the water, his ears and eyes searching for the source of the sound. Caleb whistled again, and that was enough.

Pirate came at a gallop around the end of the lake, not stopping until he reached his master's outstretched hand.

CHAPTER TWENTY-TWO

HENRY STOOD BACK AND ADMIRED THE LADDER HE'D built leading up into the barn rafters. Tomorrow, he'd do the same thing for the rafters over on the other side.

He dropped his tools into the crate where Caleb insisted they be kept and went to stand by the open door. The snow wasn't coming down as hard as before, but it was still falling. And everything in the valley was covered from ridge to ridge.

The wind whistled through the barn as he looked at the herd he'd driven up closer to the rise. The cattle were huddled together in one mass by the river, conserving their heat. Maybe they weren't so mindless after all. At least, they knew that it was a good thing, staying close to each other.

He hadn't been to Elkhorn in three days, and he was damn ready for some company. He had to admit that loneliness could get to a fella. He missed being around people. He missed ribbing Caleb about things. Hell, he even missed his friend's lectures and nagging. He hoped Caleb would finally get around to bringing Paddy out to the ranch. The constant chatter between the boy and Gabe was a noise he'd become fond of.

The days were growing shorter, and that didn't exactly make him feel any better. And this damn snow was starting to get him edgy about being stuck out here. When he was a boy and the snows fell, at least there was a camp full of people around. And the buffalo hunts always meant a lot of activity.

When it came right down to it, he and his partner in this ranch business were two completely different people. Caleb was a loner. Henry needed people around.

And he needed the freedom to move. Those six months in jail were the longest he'd ever been cooped up in one place. There were times when those walls just closed in and he thought he'd go mad. He saw fellas lose their minds in there. Twice, when a fight broke out, they put him in "the hole" for a week. Pitch dark and nobody to talk to but the rats he heard squeaking in the crumbling stonework and the rotting rafters above.

It was during those times—when Henry thought he wouldn't last another day—that his mother's Crow stories came back to him. There was one set of tales especially that kept running through his mind. It was about Old Man Coyote, who was both creator god and trickster. And it was his mother's singsong voice that kept him company:

Where Old Man Coyote came from, nobody knows. But he was, and he lived.

Old Man Coyote spoke: "It is bad that I am alone. I should have someone to talk to..."

A gust of wind came out of the west and cut through him, trying to bring Henry back to the present. But part of him stayed in a winter long past, nestled warmly in a robe made from the furred hide of a buffalo.

His mother's people traded unneeded buffalo hides at Fort Sarpy near the mouth of the Bighorn River, but he never lacked one to keep out the winter winds. She was long gone now, her face fading from his memory with each passing year. But he'd never forget her voice and her tender touch.

Henry lost part of himself when she died. So did his father. Russ Jordan had been buying and selling horses across the frontier for years, trading with tribes and settlers from Canada to the edge of Mormon country. He traveled less after he married Henry's mother. Biiwihitche was an Apsáalooke, a Crow. As far as Henry knew, she never considered taking on the white man's ways, and his father always seemed happy and content with his life. He loved her and her people deeply. That never changed, even after her death.

When she was gone, Henry traveled everywhere with his father, learning how to live in the white man's world. But the conflicts were growing sharper, and blood was being spilled all over the frontier.

He recalled the last journey he took with his father. It was eleven years ago. They'd gone to Fort Laramie to hear the Crow Chief Bear Tooth speak to representatives of the government.

Your young men have destroyed my timber and green grass and burnt up my country. Your young men have killed my game, my buffalo. They did not kill it to eat it. They left it where it fell. If I went into your country to kill your game or your cattle, what would you say? Would you not declare war?

It was on the trip back from there that Henry and his father came upon four white men attacking a Crow family who were also traveling. They had camped peacefully beside a river. Their supper was still cooking on the fire. There had been no hesitation in Russ Jordan's mind. The two of them fought alongside the Crow against the white attackers, and his father was killed in the fight. That was the first time Henry killed any man.

Bear trotted into the barn and sat next to Henry's boot, leaning against him.

"And that's one reason Caleb and I got along so good from the first day we was throwed together." He patted the dog's head. "He never asked about nothing. And some things I can never confess. Not till the day I die."

The dog abruptly stood, sniffing the air. A moment later, he ran out a few steps and stood looking across the meadow.

Henry squinted through the swirl of falling snow and saw three riders riding in past the herd. He recognized the man leading the others.

"It's all right, fella. It's only Zeke Vernon."

Henry pulled on his hat and stuffed his arms into his duster. He glanced at his rifle leaning against the wall inside the barn door but decided to leave it.

"Just a social call, Bear," he said to the dog.

He went to meet them. The two riding on either side of the sheriff were deputies Henry had seen in Elkhorn.

"What brings you out here in this mess, Zeke?"

"Nothing good, Henry."

"Why? You heard from Marlowe? Something happen?"

The deputies both had their hands resting on their pistols, and they exchanged a look.

"Nope." The sheriff batted the snow off his stovepipe hat and jammed it back on his head. "Our business is with you. And it ain't pleasant, neither. As I'm sure you already know."

"Me?"

"Get your horse, Henry. We don't want no trouble now. You're coming back to town with us."

"What for?"

"Frank Stubbs."

"What's that miserable sonovabitch complaining about now?"

"He ain't doing no more complaining," Zeke said gruffly. "His brother found him dead in that creek on yours and Caleb's property this morning."

Henry thought about that. "I'll be honest. That's one mangy dog I ain't going to miss."

The sheriff was staring at him.

"So, did the drunken fool fall in and drown? 'Cuz I ain't responsible for nothing like that."

Zeke shook his head. "Stubbs got a hole in him. Shot in the back."

"You think I did it?" Henry felt his blood firing up. "If'n you do, you're as big a fool as him."

"I got witnesses that say you done it. So let's go. And don't get cute about nothing."

CHAPTER TWENTY-THREE

In daylight and in darkness, in snow and in ice, with a clear trail or without, Caleb pushed on toward his valley. And now, after two brutal days, his ranch lay just ahead.

The journey had nearly killed him. Coming across the mountain—climbing the jagged peaks and picking his way through the deep snows in the dark valleys—he sometimes felt his mind wandering and had to make himself stay alert. He was exhausted, hungry, half-frozen. Every muscle in his body felt like it had been stomped by an angry buffalo.

By sheer force of will, he kept going.

His place lay between here and Elkhorn. The sky was steel gray, and it looked like more snow was about to barrel down from the peaks to the west. He'd been riding through the gathering gloom of late afternoon, but he wasn't stopping until he reached his cabin. Once Caleb got there, Henry would take care of Pirate while he tried to extract himself from his torn and bloody clothes. Then, a warm meal and a couple of hours of sleep. That was all he needed.

Then he'd be ready to get on with his business in town.

He still had miles to go, but the end was almost in sight. Pirate recognized home, as well, and Caleb felt the energy flow back into the noble animal.

Halfway up the valley, a blast of wind brought with it the expected snow, and Caleb fought to keep his spirits from flagging. The flakes were heavy and wet and stuck to him and to Pirate's mane. He yanked down his hat to protect his face and eyes and pulled up his bearskin coat to hide his neck from the wet, stinging cold.

"Come on, boy," he urged his mount. "There's a warm stall and extra oats ahead for you. And you've earned it all."

Night had taken the snow-covered landscape tight in its grip by the time he saw the wide, dark shape of the cattle huddled together by the rise.

Caleb smelled the trouble before he saw it. The acrid scent of smoke, pushed down and spread wide by the weight of the falling snow and the wind.

He peered ahead and saw the sky brightening and then lighting up. Flames poured out of the open ends of the burning barn.

"No!"

Caleb dug his heels into Pirate's side and pushed the mount faster up the rise. As he reached the top, he saw them. He counted four men with torches.

Yellow and orange flames completely engulfed the roof and upper walls of the barn. The roar was almost deafening, and popping explosions sent sparks fifty feet in the air. Henry's cabin was on fire as well, the open door and windows spewing fire like the gates of hell.

As he raced toward the buildings, Caleb saw the pair of horses and the mule in the corral silhouetted by the flames from the cabin. The animals were running helter-skelter, panicked by the sights and the smells, and Caleb cast a quick look at the barn, knowing Henry's horse had to be in there.

The torch-wielding villains had already heard him coming hard, and three of them weren't waiting around to see who it was. They were sprinting toward their mounts at the edge of the darkness, shooting over their shoulders as they ran.

Caleb turned Pirate toward the burning buildings, and the buckskin bravely obeyed. Reining in by the barn, he leaped from the saddle and shooed his mount away from the inferno.

Drawing his Colt, Caleb spun and opened fire on the men. One of them was still on Caleb's porch. The villain hesitated and then turned and kicked in the door. He drew back his arm to throw the flaming torch inside.

The bullet from Caleb's Colt should have killed him, but some evil angel was looking after the rogue. The slug struck the torch in his hand, splintering the wood and knocking it into the snow. Not about to press his luck, the cur left it and bolted for his horse, a bay pinto.

Seated on horses that were wheeling and rearing, the others gave up shooting in Caleb's direction, and a moment later they were all racing away into the darkness and the falling snow.

"Henry!" Caleb shouted into the night. "Where are you, Henry?"

Hearing no response, he buried his mouth and nose in his sleeve and ran into the flaming barn. Henry valued his horse more than his own life. This would have been the first place he'd go if he saw the barn ablaze.

It took only seconds to see that Henry was not here. The stalls were empty. He went out as quickly as he went in. Racing by the corral toward his friend's cabin, he yanked open the gate, and the frightened animals galloped out into the night.

A moment later, Caleb was at the cabin door, the heat scorching his face.

"Henry, you in there?"

There was no answer except for the roar of the fire and the sounds of charred wood cracking and falling inside.

Caleb took a deep breath and pushed in against the furnace-like waves of heat. Flames leaped at him like darting snakes. His face and eyes felt like they were about to catch fire, and the sleeve of his coat caught as sparks dropped into the fur. His friend wasn't in there, alive or dead, and Caleb ran out, plunging his arm into the snow.

"Bear," Caleb called out, searching for his dog. There was no sign of him. Out on the white meadows, the cattle were moving down the valley, away from the fire, and the horses had disappeared in the darkness. He hoped his dog had been smart enough to sense the danger and go into the forest or get out ahead of the herd.

Caleb moved away from the cabins and the barn toward the edge of the rise. Moving back and forth through the snow, he searched for any sign of his partner or his dog.

Every drift and shadow filled him with worry that the snow covered the corpse of one or the other. Eventually he circled back to the cabins, puzzled by the absence of both.

He looked out through the darkness, suddenly feeling every bruise and every aching muscle. His head was about to explode, and the smell of burnt wood was overwhelming his senses.

Henry's horse was missing. With any luck, his partner was sitting safely at the Belle. If he'd been here, Caleb had a good idea Henry would be dead right now.

A rafter burst, and a piece of Henry's roof sailed off into the air and fell against Caleb's cabin. The embers of the wood flared in the breeze, threatening to set the wall on fire. He went to it and kicked it clear, where it hissed as he covered it with snow.

Walking around to the front of his cabin, he picked up the torch the attacker had intended to use. Going inside, he saw it appeared that nothing had been disturbed since he left. He went back out and pushed the head of the torch into a drift.

Caleb gazed into the dark where the four men had gone. The blackguards had come, intending to burn everything, wanting to destroy all the progress he and Henry had made. He had no doubt they would have driven off what was left of the herd if he hadn't arrived when he did. Again, he hoped Henry was all right.

First, the longhorns coming from Texas were stolen. Now, his property put to the torch. He had no doubt it was all connected. His father was behind it all, determined to destroy him.

An explosive crash behind Caleb caused him to spin around in time to see the flames above the barn reach the heavens. The roof had collapsed, and a few moments later, the walls collapsed inward with another rush of spark and smoke and flame.

"On my mother's soul, you'll pay for this," Caleb swore. "By God, I'll make you pay."

CHAPTER TWENTY-FOUR

WITH THE SMOKE AND FLAMES STILL RISING INTO THE night sky, Caleb whistled, and Pirate immediately trotted up to him out of the falling snow and darkness.

"I know you're bone-tired and hungry, big fella, but the two of us got a few more miles to go before this journey is over."

Bracing himself against the pain wracking his body, Caleb hauled himself up into the saddle again. With a click of his tongue, they started out across the meadow toward the river and the trail leading to Elkhorn.

Caleb didn't take time to change his clothes or do anything else at the ranch. There was nothing he could do. The fire that was destroying the barn and Henry's cabin would just burn itself out. The herd and the horses had scattered, and that mule was probably halfway to Santa Fe. In any event, there was no way Caleb could round them up now. And no matter how many times he called, there'd been no sign of his dog.

The ride into Elkhorn passed in a weary blur, but Pirate didn't falter. Before they reached town, Caleb realized that the storm had pretty much faded to flurries, and the wind had stopped entirely.

The snow filling Elkhorn's streets didn't slow the late-night revelers at all. Drunken miners were building walls of snow and having a noisy snowball fight in the middle of Main Street outside the Belle. They looked and sounded like schoolboys on holiday. Caleb didn't see Henry's horse tied to the hitching post, but he would more likely have taken him to Malachi Rogers's livery stable.

When Caleb dismounted at Malachi's place, the sight of his dog running out of the stables and jumping up to greet him was the most welcome thing he'd experienced in days.

"Thank God, you're here. Good boy, Bear. But what in blazes are you doing in town?" Not that he was complaining.

Bear tried to answer but only managed to circle Caleb, wag his tail, and whimper happily.

Malachi Rogers appeared in the large double doors of the stable, holding a lantern.

"Marlowe, glad to see you're back." The man's voice carried the distinct sound of relief.

"What's wrong? The missus and the boys all right?" After the night he'd already had, Caleb was concerned that everything and everyone connected to him might be in danger.

"They're all fine. The boys are sleeping, being as late as it is."

Caleb had no idea how late it was. He pushed the dog down with a pat on the head. "Why is Bear here with you?"

"Gabe and Paddy didn't want to leave him out there

alone at the ranch, what with the weather. So they went out and fetched him. Brought him back this morning."

"Where's Henry?"

"You ain't heard?"

Every nerve in Caleb's body was already frayed, and cold sweat trickled down his spine. "What happened to him?"

Malachi motioned up the road toward the jail. "Your partner was arrested yesterday. Brought in by the sheriff and locked up for Frank Stubbs's murder."

"Murder?"

The livery owner nodded. "Word is Zeke's got witnesses that say Henry shot that nasty, two-legged crowbait in the back."

As far as Caleb could tell, nobody in a thousand miles would miss the miserable cur. He sure as hell wouldn't. He could see Henry shooting it out with Stubbs if their neighbor provoked him again, but his friend wouldn't put a man down from behind. Not without damn good reason.

"It ain't like Henry to shoot nobody in the back. Zeke knows better." Caleb handed the reins to Malachi. "I better see what's going on."

"If you don't mind me saying…" The livery man ran his eyes over Pirate and then Caleb. "Looks like the two of you been riding hard."

"Take care of this good fella. What with this weather and all, he's been through snowy hell this past week. And I'm gonna go and have a talk with that boar hog of a sheriff."

"All right. But maybe you oughta talk to Doc Burnett first," Malachi suggested. "Since your partner was brought in, Doc's been wearing a path between the jail and the judge's office. He's sure to have a mouthful to tell you, the two of you being friends and all."

Malachi was right. Zeke made no decisions. He did what he was told. His bread was buttered by Judge Patterson, and he wouldn't do anything to cross him. Talking to Doc first made sense.

Caleb nodded and realized Bear was ready to follow him. "You wait here. Stay."

The dog planted his butt in the snow next to the livery owner.

"That all right, Malachi?"

"'Course."

Caleb took a couple of steps and turned around. The livery man was just starting to lead Pirate into the stable. "Malachi, do you know if Elijah Starr is back in Elkhorn?"

"Don't think so. But I'd reckon Doc would know that too."

The Burnett house wasn't far, but trudging through the deep snow was harder on his worn body than Caleb expected. After two days, his left side still ached from the fall off the cliff, and it felt like at least one of his back ribs was busted and sticking into something else. It didn't matter a damn, though. He had things to do. He gritted his teeth and pushed on.

As Caleb came along the street where Doc's house stood, memories of last summer poured in. The house was the only one on the street with a porch, and Caleb's friend made good use of it on warm evenings. In the summer, he had a couple of rockers out there and a table big enough for the chess board. At the end of the porch, he'd put a comfortable bench with a woven seat and back where Sheila liked to sit and read.

He climbed the steps and noticed the porch was empty of all but the coating of snow that had blown onto it. Doc had stored the furniture away somewhere, and the emptiness of it pierced Caleb like a sharp stick.

He sincerely hoped there'd be more summer evenings for him here. But the future was definitely looking bleak.

Light was pouring out the window from the front parlor, and he glanced in before knocking. Inside, Sheila sat at the desk, writing a letter, from the look of it. Her hair draped down her back in golden waves, reaching her waist. He didn't usually get to see her hair down like that. When they were together, she wore it in a thick braid. Her face in profile was all concentration as the pen scratched hurriedly across the page. She was like a picture from the page of a book. An image to look at and admire. He knew how tough she was, but she had the gift of looking so detached from the harshness of frontier life.

For a moment, Caleb stood paralyzed by the wave of emotions that ran through him. For a few brief instances over these past months, he'd allowed himself to dream, to think he might deserve the chance of having her in his life. But he never did anything about it and never would now.

And all that talk about Paddy. Just wasted breath. Caleb had no safe life and no home to give the boy.

Something in him felt broken. Ruined. And he hated the feeling.

A breeze lifted a swirl of snow and threw it against the door. Sheila's eyes lifted from the paper, and she turned to the window. Realizing someone was on the porch, she rose quickly to her feet.

Caleb knocked on the door.

Sheila opened it, and her eyes immediately rounded. Before saying a word, she looked at him from top to bottom as he scraped the snow from his boots.

He took off his hat. "Sheila."

She took his arm and pulled him inside, closing the door behind him.

"Marlowe!" She took his hat. Words and questions bubbled out, running into each other. "What happened to you? You're hurt. Your face is cut. And bruised. That lump on your head. I smell smoke. Were you burned? Your clothes are…a mess!"

Caleb shed his bearskin and looked down at himself. He was a mess. He saw several gaping holes in the coat and charred fur on the sleeve. He now understood why Malachi kept pushing him to see Doc first.

Doc Burnett came into the front room and paused. He appeared as amazed as his daughter for a few seconds.

"Look at him. He's hurt," she exclaimed.

"You were supposed to gather your herd and bring them back," Doc said wryly, "not get trampled by them."

"Had a change of plans." This was one of the things Caleb liked about his friend. There was never panic.

Before they could say anything more, Sheila was pushing Caleb through the house toward the surgery.

Doc followed them and picked up a lamp as they went by the back parlor.

The surgery was empty and spotless as new linen. Sheila led Caleb to the high operating table and had him sit as Doc lit the lamps. The place looked quite a bit different from the night Doc took Tex Washington's leg off. Caleb asked how the young fella was doing, and his friend told him he was mending and had moved to Belle's boardinghouse this past Friday.

"But what happened to you?"

"A few things, but most of the damage come from jumping off the top of a mountain to get clear of a mama grizzly."

"Did she happen to be on fire?" Sheila asked, pulling off his boots. "Because your face and eyebrows are singed, and the soles of your boots and your pants are burned too."

"Well, I been thinking it's time for some new duds."

Doc agreed. "You look and smell like you've been rolling around in Malachi's forge while someone pumped the bellows."

"Well, I didn't want to say so, but that's exactly what happened. I might just have to take my business to the other end of town."

"You can joke, Caleb Marlowe," Sheila said with a sharp frown. "But I've never seen you in this condition."

"And you ain't never seen me rassle with a grizzly before, neither." From the furrowed brow, he knew she was worried. Caleb figured he looked worse than he felt, and that was saying something.

"Sheila, go and put on some water to heat, would you? Our patient here needs to get cleaned up."

Reluctantly, she went out.

"That girl has been pacing around here, edgy as a caged lion since you left," Doc said in a low voice. "She was pretty damn anxious about you."

No matter what Caleb thought, how he wanted to push her away, Sheila had her own mind.

He winced as Doc helped him out of his vest and his wool shirt.

"Looks like that bear got the better of you, my friend."

The physician was looking him over, silently circling around to get a good look at his back too. It was the first time Caleb had seen the results of his effort to escape the grizzly.

The left side of his body was one mass of bruises and cuts. They extended from the top of his shoulder, out over his left arm, and down his chest and ribs to the waist of his pants. He was fairly certain his hip and leg didn't look much different. The colors ranged from purple and black to green and yellow. He was glad Sheila wasn't in here to see it. He looked more like a battered plum than a human.

Doc took a hard look at the lump on Caleb's head, paying close attention to the burns as well.

"What really happened?" he asked with a quick glance at the door.

"That was a fact about the grizzly. The she-bear and her cub cornered me on a ledge two days south of here, up in the mountains. Had to jump and was fortunate to have about a hundred feet of pine tree to break my fall."

"Take a deep breath."

Caleb breathed in as deeply as he could, which wasn't too deep.

Doc was feeling his ribs, which was not a pleasant sensation, but Caleb didn't let on.

"Feels like two broken ribs. Another knot on your head to match the one in back."

"I suppose if I keep it up, I'll need to be getting a bigger hat."

Doc snorted. "You're lucky you still have a head to put one on."

He went over to his cabinet and pulled out a couple of bottles and some rolls of bandages.

"Where are Ortiz and Bass?"

Caleb told Doc everything that had happened in Pueblo and how they'd decided to split up. "I know Elijah Starr is behind all of this. He planned the whole damn thing."

Doc gestured to the burns on his face and hands. "How did you get these?"

"When I got back, some varmints were setting my ranch on fire. Four of them with torches. They burned the barn and Henry's cabin. I got there in time to stop them from burning mine."

"Recognize any of them?"

Caleb shook his head. "But I know who sent 'em."

Doc looked at the door again. "No point in bandaging you till we get you cleaned up."

"Nope, but I can't stay long. I gotta go." He paused. "I appreciate you patching me up, but I only came here so you could tell me about Henry. Malachi says you might know something."

Doc nodded grimly. "They say he killed Frank Stubbs."

"I don't believe it. Henry wouldn't plug a man in the back, even a cur like Stubbs."

"Henry denies the whole thing. And I'd take his word and yours over any of them."

Caleb appreciated him saying it. "You talked to Zeke?"

Doc gave a humorless laugh. "Zeke is no help. He says his hands are tied. I've been trying to see the judge, but he keeps putting me off. His secretary says he's too busy."

"Patterson wouldn't ignore you without a reason. He's got something up his sleeve, and he ain't about to show his hand."

"It could be the simplest of reasons."

Doc looked uncomfortable, and Caleb waited.

"I spoke to Edmond Lassiter."

"Who's that?"

"A shyster who comes through town fairly regularly. He's the only lawyer we have access to right now. He's been talking to the judge to see what Henry's chances are."

"And?"

"Lassiter says the judge hasn't had a hanging in months and is looking forward to seeing Henry with a noose around his neck."

CHAPTER TWENTY-FIVE

"If it was me that done it, Caleb, I'd fess up and take credit for gunning the skunk. But I didn't. Me and your dog were close to home, doing what we was supposed to be doing. I happened to find Stubbs and his flap-jawed brother up by that creek a few days before—and sent them running—but I wasn't nowhere near there when he was shot."

"I believe you."

Trouble and Henry were on a first-name basis. But it was always a fistfight, a bar brawl, a jag over women or bad cards. Caleb knew his partner would never shoot even someone as low as Frank Stubbs in the back. Nonetheless, trouble had come calling again.

Zeke wasn't at the jail when Caleb arrived, even though the sun had been up for hours. He figured the sheriff went out the back when he saw him coming down Main Street. When Caleb asked when Zeke would be back, the deputy had stood with his back to the office wall, shaking his head and gripping his holstered revolver like he was afraid Caleb would take it away from him.

Last night, Doc Burnett wouldn't let Caleb leave the house until he was washed and patched up. And Sheila wouldn't take no for an answer about warming some food for him. By that time, there was no question that the jail would be locked up tight for the night. There'd be no seeing Henry until morning. So Caleb accepted Doc's offer to sleep for a couple of hours and go down there fresh in the morning.

When Caleb opened his eyes, the sun was shining in. He could barely move at first from all the bruises but felt better once he managed to get his feet on the floor. Standing was an adventure. Every muscle felt like it was held together with piano wire. On a chair next to the door, he found his boots, all clean and dry. And a new pair of pants and a shirt, both his size. Someone had gone down to Wilson's General Store to get them first thing. He had a good idea who.

When he went downstairs, Doc was in his surgery with a patient, and Sheila was nowhere to be found. She'd left him coffee and some warm biscuits and a note saying she had appointments. So Caleb went down to the jail, sore as hell but feeling reasonably alive. By the time he reached the place, however, he was ready to bite the head off a rattler.

The deputy would only allow Caleb in to see Henry if he left his guns and talked to the prisoner through the bars.

Henry was not feeling too good about the situation. Seated on the bench against the wall, he held his head in his hands. Caleb had not said anything about his conversation with Doc. No mention of what the lawyer thought.

Henry already knew that Patterson prided himself on his reputation as a hanging judge. *A law-and-order man* was the way the judge liked to put it.

The way Henry looked right now, he didn't need to be reminded. Not wanting to add to his friend's misery, Caleb said nothing about their ranch going up in smoke last night. It was bad enough sharing the news that the longhorns were long gone by the time he and the two cattlemen got to Pueblo.

Henry kicked at the dirt and raised his head, the fire back in his eyes. "You hear who's accusing me? That fake preacher. Frank's own brother. And you tell me, who's gonna own Stubbs's land now? That same no-account piker, that's who. Don't that sound suspicious to you?"

Caleb nodded, giving Henry room now that he'd built up a head of steam.

"You gotta help me out, partner. Doc's been here, but nobody else is doing nothing."

"You know I will."

"I know it's been snowing terrible since that shooting, but would you go and see if you can find anything up there by the creek? Zeke wasn't looking for nothing but to haul that skunk's carcass back to town."

Henry was right. Zeke probably didn't look around at all. He had a corpse, a witness who said Henry did it, and a boss who was ready to hang somebody.

"I'll go up there first chance. Maybe there's something."

"You been a sheriff," Henry urged him. "I don't need to tell you what to do."

"I'll ride over there today."

"Also, I don't hold no faith in lawyers, but I'm thinking maybe I need one. So if you can, find me a good one. Just in case."

He could hear the anxiety in his friend's voice. Henry was in a tough spot, and he knew it.

"I'll see what I can do. Keep your chin up. We'll get you out of this."

Leaving his partner, Caleb went back into the front room of the jail. As soon as he did, the deputy jumped out of his chair like a burned hoppy toad, his hand again on the Remington holstered at his hip.

"I'm starting to think you got a bad twitch, the way you keep lighting up like that."

The deputy cocked his head like a confused street dog. He didn't know what Caleb was talking about, but he wasn't about to pursue it. "You done with him back there?"

"Yup. I blasted him out. If you go in there, you'll see there's a hole in the wall. I'm gonna get his horse now and meet him outside."

"You did?" He blinked. "You are?"

Caleb sighed. "Where's Zeke?"

"He ain't here."

"I can see that. Where is he?"

"He ain't here."

He wondered if it was worth waiting for Zeke. Caleb looked slowly around the room, trying to rein in his frustration with this dolt. A dozen WANTED posters that somebody tacked up and that nobody probably looked at since. The sheriff's desk. A rack on the wall with four rifles. Some dusty Colt Dragoons hanging from hooks. A couple of spittoons that were too small even for Zeke to hide in. "I can see he ain't here. Where is he?"

The deputy looked completely lost. "Somewheres. But not here."

This was going nowhere, and Caleb felt his patience about to slip.

"And you can't wait around here, Marlowe. I don't know when Zeke's coming back."

"I ain't waiting. Let me have my guns and my knife."

Never taking his eyes off Caleb, the deputy opened a drawer in the desk and slowly took the gun belt out. He hesitated giving them back.

"If you don't hand them over to me right now, I'm gonna plant my fist in your ugly mug."

The threat worked. His weapons landed on the desk in front of him.

The sound of shouting outside drew Caleb's attention as he slid his knife into his boot and strapped on his gun belt. "What's that?"

"Don't know."

That answer came as no surprise.

The deputy edged over to the window and shot a glance out. "It's the preacher, Amos Stubbs. Frank Stubbs's brother."

"Be sure you patch up that hole in the cell wall back there before Zeke gets here," he told the deputy as he went out. "If he ever *does* get here."

The preacher was standing on the back of a wagon across from the jail, and he'd managed to draw a small crowd of miners. He was wearing a black suit that looked shiny and new. His voice kept getting louder, building up momentum. The way he waved the Bible gave the impression that he knew what was in it. But stories from Scripture were not his subject today, as Caleb immediately found out.

"There's a sinner in that jail, brothers. A sinner of the lowest kind." Stubbs pointed with the Bible at the jail-house door. "Behind those walls lurks a beast. A monster. A man who does not deserve the appellation of *man*. Behind those walls is a man who does not deserve the *dignity* that the law in this town apparently feels he deserves."

Hearing the crowd start to rumble in response, Caleb crossed the street that was now packed with snow. Wheel tracks had cut deep grooves, and mud was starting to show in places. If it didn't stay cold, the street would be a mire in a matter of days.

"His victim was a man from your community, my brothers—not some outsider like that shiftless ne'er-do-well resting in the sublime comfort of the town's security offices—but a man you all know. A man respected by you all for his upstanding nature, his decency, and his contributions to this growing metropolis."

"Who we talking 'bout now?" someone in the crowd called out, drawing a laugh from a few others.

"I'm talking about Frank Stubbs!" the preacher thundered, shouting the man down. "Frank Stubbs, a man of property and standing. A man cut down in the prime of his life by an evil and cowardly dog who shot him in the back. In the *back*, brothers!"

The rumbling among the men started again.

"But there are some in this place who would have you believe that God's enemies deserve a velvet glove instead of the rough hemp of the hangman's noose." Stubbs's brother stared straight at Caleb. "Some who will no doubt try to use the leniency of the law to excuse the vile actions of the *serpent* lying coiled in that jail across the way."

The preacher drew a breath and laid his free hand across his heart.

"It is not for me to suggest that justice will not be served by the actions of a slippery lawyer, an easily duped jury, or a forgiving judge. Nay, and I am not suggesting that we take the law into our hands, that we drag that villain from that place and give him the punishment he so justly deserves. I would never suggest such a thing, even though God's law has been broken. And not just broken. The tablet of Moses has been shattered, brothers. Shattered!"

"Ain't you Frank's brother?" the same miner called out.

The preacher, looking as offended as he could muster, pulled back as if he'd been bitten by a rattler.

"And what of it? Don't I have the right to grieve my brother? And doesn't the Good Book say we're all brothers?" Stubbs raised his hands to the blue sky above. "Yea, I say to you that I would stand witness here for you, brother. For all of you. For the lowliest of you, if you were murdered in such a callous, unfeeling manner."

Caleb looked at the men around him and read skepticism in their faces. Perhaps later in the day, after a few more drinks, Stubbs would find a more receptive mob for his hanging talk, but not right now.

As the preacher continued to hammer away, Caleb's eye was drawn to a movement in a window above the street. In the judge's office, H. D. Patterson himself looked down at the crowd. His gaze was fixed on him.

Leaving Amos Stubbs to his task, Caleb turned and crossed to the front of the judge's building.

Maybe it was time for them to talk.

CHAPTER TWENTY-SIX

CALEB CLIMBED THE WOODEN STEPS TO THE FRONT OF the judge's building. A new plaque beside the door informed the passerby that H. D. PATTERSON, JUSTICE OF THE PEACE presided here. The judge had a larger sign above the sidewalk that could probably be seen from Denver on a clear day. But he must have had this one put up in case anyone happened to miss it.

Caleb stopped to scrape the mud and snow off his boots and started to go in. As he did, the door pulled open, and a man appeared on the threshold, checking his gold pocket watch. He didn't come out, and he didn't move back in. Instead, he simply stood there, looking Caleb over with a critical eye.

A little shorter than Caleb, he was still over six feet, tall for the majority of men in these parts. He was thin as a fence post, and his face was long and lean. Close-set cobalt eyes studied him without blinking. A reddish, waxed moustache perched beneath a long, beak-like nose. He was wearing a heavy overcoat, and a gray suit peeked from beneath. The dandy had been freshly shaved and smelled strongly of bay rum.

"Mr. Marlowe, if I'm not mistaken." His voice was

unexpectedly deep and resonant, like that of a stage actor.

Caleb was used to having people recognize him from his years on the trail. But this one was too posh to be anyone he might have crossed paths with. He'd definitely remember him.

"Who are you?"

The fellow removed his bowler, exhibiting thinning ginger hair, plastered flat across the top.

"Lassiter. Edmond Lassiter, attorney at law. I am a noted litigator, sir, well known in the highest courts of our land. I go wherever I'm needed in this fine state of ours. That is my quest. I've dedicated my life, sir, to helping our brave pioneers find justice in Colorado's rude wilderness. Indeed, sir, justice for all is my quest."

Quite the sales pitch, Caleb thought. He and that preacher in the street were a pair to beat a full house.

"You're probably wondering how I know you." Lassiter replaced his bowler, careful not to disturb his hair. "I make it my business to know important people, sir."

Caleb had heard the man's name from Doc Burnett, and he felt oily just talking to him. He recalled what Doc said about the shyster having already spoken to the judge about Henry.

"Do we have business, Mr. Lassiter?"

"No. I'm afraid we don't. I thought I could be of service to you, but no, I'm afraid we don't." The man had an annoying way of repeating himself. "I had planned to introduce myself to you once you returned to Elkhorn. I'd hoped to be of service in the unfortunate matter regarding your partner's involvement in the murder of a fellow land-owner. But sadly..."

The lawyer stopped and gestured with his eyes back into the building.

"You were talking with Judge Patterson."

"I was."

"Talking about Henry Jordan."

"I was. Again." He shook his head. "For a second time."

"Nobody has hired you to represent him."

"I know. I know. But I'm a lawyer, Mr. Marlowe. A knight errant on the quest for—"

"So you said."

"I heard of Mr. Jordan's unfortunate circumstances. I happened to be traveling through Elkhorn, and the weather forestalled my journey."

"So?"

"Your partner is facing serious charges, and after speaking with Dr. Burnett—a fine man and a pillar of this community, I should say, a fine man—I took it upon myself to seek out any information that might aid in the administration of justice."

This fella had more words than a squirrel had nuts, Caleb thought. He was a talker. By the time they went their separate ways, he figured he might know whatever it was Lassiter wanted to tell him. If the lawyer ever got around to it.

"Now that the weather is improving, I wanted to check with the judge again. In my quest for justice, I wanted to see if my services might be of any value to Mr. Jordan, for a nominal fee, of course. But alas…the road lies open before me. Other victims of injustice languish in their misery, awaiting my aid."

"You're leaving."

"I am. I am. It gives me great pain, Mr. Marlowe, to tell you there is nothing I can do for your partner. His fate is sealed, I'm afraid." A card suddenly appeared in Lassiter's hand which he pressed into Caleb's hand. "But if, in the future, you should ever be in need of my services—wills and estate documents, lawsuits, bills of sale for land or goods…"

Leaving it at that, the lawyer touched the brim of his hat and bowed. Smoothing his moustache, he pulled on a pair of gloves and stepped out onto the sidewalk.

"That was a waste of good air," Caleb muttered to himself, watching the dandy make his way along Main Street.

As Caleb went in through the large lobby, he considered what he wanted to say to the judge. More than anything, he wanted information. And that wasn't something the judge surrendered easily. Behind a railing on the right side, a trio of bespectacled clerks working at high desks were staring nervously at him. No doubt everyone working for the judge had heard of Caleb's arrest at the Silver Elk Hotel last month. He nodded curtly, and their eyes disappeared into their work.

Behind the clerks, a closed door led to the land sales office, where he'd done business when he first arrived in Elkhorn. On the left side of the lobby, a set of double doors stood open, displaying the interior of the courtroom. The judge's bench lorded over everything else, in front of a picture of Rutherford B. Hayes, flanked by Washington and Lincoln.

Wide stairs stood at the far end of the lobby. Unless he wanted to shoot his way in, there was no other way to the great man's office except through this lobby. There was a back stairway, but he always had armed guards stationed at the bottom.

Right now, Caleb didn't want to be the cause of any trouble. Henry was already occupying Elkhorn's cell. One of them had to be free to help the other get out.

Caleb started up the stairs, chewing over the conversation he'd just had with the lawyer. Something didn't set right. He didn't seem to be a fellow who would forfeit the chance of getting paid for his services.

Of course, the judge could have run him off with a threat of some kind. Everyone knew of Patterson's reputation. He was a sure hand at hanging offenses. Evidence didn't matter. Truth was a minor inconvenience. He was the law, and he used it as it suited his own interests.

Caleb had done the judge too many favors over the course of the past few months in getting Henry released from jail in Denver. The charges were only for a brawl in a bar. As time passed, Caleb came to realize that Patterson had been using his influence to keep Henry in there. That way, he kept Caleb dancing to his tune.

Now they were talking murder. And it didn't matter what Caleb might be able to find to prove Henry's innocence. None of it would matter unless the judge was willing to listen. And that gave Caleb a sick feeling in his gut as he climbed the last steps.

At the landing at the top, a pair of black-suited buffalos stood by the judge's closed door. Caleb hadn't seen these two before. They weren't among the mob guarding the judge over at the hotel the day he went after Elijah Starr. But after the betrayal of Frissy Fredericks, Patterson's trusted former bodyguard, he wasn't surprised that these bruisers were continually changing.

"Hold it right there," one of them growled. "I mean, can I help you?"

"All that practicing for nothing, huh?" Caleb replied.

"You got business, smart guy?" the brute asked, tucking his thumbs into his waistcoat pocket and displaying a brace of short-barreled Colts in cross-draw holsters.

"I'm here to see the judge."

"And who might you be?"

The snort of amusement from the bull standing on the other side of the door told Caleb they were playing with him.

"Nice irons," Caleb said. "While they were teaching you that polite 'howdy,' was that when they taught you boys to stand on your hind legs?"

"If you're looking for trouble, Marlowe, you keep at it."

"There you go. You knew me all along." Caleb held his gaze. "I'm here to see the judge."

"Got a...appointment?" the other bruiser said.

Caleb turned his attention to him. "New word? Practically rolled off the tongue, fella."

Both of them bristled. It didn't take much to stir them up. Unhappy in their work, probably.

"I'm here to see the judge."

"You ain't got a appointment, you ain't going in."

"You're making a mistake. The judge wants to see me."

The two knotheads glanced at each other. They didn't believe him.

At least, Caleb hoped Patterson wanted to talk to him. There used to be a day, not too long ago, when the man behind that door would do plenty to talk Caleb into pinning on a tin star. Cleaning up the town and running off troublemakers were a priority for him.

But hiring Elijah Starr had put them on opposite ends of a pointed stick.

"Don't think he wants to see you, Marlowe. We woulda heard."

"Good thing you don't get paid to think, I reckon. But if you wanna keep getting paid, you'd best ask."

The one standing on the right shook his head but turned and knocked once. A voice inside answered, and the big man went in.

Caleb and the other one stood staring each other down in not-so-companionable silence for a very long time. Finally, the door opened, and Buffalo Number Two emerged.

"Judge says you gotta give up your guns and your hunting knife. Then he'll see you."

Caleb figured that would be the case. Patterson had good reason to be feeling jittery about armed men who might not be feeling too partial to him. He unbuckled his gun belt and handed his weapons over. This was the second time today he'd done it, and these fellas were only slightly more relieved than the deputy had been.

The two bruisers separated, and Caleb went in.

In the small outer room, the judge's secretary sat behind a desk piled high with papers. The overworked fella lifted his balding head and gestured to the open door beyond. Caleb went through and paused inside to take in the view. It never failed to impress him, in spite of knowing that was surely the judge's intention.

The first time he came in here, the thought occurred to Caleb that the man's office was big enough to house an entire cavalry unit and their horses. Though they'd have to move some of the furniture out to make room for everyone, he still thought so. A long, heavy table with matching chairs of carved oak took up one end of the dark, wood-paneled room. That would have to go. And the chandelier of gleaming brass and crystal hanging above the table was a little fancy for cavalry quarters, but they might want to leave it. Velvet drapes, red as blood, hung in the windows, held back by gold ropes. Might want to take them down and roll up the fancy carpets. The shoes of all those horses would do considerable damage to the rugs.

Horace Patterson, Justice of the Peace, sat at a desk nearly as large as Caleb's ranch. Behind him, he had a handsome cabinet with a nice display of law books. On his desk, he'd carefully arranged a pair of oil lamps, a desk set of pen and ink, a writing blotter, and a bronze sculpture of Napoleon with his hand resting on the head of a very sorry-looking lion.

"I see that nothing has changed, Judge. It's good to be the king, I reckon."

The judge stood. One thing about him, he always looked ready to dine with President Hayes himself, should the situation present itself. This morning he was wearing a charcoal suit, silver-gray waistcoat, white silk shirt, and black tie.

"Marlowe, if you've come in here to offend me, then you can turn right around and show yourself out."

"Nope. Just the opposite."

Patterson slid his hand inside the lapel of his waistcoat, eyeing him and taking his measure. "So, then, you've come to apologize."

"Apologize?"

"For your barbaric behavior in the dining room at the Silver Elk Hotel."

Caleb would have liked to confront the man and accuse him of being in with Starr on the theft of his herd and the burning of the ranch. But he was here to save Henry's neck from the noose. That required diplomacy, and that was not Caleb's usual way of doing business.

"You want me to apologize for what happened at Silver Elk Hotel?"

"I do. Or our business is done here."

Patterson had a kind of energy to him, like a timepiece wound too tight. And he was a killer. Caleb had known it the first time he met the man. And right now, the cold,

hard look of a gunman—a look that he knew so well—
was there in the judge's hawklike eyes.

"Judge, there's a lot of things about what happened
over there that I'm sorry about."

Such as not killing his father when he had the chance,
Caleb thought.

"And I suppose ruining your lunch would be among
'em."

The judge gazed at him for a long moment, as if trying
to decide if Caleb meant it or not. "You need to end the
hostilities with Elijah Starr."

He wasn't about to agree to that. "Is he back in Elkhorn?"

"No."

"Good. Then you and I can do business."

"You're here to do business?"

"Yep."

There was that long look of appraisal again. Caleb
stared back, not willing to show his hand. Patience, he
told himself.

Finally, the judge shrugged, waved him into a chair by
the desk, and sat down as well. "You look like a man who
could use a drink."

"I could use a drink," Caleb replied.

"Let's hear what you have to say, and I'll see if we have
reason to drink together."

He ignored the comment, knowing that the judge
was a master at this. The man always wanted to control
things—a conversation, a negotiation, a whole town. And
people, most of all.

"I'm here about Henry."

"I figured as much." Patterson sat back and steepled his fingers, looking intently at Caleb. "He's going to hang."

"What if I could prove that he didn't do it?"

"My sheriff has given me all the evidence that I need, and everybody knows there was bad blood between them. He's going to hang."

Caleb clenched his fists to stop himself from climbing over the desk and grabbing the man by the throat. He took a breath to stay calm. "We both know that Zeke is no lawman. He never wanted the job. He'd be the first to tell you he's no good at it."

"I hired him on your recommendation. He's doing fine."

"This ain't Denver. One of these days, a gunslinger is gonna roll into town, and Zeke will be lying dead in the street."

"He knows the risks that go with the badge and the money."

Caleb paused and then dove in. "You always say you want a town that's safe and civilized."

"So?"

"I'll pin on that tin star, like you asked me before. But you gotta give Henry a chance."

The judge looked steadily at him. They both knew he had Caleb over a barrel, but he had the decency, at least, not to gloat openly.

Still, he shook his head. "That ship has sailed, Marlowe. I recall you rejected my offer repeatedly. No. Zeke will do. But..." He drummed his fingers on the desk.

Caleb waited. He was about to feel the lash fall, but he waited. He kept telling himself that his partner deserved to live.

"I'm willing to make a deal." He sat back in his chair, the emperor of his world. "I can use a strong arm at my side. A gunhawk of your caliber. Someone who can eliminate the nuisances that stand in my way. Someone who will smooth the difficulties that my man, Elijah Starr, might face in building my railroad."

Caleb's blood came to a boil. "You want me to do the killing for Elijah Starr."

"I want you to do what he says." The judge waved a hand in the air. "My time is too valuable to get involved with the small details of the daily operation. He knows what to do and how to get me there. I want results, Marlowe."

"Is stealing my herd one of them small details? I'm talking about a thousand longhorns and nine men dead outside of Pueblo. Does that figure into your idea of results? How about putting my ranch to the torch? More small details?"

Patterson leaned forward, his eyes flashing with anger. "Are you saying I had something to do with stealing cattle and destroying your property?"

"Elijah Starr did. There are fellas in Pueblo who identified him as the man responsible for the taking of that herd."

"Those are serious charges, Marlowe. Serious and unsubstantiated. I have seen firsthand the hostility you harbor toward your family. So I give no credence to what you say. In fact, I know for a fact that the man you reck-lessly accuse is in Denver, serving my business interests. Elijah Starr has no time and, I would wager, no interest in playing these paltry games with you."

The judge looked at the door, and Caleb glanced around. Buffalo Number Two was standing behind the partially opened doorway, his hand at the ready on the grip of his shooting iron. He wondered if the man had been in the outer office the entire time.

"So there you have it, Marlowe. What's your answer? Will you work for Starr?"

The judge was asking him to kill for him. To sell his soul to the devil.

"Hell no."

"So be it. There is the door."

Caleb stood so quickly that the chair skidded back-ward across the floor. He had no idea what choices were left to him now, but the answer clearly didn't lie here. Not with the judge.

As he turned to go, Patterson called out to him. "Wait. There is one other possible solution."

It took great effort to look back at the man. Caleb's distrust had become an intense loathing.

"You and Jordan sell me your ranch."

Sell out. This was the bottom line. The judge wanted his land. And the reason came to him like lightning out of a clear sky. It was the railroad. Not only would he have a straight line south from Elkhorn for his tracks, he'd have open land for a siding and for stockyards. He'd be free and clear to supply beef for everyone in these parts.

Caleb clenched his jaw tight. "And Henry's murder charges?"

"They'll be dismissed." Patterson shrugged. "Lack of evidence."

With the money from this one, Caleb figured they could buy another place. They pretty much had to start over anyway, and Henry's life was worth it. "All right. How much?"

"Two thousand dollars."

Caleb wasn't sure he'd heard correctly. "That's a quarter of what we paid."

"I know. But you have the added value of your partner's life," the judge reminded him. "And there is one more condition."

"What's that?"

"I won't have you standing against me, interfering with my plans. You and Henry Jordan will leave Elkhorn. And if you ever show your faces again, I'll put a bounty on your head and on his. Those are my terms, Marlowe. You can take it or leave it."

CHAPTER TWENTY-SEVEN

Caleb stood with his back to the smoking ruins of the buildings and looked down the valley to the south. Patches of cloud scudded across the afternoon sky, here and there casting large swaths of moving gray across the snowy meadows. It was cold, but the storms had passed to the east, for the time being.

The pain that dragged at his gut surprised him when he rode up the rise from the river. He reasoned that it was because he'd never put so much of himself into a single place, and seeing the blackened timbers of the barn sticking up from the ashy, gray snow physically hurt him. Even now, staring out at the valley, he was in no hurry to turn his gaze to the devastation again.

Down below, a few dozen head of cattle crowded along the icy river, stomping the edges into a brown mush. The rest of the herd was nowhere to be seen. Probably up in the forest or much farther down the valley, searching out protected patches of grass to feed on. Before leaving Elkhorn, he'd made arrangements with Wilson and with Malachi to have hay and feed carted down to the ranch. He wasn't sure why he'd gone to the trouble. The place wouldn't be his much longer. Still, the animals needed to be fed.

He'd left his damaged bearskin in his cabin and donned his elk-skin coat, but neither one could stop the bitter cold from seeping into every crevice in his body and soul, numbing everything it touched.

"Don't be a fool," he muttered to himself, fighting it off. "It's a damn *place*. That's all."

Bear trotted up from behind him and planted his butt in the snow. He leaned against Caleb and pressed his large yellow and black head against his hip.

"I know, fella," he said, patting the dog's head and stroking the soft fur covering his ears. But the truth was, Caleb didn't know. He didn't know a damn thing.

He blew a deep breath of air out of puffed cheeks. The steam drifted off and disappeared quickly in the cold, clear air. There was probably a message in that—here today, gone tomorrow, or some such thing—but he wasn't in any mood to think about it now.

He turned and trudged toward the barn. Ash coated the top of the snow, making it look as dirty as a city street in winter. Charred pieces of wood stuck out of the surface and made patterns in the snow where they'd melted through as they landed.

Some things made him feel even worse about it all. The cattle had scattered hither and yon, but the two horses and the mule had returned to the corral on their own. In spite of the acrid smell of burnt wood poisoning the air, they stood there with Pirate in one corner against the fence, waiting for life to somehow return to normal, he supposed.

But life would never return to *normal*…whatever that meant.

Caleb didn't bother to close the gate on them. Hell, if they wanted to take off for greener pastures, he wouldn't blame them.

He stood on the threshold of the barn, looking in. The air was still hot and sharp with smoke, and he put a gloved hand over his mouth to breathe. Charred timbers still glowing red in places lay in a jumbled heap where they'd fallen. Some lay crisscrossed, cluttering the dirt floor, and some lay on an angle against a lower portion of the wall. The roof was gone, except for one corner. And a few lower sections of the walls were only scorched. But there was no saving any of this. If anyone rebuilt, they'd have to pull the whole thing down and start again.

After his talk with the judge, Caleb had gone back to the livery. There was no point in going and explaining everything to Henry. Not yet. Not until he had his temper under control and some kind of plan in place.

Bear had been curled up in front of Pirate's stall, waiting and watching for his master to return. Caleb was not leaving Elkhorn without him, no matter what. And no matter how dark Caleb's thoughts were on the ride out, he couldn't help but feel his spirits lift—if only for a moment—at the sight of the dog romping happily through the snow on either side of the trail, scaring up rabbits and once a pheasant as he ran.

Caleb had stopped once or twice to look for signs of the men who had come to burn the ranch. In a few places beneath the protective boughs of the conifers, he'd found tracks showing that the four riders had been joined by a fifth man who hadn't shown his face. But they'd all returned to town together.

In the ashy rubble, Caleb spotted one of the iron hinges fashioned by Malachi. Stepping into the barn, he picked it up with his gloved hand and tossed it out into the snow. It was still hot from the inferno that had claimed the stables. He saw no sign of the other iron pieces.

He and Henry built this barn with their own hands. This ranch was home. It was meant to be a place to put down stakes and settle. Henry had been downright sentimental, arguing for finding this land. He'd talked Caleb into it. And once they bought the property and Caleb started it as he waited for Henry to join him, the pieces seemed to fall into place. All of a sudden, staying in one place began to rub off on him. Caleb was getting used to seeing familiar faces, having a few friends, going into Elkhorn for his chess games with Doc. The conversations and flirtations with Sheila had become damn appealing. Bit by bit, he was changing.

A long chunk of timber near his foot flared up, the flames blue at the base and yellow above. Caleb stamped on it, trying to snuff the fire out. The flames disappeared, but only for a moment. Immediately, the wood smoked, and the flames rekindled again.

"Why the hell bother?" He kicked at the timber, but it didn't move. Nothing he did mattered anymore.

What choices did he have? Whatever he'd been

thinking, he now had one choice only. He had to sell the ranch to free Henry.

He wondered for the hundredth time how much the judge was involved. The entire series of disasters—from the loss of the cattle, to Henry's imprisonment and charges of murder, to the fire here last night—all of it had to be related. Caleb strongly suspected Elijah Starr's twisted thinking was behind it, but the judge wanted Caleb and Henry gone. However he got there didn't matter.

Somewhere in the distance, Bear let out a playful bark. Caleb walked out of the barn to see Sheila riding up, the dog prancing along beside her. She was wearing her black, wide-brimmed hat and a heavy wool coat that Caleb had seen her father wear last winter. Around her waist, she'd strapped on the gun belt with the Colt Gunfighter he'd given her.

Sheila stopped by the corral, dismounted, and tied her horse to the fence. As he came up to her, she eyed the open gate but made no comment. The sad expression on her face was greeting enough.

"What are you doing out here?" he asked.

She ran her gaze around the scorched buildings, taking inventory of the destruction. She cursed under her breath.

"They're still out there, the coyotes who done this. You shouldn't ride around alone."

"Did you see Henry?" As always, she was ignoring his warnings.

"Yep."

"And you talked to the judge?"

"Yep."

"So what did he say?"

Sheila knew more about Caleb and his past than anyone else in Elkhorn. He had no reason not to discuss what Patterson said.

"He wants this land to run his railroad through. I got to sell him the property. That's the only way he'll let Henry go."

"This abominable railroad!" She kicked at the snow. "How many lives must be destroyed?"

As she stood next to him and looked out at the valley, Caleb realized she was wearing no gloves. He took his off and held her cold hand, telling himself there was no harm in it.

After all, he was going.

She entwined her fingers with his. "So you buy again. Build again. There must be another piece of property that would suit you both."

He considered telling her about the judge's demand that they leave town and never return.

"Back East, they call it progress. Imala has been telling me about the damage the railroads have caused. She has many stories of how they've killed the way of life for so many tribes."

"What we're losing here is nothing compared to them." He gave her a look. There were icicles on her eyelashes. Her cheeks were bright from the cold and fresh air. "What did she tell you?"

"She said that her people, the Arapaho, are starving on a reservation to the north."

"You know that Imala was a survivor of the Sand Creek Massacre," Caleb said.

Sheila nodded. "She told me all about what happened there. About what the soldiers did to the old people and the children." She looked away from him, composing herself. "And it was done to secure land that belonged to the Arapaho for railroads. She says the tracks go right across the land where they lived, and the buffalo are now gone."

Her eyes were flashing when she looked back at him.

"The Lakota, the Cheyenne, the Arapaho, and other tribes have a way of life that depends on following the buffalo herds. That is being destroyed every time another railroad divides the land and brings more towns to property that belongs to the tribes."

What she was saying wasn't the common view of folks coming to the frontier. He thought of the travelers being led out West by Bill Clark. They only thought of themselves. Caleb was impressed that in half a year, she'd made it her business to learn so much.

"Do you know that our government deliberately targets villages and burns the food tribes need to survive these winters?" she asked, becoming more agitated. "Just as they did at Sand Creek, they are still destroying entire villages and defending their actions with lies."

He knew all this very well. That was exactly what the army was doing in the Dakotas and in Wyoming. That's what Custer was doing two years ago when Crazy Horse and Sitting Bull cut him down. All that was to make things easier for railroad companies to put tracks across land that didn't belong to them. He'd seen the bloody work firsthand.

"All the reading I did when I was back East told one side," she said. "But the truth is the government takes land that belongs to the tribes. They just take it. And when tribes protest, when they demand that the treaties be honored, when they fight against the intruders, they're called savages."

The railroads were making it easier for moving troops and supplies around, no matter what time of year. When an uprising happened, the army's response was getting swifter and harder. Caleb knew tribes were being busted up, leaders killed or shipped off to prisons, children being sent away to Christian schools.

Schools like the ones Elijah Starr had run, filled with those children. His favorite saying was "kill the Indian and save the man."

"My father told me about the summer when the Cheyenne cut off Denver from everywhere. He said the fighting was fierce, and it was all about the railroads."

Caleb wasn't there, but he'd heard plenty about it. Cheyenne and Lakota raiding parties were doing everything they could to stop the Union Pacific from building across their lands. They attacked military outposts, settler communities, and the overland trail. But the response was brutal and bloody. And later, even after the transcontinental railroad was completed, the Lakota kept fighting. And the Cheyenne fought alongside them at Little Bighorn.

"They're all still fighting," she said. "It's in the newspapers every week."

Still fighting. A hawk circled above his cabin, drawing Caleb's eye.

"And you and Henry are about to lose your land. Tell me about this deal the judge is giving you."

Far down the valley were the snow-covered fields. Caleb caught a glimpse of something down by the river. He wondered if it was some of the cattle, finding their way back to the herd.

She tugged his hand to get his attention. "Is he giving you enough to buy and build again?"

"No." He decided to tell her the rest of it. "But what he's stealing from us is only part of it. He wants us gone. The two of us. And we can't come back."

"Gone? He can't do that!" she blurted out, angry. "Why is he doing this, saying this? You've done everything he's ever asked you to do. You saved his life. You saved my father's life and brought him back to Elkhorn. You recovered strongboxes from stagecoach robberies. You're the best thing that ever happened to him."

If nothing else, Sheila was a loyal friend. "It was either sell and go or become a hired gun under the lash of my father. And I ain't doing that."

"He wants you to work for the man who killed your mother? Who stole your herd? And did this?" She motioned to the burned buildings around them. "What's wrong with him? Is the judge ignorant to what that man has done to you? What he continues to do to you? The evil he's capable of?"

"The judge don't care."

Sheila turned her face away for a moment, and he realized she was real upset. The two of them had been playing a tug-of-war with their hearts for some time now, but Patterson had cut that rope. When she finally turned back to him, Caleb thought her face was about the prettiest thing anywhere.

"What happens if you and Henry come back someday? A month or a year? What about then?"

"Henry'll hang. And I don't reckon it'll be too pretty for me either." Not that he cared for himself. But his partner's life mattered.

She took her hand out of his grasp and turned to face him. "And you're going to let him do this to you? Tell you what to do? Force you to run away?"

"I gotta think about Henry's life."

"Henry is in jail for a murder he didn't commit. But the judge is going to hold that over your heads forever."

"That's about right." Caleb rubbed the back of his neck. He was tired. He felt like he'd been beaten with a stick.

"Look around you, Marlowe. Look at what they've done."

He didn't have to look. He knew the destruction that surrounded him. He was well aware of everything that they'd lost.

"The judge and Starr want you to go because they're afraid of you," she said. "They see raw courage and independence in you. They know what you're capable of."

Caleb knew they were afraid of him.

"Proving Henry's innocence, finding the men who burned your ranch, discovering for certain who was behind the theft of your longhorns and the deaths of Ortiz's men. You can't do these things if you give up and go." She wasn't giving up.

Caleb looked up at the sky, letting Sheila's words break through the fog clouding his thoughts.

"You can only do them if you stay and fight." She turned to face him. "Do you remember the words you said to me before going after your herd? You said, 'When you know the right thing to do, only a coward or a villain ignores it.'"

"I was talking about my responsibility to Paddy."

"Paddy still needs you. Henry needs you."

Caleb ran a hand down his face.

"We all need you. We need you to fight."

She was right. He had to fight. He was no longer Caleb Starr, that whipped boy back in Indiana.

He was Caleb Marlowe.

CHAPTER TWENTY-EIGHT

THE BRAYING OF THE PREACHER OUTSIDE WAS LOUD enough to draw Judge Patterson to the window. He glanced down at the crowd gathered around the makeshift pulpit on the back of the wagon out in front of the jail.

Frank Stubbs was a drunken lout and boor, but at least he contained his antics largely to the saloons and brothels. This loudmouth brother of his, however, was starting to get under the judge's skin. It was high time for him to be moving on.

Patterson looked over and found Elijah Starr had positioned himself at the next window of the office and was also looking out at the commotion. His new director of rail construction had returned from Denver late yesterday.

"This Amos Stubbs fellow can draw a crowd," Starr said.

"I believe there are twice as many people listening to him today."

The judge had wanted to meet with Starr last night, but the members of the Ladies' Event Planning Committee wouldn't be put off about the Christmas gala. Unfortunately, the prettiest flower in that particular bouquet, Doc Burnett's daughter, had been absent from the dinner meeting.

"He's starting earlier than usual today," the judge said. "Has the transaction been completed regarding the property he inherited from his brother?"

"The deal is done."

"At the price I wanted?"

Starr nodded, still watching the street. Something had caught his eye. "It's all done just as you wanted. He's planning to get back on the road right after Jordan's hanging."

Patterson tried to see what Starr was so interested in. The answer was what he'd expected. A tall rider in an elk-skin coat was coming slowly down Main Street.

About time. It had been two days since they spoke. Marlowe was taking his time. Another annoyance, but perhaps the gunman needed the extra day to think everything through before accepting the offer.

"When is it going to be, Judge? The hanging?"

Patterson looked across at his man. Starr had taken a step back from the window, but his attention was entirely focused on the street—watching Marlowe's every move. The hate that existed between father and son was unlike anything the judge had seen between blood relatives. He couldn't understand it. They both had such formidable talents. The son had lightning speed and accuracy as a gunman, along with peerless tracking skills. The father had the ability to enact a plan, and he was ruthless in seeing it through. Together, those two men would be a force to be reckoned with.

He stifled a sigh. He'd tried, but Marlowe would have none of it. It had been an interesting and productive conversation, nonetheless. If the gunman didn't want to work for him, the judge didn't need Marlowe's righteous attitude around once their plans firmed up and construction started.

Looking out at the gunslinger, the judge recalled the accusations Marlowe had made.

"Starr, do you know anything about a thousand head of cattle being stolen around Pueblo?"

"I'm not in that business, Judge. Cattle doesn't interest me...unless it's sitting on a plate in front of me at supper."

That was not really an answer, Patterson thought. "How about a fire at Marlowe's ranch this past week?"

"Fire?" Starr turned to him, his one eye piercing. "I wasn't in town. I was in Denver conducting *your* business."

"You weren't in town when your gunmen tried to shoot me on Main Street this past summer."

A deadly silence stretched between them, and Patterson thought about this man he'd hired. He had that lean and hungry look that Julius Caesar warned about. *Such men are dangerous.*

He glanced over at his two guards, standing inattentively by the door. Moments like this made Patterson think that perhaps he'd acted too quickly and recklessly in coming to terms with Starr.

"I had nothing to do with any fire. Caleb is not worth my time."

Patterson turned his attention back to the street.

Marlowe had dismounted in front of the jail, and the preacher was directing verbal attacks at him.

"I want you to leave him alone," he told Starr.

"Caleb could ruin our plans. He's dangerous."

He fixed his gaze on the other man. "So are you."

A smile pulled at Starr's thin lips, but it never reached his eyes. "But I work for you."

"So you say," Patterson replied, not trusting a single thing Starr had said or done for him so far. "And I'm telling you to leave him be."

"Whatever you say, Judge."

"And for your information, Marlowe is selling his ranch to me. He's leaving town."

"Same old coward, that boy of mine." Starr snorted. "Leaving his partner to hang."

"No. I'm letting Henry Jordan walk as soon as they sign the papers."

CHAPTER TWENTY-NINE

CALEB LOOPED PIRATE'S REINS OVER THE HITCHING rail and stepped up onto the sidewalk outside the jail. Behind him, Amos Stubbs was shouting taunts and accusations at him, as he had been doing from the moment Caleb turned down Main Street. The man was no longer concealing his intentions behind half-baked references to Scripture.

Caleb considered crossing the street and dragging him off the back of that wagon, but he had more important things to do at the moment. He needed to see Zeke and square things with Henry. And he needed to talk to that sonovabitch Patterson, who right now was standing in his office window.

Spending the rest of the day yesterday trying to put things in order at the ranch—at least as well as he could—had been something he needed badly. He was still aching from his jump off the cliff, but his mind was clearer, and he was feeling stronger and better rested.

After Sheila left, Caleb had saddled Pirate again, then taken Bear and ridden down the valley to hunt up his missing cattle. Even though the creatures had an amazing resiliency when it came to surviving in the snow, he knew it was only good for a short while. They needed care, and they needed to stay in a herd.

Caleb had seen the remains of mule deer and elk and other signs of wolves in the forests along the ridges. Many a night, he'd heard their howls, as well as the yips and barks of the coyotes and the occasional mating cry of the mountain lion. A hurt stray stuck in a thicket was always a tempting meal.

The light had been nearly gone by the time the herd was rounded up. His muscles were tired, but as he'd worked, the looseness and power had returned to them.

Nothing like hard work to set a man straight.

Later, the smell of smoke still hung heavy in the air as he and Bear had shared a meal in his cabin. But he'd forced himself to think about the future rather than the past.

Before settling here, he and Henry had considered Montana or Wyoming. But they'd decided on Elkhorn, and now it was home. Sheila was right. He was not about to be run off his own land, not without a fight.

Accepting the judge's offer would be a coward's way of dealing with his troubles. If he took that deal and left, one day soon he'd be sorry he did. And by then, there'd be no coming back. All the roads and trails back here would be washed away. There'd be a bullet or a noose waiting for both him and Henry. That was no way to live.

There were things he could do something about and things he couldn't. Pretty much the only kind of luck he'd been having lately was bad luck, but that had to change. He just had to keep bulling his way forward and stay alert.

He'd lost that herd of longhorns. He figured they were gone, and he knew in his heart who was behind it. But he'd wait and see what Duke and Bass could come up with as to proof.

Henry was looking at a dance with the hangman, but there was still a chance for him to get out under the law. Caleb wouldn't let his partner hang, no matter what. Even if he had to bust him out.

While Caleb had been hunting up his strays, he'd gone up to the creek, as Henry had asked him. Even with the snow that had fallen, he'd found the spot where Frank Stubbs was found. Of course, there were plenty of tracks, more than Caleb could make sense of. He needed to talk to Zeke.

Then there was the matter of finding the four men who set fire to his ranch. Tracking them down and digging them out of whatever hole they were hiding in wouldn't be too difficult. Somebody in town would remember that bay pinto one of them was riding. And once he found them, making them talk about who put them up to it would be a pleasure. He was looking forward to that immensely.

Now, standing on the sidewalk in front of the jail, Caleb looked up at the judge's window. The great man had disappeared.

"Look away," Amos Stubbs called out. "Look away from the servant of the lord of justice, heathen. Yes, you across the way."

Oh, hell, Caleb thought. Once again he was the object of Stubbs's nonsense. Now the preacher was pointing his Book at him and calling him out directly.

"Yes, you see me now, villain. You see the one who stirs up the righteous. The one who fears no heathen, no villain, no devil. A man of God who fears no one who stands in the way of justice. For the sword of Him above is keen and swift. His arm is all-powerful. His enemies will be cut down by his own chosen army."

Stubbs swept his hand out over the miners and loiterers who'd stopped to enjoy the show.

"Yea, I say to you, devil, the fists of his virtuous servants will prevail once again. What say you, brothers? Will you be cowed by one villain? Will you have the sword of honor and decency dashed from your hands like weak and mewling children?"

Caleb ran his eye over the crowd. It looked like a few fellows were siding with Stubbs. There were always a few. They were same ones who would jump in to wager how long a decrepit three-legged dog would last against a young fighting dog in his prime. The rest seemed mostly unimpressed by the preacher, but they had nothing else to do. And if a hanging party got started, who were they to miss the excitement?

As Caleb started to turn away, Stubbs launched a fresh attack.

"Heathen, devil, coward! You, Marlowe. Partner to the foul and evil one. Turn your back on His servant. Turn and run from the instrument of divine justice. Run away, Marlowe. Run away, coward!"

"You're a no-good, lying polecat!" A youngster's high-pitched cry cut through the preacher's taunts. "Marlowe ain't no coward. He ain't none of them things coming out of your dirty, lying mouth. And Henry Jordan ain't no murderer, neither!"

Paddy was standing with Gabe by the edge of the crowd, and Stubbs reared back, his face reddening with rage at being contradicted.

"Someone stop that little heathen's mouth."

Two miners next to the boys turned amused faces toward them.

"I ain't no heathen," Paddy shouted. "You're a heathen. And a damn skunk too."

A short fella in front of them turned and cuffed the boy solidly, knocking him down. Gabe dove at the man, and immediately, all hell broke loose.

Caleb raced across Main Street, pushing into the crowd around the boys. Quickly, shoves escalated to punches being thrown. In a matter of seconds, a riot had started. There were no sides being taken in the battle. Everyone was punching and shoving the man next to him in a general melee. From the safety of his wagon, Stubbs was watching, his face lit with gleeful enjoyment. His words had started it all.

Caleb shoved through, clearing his way toward Paddy, who'd been yanked to his feet. Gabe, bleeding from the corner of his mouth, was pulling the ginger-haired boy toward the edge of the crowd, and his face showed his relief when Caleb broke through to them.

"Hold on to Paddy. I have to get you two out of here."

Gabe nodded, and they started back in the direction of the jail. Punches landed on Caleb's face and shoulders as he batted and elbowed others away. His only thought was to get the boys clear.

Suddenly, the broad, whiskered face of a gigantic miner reared up in front of him, roaring curses. The smell of whiskey spewed from a mouth that was missing more than a few teeth. He'd already taken a shot from someone, for his left eye was swelling shut. The giant was easily half a head taller than Caleb, and he was clearly totally committed to this battle.

Not wanting to let go of his grip on Gabe or lose his momentum through the crowd, Caleb had few options. Reaching up with his free hand, he took hold of the miner's beard and shoved his face straight up. At the same time, his knee connected sharply with the man's balls. A whoosh of more foul air came from the miner's mouth as he doubled over. Caleb's fist flashed toward the descending face, finding the point on the jaw that dropped the giant into the muddy snow at their feet.

A tight circle had formed around them during the confrontation, and from the side, another blow landed, striking Caleb's ear. He ignored it and pulled the boys around the fallen fighter.

The men at the far side of circle appeared to be dead set against him leaving with Paddy and Gabe. Hands grabbed at the boys, and Caleb lashed out, driving his fist into the faces around him.

A revolver fired twice from just beyond the crowd, cutting through the air and causing a momentary cessation in hostilities.

As he straightened up and tugged the boys closer to him, Caleb realized it was a minor miracle no guns had already been drawn. He glanced in the direction the shot had been fired, expecting to see the sheriff on the sidewalk with his deputies.

No Zeke.

Instead, it was Red Annie O'Neal—sitting astride a good-looking palomino mare, revolvers in each hand, cocked and ready.

"That's enough, boys." Looking at her hard, piercing eyes, no one could doubt she meant business. "I am the first one to enjoy a good fight, but this one don't appear to have much of a point. So just settle yourselves down."

Red Annie was a tall woman, taller than most men, and as tough as buffalo hide. She kept her fiery-red hair cropped short and covered with a wide-brimmed hat the color of night. Caleb guessed she'd once been fair-skinned, but sun and wind and cold had weathered her face to a tawny gold, and wrinkles spider-webbed from the corners of her gray eyes. When she smiled, deep creases formed at the corners of her mouth.

She could be as intimidating as hell when she chose to be. When she was angry, those smile lines disappeared, and her eyes narrowed to slits. That's what he and the crowd were looking at now.

For as long as Caleb had known her—about five years—he'd never seen her in anything except men's clothes, with a brace of Colts strapped to her hips. Right now, she was wearing buckskin trousers tucked into her boots and a jacket of elk skin that would keep out all kinds of weather. More often than not, she was carrying the Winchester '73 that was sticking up from its scabbard on the right side of her saddle. An important tool of her trade. She could drink most men under the table, but she could also put a bullet though the back legs of a horsefly at two hundred yards.

And as Red Annie was the only Star Route carrier in this area, most everyone knew her.

"Did they close all the saloons in this here metropolis?" she called out. "'Cuz I'm ready for a drink. Hell, you boys must've worked up a righteous thirst, and I see the Belle's doors are open wide. So why don't y'all get to it?"

The men in the crowd knew a good idea when they heard one, and the combatants began to head off arm in arm for the bars to lie about their prowess in the fight.

Pouching her irons, Red Annie swung down easily from the horse and turned her gray eyes on Caleb. One of those creases formed at the corner of her mouth.

"You need me to follow you around and save your carcass regular, Marlowe?"

"I was handling it."

"You keep saying that, and one of these times I won't be around to watch your back." She motioned behind him. "Like now."

Caleb turned in time to see the flash of a knife. It was the short fella who'd cuffed Paddy and been shoved back by Gabe. He was lunging toward them from the receding crowd, but Caleb was too quick for him. Sweeping the boys to the side, he caught the wrist with the knife with one hand as he planted his right foot in the snow. Dropping his shoulder, Caleb came up with a fist, connecting squarely under the man's chin. The attacker's head snapped back, and he left his feet, flying a yard or two before landing unconscious in the packed snow. The knife sailed off and dropped harmlessly beside him.

"See? You oughta get yourself another set of eyes for the back of your head."

"Who am I to argue, Red?"

As far as Caleb knew, there was only one other woman who worked the Rockies as a Star Route carrier for the U. S. Postal Service. An independent contractor, Red carried mail for them from town to town along established routes, sometimes using stagecoaches but often by horseback.

She was a woman who liked her life the way she lived it and was damn good at what she did. Caleb had heard a number of stagecoach drivers say they liked having her along for the ride. She was good company, a dead shot, and road agents gave her a wide berth if they knew she was coming through.

The four of them started across the street, and Red Annie tied her mare beside Caleb's buckskin.

"So how'd that lively little dance get started?" she asked, gesturing with her chin at the man just starting to stir in the middle of Main Street.

Caleb looked back at the wagon where Amos Stubbs had been holding forth. The clown responsible for it all had disappeared. He put his hand on Paddy's shoulder.

"This fine fella and his friend here felt the need to stand up for my character, Red."

"Questionable as that is," she replied with a laugh. She took both of their chins in her gloved hands and inspected their wounds. "Looks like they got their licks in without too much in return."

"I'll have these two beside me in a tangle anytime," Caleb said.

The boys grinned at each other.

"Glad you're back, Mr. Marlowe," Paddy said. "Miss Sheila said you rassled with a bear when she came over to the livery yesterday."

Red Annie pulled the saddlebag from her palomino and slid the Winchester from the scabbard. "That's where I know you fellas from. You're the son of Malachi Rogers."

The boys removed their hats.

Gabe nodded. "Yes, ma'am."

"I work there," Paddy chirped. "And you're Red Annie O'Neal."

"That's right. So then, why don't you two take my lady Argo here over to the stable and see that she gets everything she needs." She ruffled Paddy's hair. "I need to talk to your pa."

"Marlowe ain't my pa," the boy said, his face reddening.

"That's what they all say."

As the boys led Argo away, Red Annie turned to Caleb. "Whoever's boy that is, you and me need to talk. I got a message for you from Duke Ortiz."

CHAPTER THIRTY

MANY SALOONS IN ELKHORN WERE NOT SO CHOOSY AS to exclude women from their clientele, but the Belle Saloon was Red Annie's favored place to drink when she was in town. Before going in, however, she needed to drop off the mail at Wilson's General Store.

As they passed the judge's building, she went in and dropped his mail with the clerks in the lobby.

"Always gets his mail delivered separate," she told Caleb with a shrug.

Once they reached the Belle, the two of them found a table near the door, where Caleb sat with his back to the wall. Though the Belle wasn't exactly famous for serving breakfast, quite a few miners were in, drinking theirs.

The stove was warming the place nicely, and the two of them shed their coats as the barman called to them, asking what they'd like.

"Brandy for me," Red ordered, putting her saddlebag and rifle behind her.

"That coffee I smell?" Caleb asked. The Scottish bartender raised his eyebrows, exchanging a look with Red Annie.

"Look, the fella's got a lot on his mind," she said.

"Rassling bears. Knife fighting with preachers." She sat back in her chair. "Just get him his damn coffee."

The barman tugged at his collar, displaying the tattoo of an upright lion with the claws extended. Then, without another word, he shrugged and went to get the drinks.

"Going soft on me, Marlowe?"

"Like you said. Got a lot on my mind."

"'Cuz if you order buttermilk the next time we come in here, we ain't drinking together no more. A girl can get a reputation in this town, you know."

He tapped the table. "Duke Ortiz found you?"

"I ain't too hard to find, even in a place like Denver."

"I told him the places where you usually boarded and drank when you were there."

"He found me." She reached inside her coat and produced a letter that she handed over. "Every time I think I got you figured out, Marlowe, you surprise me a little more."

"How's that?" Caleb stared at the letter in his hand.

"For one thing, the company you keep. You're the best of friends with all sorts of fellas."

"I've known Duke Ortiz for a long time. We been in some fearsome scrapes, as I'm sure he told you if you gave him ten minutes. And Bass Dart? That fella is a good man. We've traveled some hard miles together."

"I liked both of them. They actually drink hard liquor. Surprisingly, they talk real good about you."

Caleb nodded, impatient to open the letter.

"And that Chinese family you paid me to take to

Denver this past summer." Red Annie smiled. "They all but made me a member of the family. I got a real warm feeling for that bunch."

The barman put her brandy and Caleb's coffee on the table in front of them.

"Hell, Marlowe. You even call *me* your friend."

The first time Caleb met Red Annie was at a stage-coach way station up in Wyoming. He'd come in as she was going to war with two fellas who'd taken exception to her wearing trousers and riding as a guard for Wells Fargo. She had no trouble handling them. Caleb had only stepped in when a third, in the solemn defense of man-hood, tried to jump her from behind.

He couldn't wait any longer and opened Duke's letter. It was brief, and Caleb struggled with the handwriting. The gist of it was that they were in Denver, as if he didn't know that, and the herd of longhorns had arrived by cattle car and got shipped north to Cheyenne City. Addressed to a Mr. Eric Goulden. They were following.

Caleb shook his head, trying to figure out why a rail-road baron would be interested in stolen cattle. Elijah Starr had surely cut his ties with Goulden when he went to work for the judge, Goulden's sworn enemy.

When the answer came to him, it was like seeing a rat-tler slither into a privy. Starr was working for both sides. Or rather, he never stopped working for Goulden. Maybe that herd of longhorns was a gift to his boss to smooth over any rough patch that had come up when Caleb thwarted his plans in Elkhorn. Four dollars a head in Texas brought as much as forty a head by the time they reached St. Louis. More in Chicago. Even for a fella as well-heeled as Eric Goulden, a forty-thousand-dollar gift had to be considered a serious apology.

"Did you hear one word I said?"

Caleb looked up at Red Annie. "What did you say?"

"I said, you even call *me* your friend," Red repeated, banging a hand on the table.

"Of course, I heard that."

"Well, you was supposed to answer before burying your nose in some damn letter."

"Hell, Red. We got history. We're friends. What else is there to say?"

She rolled her eyes. "You're supposed to say something. We're having a conversation."

"About what?" he asked.

"We were discussing the kind of friends you keep."

"Oh." Caleb realized what she was getting at. "Red, your idea of a conversation is like going to San Francisco by way of Mexico. If you got something on your mind, go ahead and say it."

"I do not understand Henry Jordan."

"Henry again?" Caleb asked. "Why are you so interested in him?"

"I ain't interested."

"Sounds like you are."

"Well, I ain't." She drank down her glass of brandy and waved for another.

With all Caleb had on his mind, he didn't want to get

involved in this. But for someone who wasn't interested in Henry, she always asked about him.

The two of them had been at odds from the day they met up north. At the time, Henry had a woman on his lap while he was playing poker and putting down red-eye faster than a city barber goes through hair oil. She took exception to his lack of attention to the cards, apparently.

Something about Henry tickled Red, though, whether she was willing to admit it or not.

"But, just for conversation," she continued, "where is the chucklehead? The last time I come through, he was out of jail and trying out his new life on the ranch. Is he staying out of trouble?"

"Hate to say it, but he's back in jail."

Her drink arrived, and she frowned at it for a moment before her gray eyes lifted to his. "Drunk and disorderly again?"

"Nope. Murder."

"Hats and horseshit! Murder? Henry? He ain't the type."

Red Annie tried to say it casually. But there was something in the way she pushed her glass away that made Caleb think she was more upset than she was letting on.

"You're right, Red. He ain't the type. He didn't do it."

"You helping him?"

"Doing my best."

She thought about it. "But you ain't wearing the badge, are you?"

Caleb pocketed Ortiz's letter. "No. Zeke Vernon is still the sheriff."

"Maybe I'll go by and say howdy to Zeke. And while I'm there, say howdy to Henry. Just to be friendly."

Caleb nodded. "I think he'd like that, Red."

She took a drink and shrugged off the cloud hanging over the table. "But he's still a damn fool. And you're a damn fool taking him on for a partner."

"If you say so," he replied into his coffee cup.

They both looked up as the door to the saloon opened, and Sheila sailed in. Regardless of how much she tried to fit in to the frontier town, there was something about the way she carried herself that said she came from old money. Caleb had decided long ago that it was the confidence.

"Uh-oh. That who I think it is?" Red asked.

"You be nice," he said, rising to his feet.

One of the Belle's girls was standing by the bar, chatting it up with the tattooed Scotsman, and Sheila went straight to her. The saloon girl looked downright shocked at being addressed but then smiled and replied to whatever was asked.

Caleb immediately realized that he might have jumped the gun, thinking she was here to see him. He remembered that she and Belle Constant were on speaking terms. He knew she'd been here before.

Sheila turned, and her eyes settled on Caleb and Red Annie.

Her face glowed, and her eyes shone from the cold outside and exercise. She had snow at the hem of the long, blue dress that hung below the heavy wool coat. She'd apparently left her wide-brimmed hat at home, along with her gun belt.

He watched her every step as she approached. To give her credit, she had no trouble weaving her way through the gawking miners. He hadn't jumped the gun. Sheila came directly to him.

"I heard there was a fight," she said in greeting.

"Nothing compared to Bull Run or Antietam."

"And the boys were involved."

"They tell you that?"

"They said that horrid Amos Stubbs was slandering you."

"Hard to imagine Paddy using the word *slandering*, but I reckon that's about right."

It was impossible for Caleb to ignore the way Red Annie was staring at one of them and then the other, a smile lifting a corner of her mouth. Finally, she couldn't restrain herself any longer.

"Marlowe, are you going to introduce me to Mrs. Marlowe?"

A blush colored Sheila's face instantly. "We're not… I'm not…"

"Not married yet? Well, then, when is the happy event?"

"No! You're mistaken."

"That ain't what *he* tells me."

"Hold on there, Red," Caleb warned.

"Now, don't you get no bee up your bumble chute. You didn't say it was a damn secret."

Sheila was clearly at a loss as to what to say. Red seemed to be just getting started.

"Don't believe nothing she says. She had a mule kick her in the head as a child," Caleb said. "I know I'm going to regret this…but Sheila Burnett, let me introduce you to Red Annie O'Neal. She's the—"

"Star Route carrier for the U.S. Postal Service," Sheila finished for him, holding her hand out for a handshake. "I've heard so much about you."

Red looked past the outstretched hand at its owner, not taking it yet. "From this one?"

"No. From my father, Doc Burnett. He sings your praises all the time."

"Well, in that case…" Red Annie shook the hand and motioned to a seat. "Now you *got* to join us. Marlowe ain't much of a conversationalist, as you probably know. I've been on the road for a week, and I talk to my horse plenty, but I don't get much in the way of replies. She's a pretty thing, but a whisker less chatty than this one."

"Thank you." Sheila took off her coat and sat down.

"And to keep the record straight, that weren't no mule." Red motioned to the bartender to come over. "It was a small pony."

Caleb was starting to wish some animal would come by and kick her again.

"What do you drink, missus?" she asked Sheila. "Whatever you like. Marlowe is paying. What's your usual? A hot Scotch? A horn of forty-rod?"

"What are you having?" Sheila asked.

"Brandy."

"I'd like the same, thank you," she told the bartender.

Caleb had to bite his tongue. All the times he'd gone to Doc's house for dinner, he'd never seen Sheila drink brandy. He didn't think they even had it in the house. She might have a bit of wine, occasionally a little cider. That's all.

"So, missus—"

"My friends call me Sheila," she said, touching Red Annie's hand. "I'd like it if you would do the same."

"Well, I like that. I'm just Red Annie to one and all."

Caleb couldn't help but notice the difference between the two hands. Red's showed the rough wear of the trail and the weather. She had several scars on the back and strong, tanned fingers. Sheila's was smaller and paler with glimpses of blood vessels running beneath the surface of the soft-looking skin. But he knew this was not a weak hand. The strength of her grasp was equal to the strength of her character. And while it was a hand that was rarely quiet, there was no nervousness in it. Sheila Burnett was as sure of herself as Red Annie O'Neal. Two different hands belonging to two different but equally strong women.

Their drinks arrived, and he eyed them. He was not about to say a word.

Red sent a sly look at Caleb and lifted her glass to her new friend. "Sheila, old girl, here's to you."

"And to you," she replied.

The two women tipped up their glasses, and Caleb sipped his coffee. He was waiting for Sheila's mouthful to spray across the table, and he realized Red was watching for it as well. But once again, Sheila Burnett was a surprise to him. The color of her face slipped a little, but the liquor stayed, and she managed a smile as she put the glass down.

"So what are you two naming your future babies?" Red asked.

"Too early in the day for that talk," Sheila said, not skipping a beat this time around. "It's not too many times I get a chance to sit across from a legend."

"A legend?" Red asked. "You clever girl. You're trying to distract me from all this talk of matrimony."

"No, you'll be the first to know, whenever Marlowe gets around to asking."

Caleb almost spewed out a mouthful of coffee.

"But, to more interesting conversation," Sheila continued, warming to the company. "Is it true that you've ridden as a coach guard everywhere from Denver to Carson City?"

Red Annie sat back. "Actually, I'd say from Topeka to San Francisco."

"Did you single-handedly drive off Dirty Dave Rudabaugh and his gang when they tried to rob a Wells Fargo stage you were riding on?"

"How do you know about that?"

"You'd be amazed how much I know about you."

"In that case." Red turned a shade of pink. "That story's done got blowed up some. It weren't just me. There was a young greenhorn riding below that I don't think knew one end of his Remington from the other. But he made some noise with it and managed to not shoot himself."

"And you won a marksmanship contest in Dodge City judged by Buffalo Bill Cody himself. You defeated forty of the best riflemen in the West, including Ben Thompson, John Wesley Hardin, Mysterious Dave Mather, and Bat Masterson himself."

"How d'you *know* all this?"

"I told you, I know things."

Caleb wondered who'd been the source of all this information. He didn't think he'd ever seen Red Annie actually glow before, but she was practically lit up now. She reached behind her and produced her Winchester '73.

"Well, that's true," she replied proudly. "Except for Hardin. He weren't there. But I won this pretty thing in that contest."

She held out the rifle with an inscription on the side plate.

Sheila took it and read the inscription out loud. She held the weapon to her shoulder and sighted along the barrel, pointing it at the elk on the wall behind the bar. She ran her hand along the smooth stock then handed it back to Annie.

Caleb chuckled to himself. He was actually feeling a little left out. After all, he'd given Sheila a lesson with his own Winchester.

"Some of them boys were damn sorry losers, let me tell you. Thought I'd have to fight my way outta Dodge that day."

"I'd love to hear more about your life. Why don't you come and have dinner with me and my father?"

"Marlowe going to be there?"

"I haven't invited him yet."

"Good. Then I'll be there."

"Well, now I know where I stand with you two." He pretended to sound offended, but neither of them seemed to buy it.

"I do love making new friends, Annie."

Red glanced at Caleb. "Funny thing. Just before you come in, him and me was talking about friends."

As Red was talking, Belle Constant came into the saloon through the side door. As she pulled off a heavy shawl, she spotted them and immediately glided up to the table, standing across from Caleb.

He was not one to notice such things, usually, but the proprietor was not dressed in her customary silk gowns. Her black hair was done up with curls and her face looked the same, but she was wearing a fine dress of linen or some such material, of a style similar to what he called Sheila's "New York dresses." The color of the thing—like ripe chestnuts—was surely intended to set off her dark skin to advantage. She was carrying a small, fancy bag along with her shawl.

"Miss Sheila. Red Annie," she said, acknowledging the women before fixing her black eyes on Caleb. "How is your partner holding up, Marlowe?"

This was the first time she'd ever spoken to him. And he was impressed that she even knew his name or what was happening to Henry. "He's a fighter, Miss Belle, but the odds are stacked against him at the moment. I'm trying to change that."

"Good. Before you leave, stop upstairs and see me. I have some information that might help."

Caleb could definitely use someone with her connections on Henry's side.

"Miss Sheila, I'll be seeing you at the next Christmas gala event meeting." Receiving an affirmative response, Belle took her leave and swept up the stairs.

Red Annie finished her drink and pushed the glass away from her. "Well, I'd like to spend all day with you two lovebirds. But you have some place to be, Marlowe. And I have a hundred things to do."

"Dinner tonight?" Sheila asked her.

"I'll be there."

They all came to their feet. "I'm so glad I stopped in to ask Marlowe about his clash with that so-called preacher."

Red's face clouded over. "Now that you mention it, it was funny seeing that fella here, stirring things up."

"Seen him somewhere?" Caleb asked.

"Up in Denver. Though I didn't take him for no preacher."

"When was that?"

"A few weeks back. In a snake hole by the railroad depot. He was putting down the 'oh be joyful' by the noggin full. Couldn't help but notice him. He had his hand on every saloon girl in the place."

"Some preacher," Sheila said.

"Like I said, he weren't waving no Bible around." Red Annie stared at Caleb. "As I was getting ready to move on, though, another fella joined him. That got my eye. Didn't think of it till now, but it was that big shot you was looking for in Bonedale last summer. The one that left before you got there."

"Elijah Starr?"

"That's the one. A one-eyed, pirate-looking fella. You know, I didn't make the connection, but it just come to me. Elijah Starr." She paused. "But ain't he the one that was in jail here for a while, waiting to get strung up?"

"The same."

CHAPTER THIRTY-ONE

CALEB KNEW ALMOST NOTHING OF BELLE CONSTANT, but he'd sensed that she was tough and enterprising. Her corner office above the saloon confirmed his suspicions, but it also showed a side of her that he guessed very few of the brandy-guzzling miners downstairs ever saw.

A strongbox that must have required six men to carry up the stairs dominated one corner. A small stove kept the room comfortably warm. Two straight chairs sat facing a desk cluttered with papers and ledgers. Crates of good wine and whiskey were stacked high against the walls, and there was one small mirror, hung low enough to suit the height of the proprietor.

The office was not entirely dedicated to business, however. Pale-yellow curtains were draped around an east-facing window, brightening the room, and the sun's rays were angling in across the desk. More surprising than the curtains, a row of open shelves had been built in front of the south-facing window. Each shelf was filled with pots of plants. Considering the encroaching winter, Caleb was more than a little surprised at the brilliant show of colors amid the lush, green foliage.

And on a small table behind Belle's desk, three books

stood between bronze bookends depicting half-naked angels or goddesses. On the spines of two of the volumes, *Don Quixote* was embossed with gold lettering. On the third volume, *Los Trabajos de Persiles y Sigismunda*. Caleb had heard of the first books—about a knight who rode around fighting windmills for some reason—but he had no idea what the other book was, except that the title was in Spanish.

Caleb had more important things to think about, however, so he was glad when Belle motioned for him to sit and started in directly.

"I believe Henry Jordan is innocent, Marlowe."

"What can you tell me to prove it?"

"This brother of Frank Stubbs—the preacher who's been making a nuisance of himself and trying to stir things up against your partner—I have some information about him that might help."

As she started, Caleb realized that Belle and the judge had a few things in common. Like Patterson, she was a person who knew the value of information. It gave her leverage that she needed as a woman in a rough business. Just as when he dealt with the judge, he wondered for a moment what she'd want in return.

"I have a young woman who works for me named Mariah. Henry got himself into two separate dustups with Frank Stubbs over her downstairs."

"I've heard."

"Mariah wants more for herself." Belle frowned. "She grew up in Independence, Missouri. Had a father who was apparently a strict, God-fearing cloth merchant. When she was sixteen, she ran away with a man coming to Colorado to find his fortune. He left her here in Elkhorn and moved on. She's been with me for almost three years now."

Caleb had heard Mariah's name mentioned a few times around the ranch, and he knew Henry didn't have a soft spot for her. For any woman, for that matter.

"From day one she's had an eye out for some fella with enough money to take her to a big city. She's made no secret of it. A lot of girls think San Francisco is the Promised Land."

"Henry Jordan ain't that fella, though."

"I know. Nor was Frank Stubbs. But he had money, so she put up with his rough treatment."

Women were in short supply on the frontier. Caleb had seen other saloon girls who'd married clients. Maybe that was Mariah's plan.

"Once your partner showed his face around here, the silly girl had the bright idea of using Henry to make Frank jealous. That plan blew up in her face. And after Stubbs was beaten and humiliated in front of everyone, Mariah became terrified that he would kill her."

Belle opened a bottle of her good whiskey and poured two glasses, pushing one in front of Caleb.

"I banned Frank from coming into the saloon. But then the brother, Amos—new in town—started showing up. When he wasn't preaching against me on Main Street, he became Mariah's shadow." She drank down her glass. "A couple of the other girls told me Frank had been sending his brother here, trying to lure her out to Frank's place. But apparently, she decided the preacher held more promise."

This *was* news.

"Amos Stubbs has been romancing her for two weeks. It started before Frank ended up facedown with a bullet in his back. And now I hear the preacher is about to take Mariah out of here."

"Frank's brother killed him for the girl."

"And the money. I heard the preacher sold Frank's claim to the judge."

Caleb downed the drink in front of him. "You think Mariah is in on it?"

Belle took a sip of her whiskey and gave him an enigmatic smile. "That's for you to find out, Marlowe. I'm just a woman selling drinks and entertainment to miners."

CHAPTER THIRTY-TWO

THE ALLEY STARTED AT MAIN STREET BETWEEN TWO substantial wood-frame buildings, the Belle Saloon on one side and Smith's Haberdashery on the other. On the west side of the passage, which was wide enough for little more than a wagon, the Belle went back almost two hundred feet. On the other side, the clothing store went back nearly as far. From there, a shadowy, haphazard jumble of shacks and shanties and sheds followed. Some of the buildings were still inhabited, and some were no more than yawning cavities, left to the forces of winter cold and summer rains and filled with decaying wood and rotting trash.

At the far end, a row of newer wood-frame houses faced a road running parallel to Main Street. Caleb knew that from there, the streets became wider and more dignified. Predictably, only a few blocks farther on, the judge and the other pillars of the community lived in a row of wood and stone structures that rivaled the finest houses in Denver.

The boardinghouse Belle Constant used to house some of her employees—the same one that Tex Washington was currently recuperating in—was located around the corner just beyond the end of the alley.

The conversation with Belle gave Caleb direction. He knew exactly what he had to do.

After leaving the side door of the saloon, Caleb picked his way past snow-covered crates and barrels of all sizes that had been dumped along the edges of the lane. He stayed as much as he could to the packed-down tracks of carts and walkers. Caleb went as quickly as he could manage, dodging obstacles and icy patches. Smoke from nearby chimneys drifted on currents just above the alley, giving it a roofed-in feeling, closed off from the sky and fresh air.

Beyond the Belle, however, he occasionally caught glimpses of bright, sunlit lots between and behind the derelict buildings. There, piles of broken bottles, boxes, dishes, door frames, shoes, and animal bones poked up through a most unlikely blanket of the purest white, as if they were an early spring crop caught by an unexpected snowfall. But even in the cold, the smells wafting from them were hardly garden-like.

Caleb was about halfway down the lane when he paused and then ducked into the shadows of an abandoned stable. Coming toward him at a slow and deliberate pace were the very people he was going after.

All the things he intended to do this morning had been put aside after his meeting with Belle. He'd planned on speaking with Henry, Zeke, and the judge. Caleb had even decided to track down Elijah Starr, for he'd heard his father had returned to town. All of that would have to wait.

Red Annie's information about seeing Amos Stubbs

and Elijah Starr together in Denver was some of the best news Caleb had heard in days. That meeting had taken place just before the preacher showed up in Elkhorn.

Now, standing in the shadows in the ruined shell of the old stable, he unbuttoned his coat and unfastened the thongs over his twin Colts. As he waited, the cold curled in around him, but it didn't bother him at all. For too long, he'd been feeling the foul breath of ill fortune breathing down his neck. For a change this morning, Caleb felt that he had a chance of facing it down.

The two people were drawing closer, arms linked as they moved slowly through the snow and ice. Amos Stubbs's voice was clear enough. Caleb had heard it already this morning, but right now he wasn't quoting Scripture or trying to stir up a mob against him and Henry. Instead, he was speaking to the woman beside him.

Caleb moved farther into the shadows as the two drew closer.

"You promised me," the young woman said, a whining note in her voice. "Come on, Amos. Let's go now. This week. I'm telling you, I can't do it no more!"

They were nearly opposite Caleb, and the preacher was pleading with her. "Look, Mariah. I told you I'll take you away. I'm going to marry you. But first, I have to collect the money."

She stopped short and planted her feet in the snow. Pulling her arm from his, she put a fist defiantly on her hip.

"How long does that take? Frank is dead. What else do they want from you?"

"I have to wait for the hanging."

"Why?" Mariah snapped. "What's one thing got to do with the other?"

"The money's coming, but I have to make sure Jordan takes the blame."

"So you got to wait around for them to hang the man you lied about? That makes no sense. Ain't you afraid of getting caught?"

Stubbs lowered his voice a little. "Those killers that gunned Frank will come after me for sure if I don't do what they say. I've *got* to wait. And once I have the money, we'll go. And I won't get caught."

Caleb had left the Belle with the full intention of beating Amos Stubbs until he admitted his involvement. But this was all he needed.

"You're already caught," Caleb said, striding out of the shadows.

Mariah immediately paled and shrank against the preacher.

Stubbs fumbled inside his coat, and Caleb cleared leather, pointing the Colt at his chest.

"Don't."

The preacher stopped reaching and slowly withdrew his hand. Caleb went up and yanked a small revolver from Stubbs's belt. Backing away, he stuck it in his pocket and pouched his own iron.

"I'm not afraid of you, villain. You be on your way." Stubbs looked around him to see if there was any escape or anyone close enough to help.

"Save that for your mob. I've already heard everything I need to hear." Caleb gestured to Mariah. "Let's go. You're both coming with me."

"Where?" she asked, holding tightly now to her man's arm.

"We're going to the judge. You're gonna repeat everything you just said."

"I won't," she cried out. "I didn't say nothing."

"Have it your way. You'll hang with this one for being behind the killing of Frank Stubbs."

"Killing?" she gasped. "Why would I kill Frank?"

"For beating you. You told anyone and everyone who would listen how you planned to get Frank to take you away from here, in spite of how much you hated him. And then the tables turned, and you knew that wasn't going to happen." Caleb turned his gaze on the preacher. "And then you came into it."

"You've got nothing on me. I'll deny everything."

"Seems believable to me. You come to town, steal your brother's woman, and the only thing left was to get rid of him. Then you've got it all: his girl, his land, and his mining claims."

"I didn't steal her."

"And yet, here you are. But if you think she ain't gonna turn on you when she's looking at the noose, you're as crazy as a shithouse rat."

"She loves me, and I love her. We're going to be married. She'll never betray me."

Maybe that was right, but Caleb could see the cogs

turning in Mariah's head. All he had to do was keep the pressure on.

"What did Frank do when he found out you were taking his woman?" Caleb asked Amos. "I forgot. He didn't do nothing. He couldn't, because you killed him first."

"Amos didn't kill nobody!" Mariah squeaked.

"I went up to the creek where you and your helpers dumped Frank's body. There was plenty of tracks left up there. Once I sorted it out and saw where they all come from and led back to, I went up and told the judge what had really happened."

There were times when stretching the truth—or making it up—was justified. Saving a man's life was one of those times.

"As you know, Mariah, I've worked as his deputy before, and he was more than willing for me to wear the badge again. And you just told me why, Stubbs. It's about that property. With you going to the gallows, Patterson won't have to pay nothing for Frank's land. He just takes it, free and clear."

"Tell him, Amos. Tell him. You can't let them do that to you. To us."

Caleb turned to Mariah. "You've been around long enough to know Judge Patterson owns this town. He sure can sure as hell do anything he wants."

"He's right, Amos." She had panic in her eyes. "Patterson is a hanging judge. That's why you ain't seen the money. It's cheaper to get rid of you. And then what happens to me?"

Being patient was difficult, but Caleb waited. Mariah was doing a better job of prying Stubbs open than he'd have ever expected.

"I didn't kill Frank," Amos said again.

"I say you did. You reckoned you'd get everything when he was dead. And everything points back to you."

"I tell you I didn't kill him. I…" His voice broke.

"I say you gunned him in the back. Let's go talk to somebody about that 'sword of honor and decency' you like to spout off about."

"He didn't do it, Marlowe," Mariah almost shrieked. "But he knows who did."

"Unless he finds his backbone and talks, there ain't no way that noose ain't going 'round both of your necks."

"He'll tell you. Tell him, Amos. But you have to let us go. Him and me both…and with the money from the land."

Mariah was the sharper of the two of them, but desperation wasn't the strongest place to negotiate from. Still, whatever deal the judge made to buy Stubbs's land, that was none of Caleb's concern. All he wanted was to get Henry out of jail.

"Who killed Frank?" he snapped.

Amos Stubbs stared at Caleb's twin Colts and made up his mind. "There were five of them. And I can show you where they are."

CHAPTER THIRTY-THREE

CALEB WATCHED AMOS STUBBS RIDE BACK DOWN THE trail toward town. It wasn't that he was sorry to see him go. He wanted to make sure the knothead didn't try to circle around and warn the five killers hiding in his late brother's cabin.

He didn't think he really needed to worry. After nervously showing Caleb where the killers were holed up, the preacher had been visibly relieved and vocally grateful at being turned loose. It took Stubbs only a few moments to descend the hill, cross the creek, and disappear around a wooded bend.

A cold, white sun had been hanging high in a sky of washed-out blue when they left Mariah at the Belle and rode out of town together. The trail took them through groves of aspen that had shed the last of their golden leaves in the storms and dense forests of conifer. It led them close to the ridge that served as the border with his own property, and they splashed across icy streams, occasionally dammed up into ice-covered ponds by industrious beavers.

Satisfied that the preacher was long gone, Caleb turned his attention back to the cabin. It was still early in the afternoon.

Frank Stubbs's place was little more than a mile from town. Smoke was rising from the chimney of the low log cabin. Near it stood a lean-to stable and a small corral. Not far from the cabin, two dilapidated mining shacks stood, forming a U-shape with the house and the stable. The shacks were three-sided affairs, constructed of weathered, gray planks. Shovels and picks, barrels, buckets, and a wheelbarrow stood in the shadow against the outside walls. Inside, ladders stuck up from shafts that were topped with hand cranked pulleys for removing earth.

Something about them gave Caleb the feeling that they were not working mines, and he wondered if the claim was pinched out. It occurred to him that if that were the case, it would explain Frank's interest in gold beyond the ridge on Caleb's property. This past summer, he'd even run into the murdered miner prospecting for gold in the hills far to the west of Elkhorn.

Mounds of dirt and rock from the mine shafts had been piled up, forming one long wall that encircled the entire group of buildings and the piles of discarded and busted mining equipment. An old wagon with a missing wheel sat amid unstacked piles of firewood. Gray snow covered everything, giving the place a dismal, unkempt look. It was like a fortress built by some drunken, undisciplined reprobate. Frank Stubbs exactly.

From behind a fallen tree that served as the base for a snow drift, Caleb looked again at the five horses in the corral by the stable. He'd fully expected one of them to be a bay pinto, and he wasn't disappointed. Not only were these the men who killed Frank Stubbs, they were also the men who set fire to Caleb's barn. The night of the fire, he'd seen four of them, but the tracks of a fifth horse had joined the others on the trail back to town.

Caleb considered his choices. He could drag some of the hay from the stable to the back of the cabin and set fire to it, smoking the men out. Or he could kick open the door of the cabin and go in with his Winchester blazing. Or he could wait patiently for them to come out and hope he didn't freeze to death sometime during the night. He dismissed the last option immediately and was about to dismiss the first when the door opened and all five of the killers came out, laughing at something one of them had said.

They appeared to be cleaned up for a trip to town. The identities of the first three were unknown to Caleb, but he knew the last two instantly.

John Rivers looked better than the last time Caleb saw him. He was still short and stocky and had the same scraggly wisp of beard, but he wasn't whining or even limping from the bullet that had taken a chunk out of his hip.

The outlaw had been sitting in the Elkhorn jail until he was shipped up to Denver, but Caleb could see that he'd never made it that far. He had to assume the cause of his escape was the fifth man to exit the cabin.

It was a toss-up whether Mad Dog McCord looked any better. He was wearing a new set of clothes, but he was still big and burly and ugly. When he came out the door, his shaved head gleamed in the watery afternoon sun, and he immediately covered it with a new fawn-colored hat, decorated with the same ornate, beaded band at the base of the crown.

All of them were armed with six-shooters, and they were carrying rifles as they made their way toward the stable.

Cocking his Winchester, Caleb raised it to his shoulder. "Stop right there," he shouted. "Throw down them irons. Now!"

The five men froze, but none of them dropped their weapons.

Caleb knew that this was one of those critical instances in a man's life when he must balance the value of freedom against the chance of dying. He understood it. He'd faced it many times in his life.

He could see each of them wrestling with the choice, all the while scanning the terrain to see if Caleb was alone or if there were others ready to gun them down. Seeing only him, they were now weighing their odds of catching the first bullet or successfully diving for cover. If they could make it, they were thinking, they could return fire and eventually overwhelm the single gunman simply by virtue of sheer numbers.

Almost simultaneously, all five made the wrong choice.

The first two men jerked their rifles to their shoulders and opened fire, their bullets whizzing by Caleb and thumping into the log in front of him. Caleb's rifle barked in response, catching the first man square in the chest. He staggered and took a step back, dropping his gun as his mouth dropped open, forming an O. He sank to his knees and fell onto his face.

Caleb didn't wait for the end, however. Swiveling his rifle a degree, he fired at the second man as the outlaw went down into a crouch. The bullet struck him in the throat, and he clutched at his neck as the blood sprayed from the severed vein. He sat down heavily, watching with disbelieving horror on his face as his life spewed out onto the reddening snow around him.

The third man dove forward to take cover behind some broken crates. Because of the mound, he rose to get a clear shot. But as he sighted along the barrel of his Sharps carbine, the slug from Caleb's Winchester buried itself in his left lung. He staggered, and his rifle tipped forward slightly, but he was a determined fella. He began to lift the carbine again, but Caleb finished him with a shot directly to the heart.

He didn't want to kill these fellas, only bring them to justice and, in so doing, free Henry. But fate generally tended to take a hand in things, and men didn't always help themselves.

Bullets were *thupping* by Caleb's ear and raising puffs of snow as they glanced off the log or passed through the drift. He dropped down behind the log and replaced his spent cartridges.

Three down.

The two remaining killers continued to shoot, the reports from their rifles echoing off the ridge. He didn't need the smoke from their rifles to know where they were.

John Rivers had planted himself by the stack of firewood, and Mad Dog found cover behind the old wagon.

"Rivers," Caleb shouted when there was a momentary break. "McCord."

Mad Dog's voice boomed across the snow. "We know that's you, Marlowe. And you're a dead man. We could wait you out, if we needed to. But we won't need to. You might as well give it up now."

"I expected you to play the fool, McCord," Caleb shouted back. "But you, Rivers, I never took you for being as stupid as Mad Dog."

"What do you mean by that?" Mad Dog bellowed. "Who're you calling a fool?"

Caleb let that hang. "Rivers, I know you're the real brains in this outfit. It probably didn't take no time for you to figure out that your cellmate Elijah Starr was your ticket out of that date with the hangman."

"I don't know what you're talking about," the outlaw called out from the woodpile. "And I don't know nobody named Rivers."

Caleb chuckled. That fella never could quit.

Mad Dog couldn't keep his mouth shut. He was not about to play second fiddle to anyone. "*I'm* the boss of this outfit…and the brains too. Rivers works for me. You got that, Marlowe? Now who's stupid?"

"Shut up, Mad Dog," Rivers barked.

Staying low, Caleb moved ten feet to his right to the end of the fallen tree. He judged that from there he could get a better angle on John Rivers.

"Who you telling to shut up?" Mad Dog growled.

"You," the other outlaw hissed. "You ain't got the brains of a busted axe handle. When we get out of this, I'm cashing in my chips, and you and me are going our separate—"

Four pistol shots came from behind the wagon, cutting off the rest of Rivers's words. Caleb peered over the top of the log and saw the smoke hanging in the cold air above the wagon.

"Why wait, you scrawny little shit?" the burly killer spat, firing two more from his short-barreled Colt for good measure. "Cash in *them* chips."

From this angle, Caleb could see where Rivers had fallen. His boots extended beyond the edge of the woodpile. One of them twitched and then went still.

Four down, one mean sonovabitch to go.

"Brilliant," Caleb shouted. "Now you're the undisputed boss, ain't you? Boss of nobody."

"I don't need nobody, Marlowe." He fired twice at the log where Caleb had been before. "You hear me? I'm Mad Dog McCord."

The problem was Caleb wanted this mean sonovabitch alive. He slid the barrel of his Winchester over the top of the log and waited for his shot. He didn't have to wait long.

Mad Dog poked his head up quickly and then dropped down again. A moment later, the outlaw's new hat appeared above the boxboard. He rested it there and fired another round. Almost immediately, he appeared at the front corner of the wagon, ready to blast Caleb when he shot at the decoy.

"Well, hell," Caleb murmured to himself. "That ain't gonna work."

He had a clear shot at the killer. He could put one right in the middle of that big, gleaming forehead. Sighting carefully, he squeezed the trigger.

Mad Dog howled as the bullet grazed the side of his head. Dropping his rifle, he leaped back, slapping his hand against the place where his ear had been. Blood was streaming through his fingers and down onto his arm and new coat.

Suddenly realizing he was standing in the open, Mad Dog ran in panic back toward the cabin and barreled into the closed door, smashing it open and tumbling through.

"Damn. Gotta make things difficult," Caleb muttered. "You coulda just gave up, you know."

Going around the log, he moved quickly and stealthily to the snow-covered mound of dirt and rock. Positioning himself where he'd have a decent shot into the door, he dropped down out of sight.

"Give it up, Mad Dog. You wanna keep shooting this out? You make that choice—smart as you are—and you ain't getting outta this alive."

"I can't hear nothing! You shot my damn ear off!" The outlaw punctuated the words with six straight shots at the fallen log from his Colt.

Caleb stood up and took aim. The burly figure was only a silhouette in the doorway, hurriedly trying to reload, but that was enough time.

The bullet went through the door and caught Mad

Dog high in the shoulder, spinning him away. He went down and out of sight onto the cabin floor, but Caleb was already at the door.

With his smoking Winchester pointed at the outlaw's ugly face, he kicked a fallen pistol out of reach across the packed-dirt floor.

"You got me, Marlowe." Mad Dog was bleeding from the former location of his ear and from the bullet wound in his shoulder. "I'm dying, man. Shoot me, and get it done with."

"Not yet. I ain't close to being done with you."

CHAPTER THIRTY-FOUR

As the afternoon had progressed, the sun had become a pale disk, eventually disappearing behind the clouds building in the west. With the smell of snow again in the air, Main Street was even busier than usual. Men on horseback and wagons crowded the street, and folks rushed around, intent on getting their business finished before dusk settled in.

Caleb rode slowly down the thoroughfare. He was holding the lead of a bay pinto that trailed behind him. In the gelding's saddle, a wounded man sat with his hands tied behind him.

They couldn't help but attract attention, which was exactly what Caleb wanted.

Pedestrians paused on the sidewalk, conjecturing with one another about the spectacle as they gawked and pointed. Those crowding the street pulled aside to make room for Caleb, casting inquisitive eyes at him and his captive.

Caleb glanced around just once at Mad Dog. The wounded man searched the crowds and the sidewalks fearfully. He was pale as a ghost and wore no hat. His bald head and neck were caked with dried blood.

Caleb reined in Pirate, slowing the buckskin. He wanted to be sure the news of their arrival had spread through town before they reached their destination.

One of Zeke's deputies stood in the door of a saloon as they passed. Seeing Caleb and his prisoner, he dropped the stub of his cigar and ran up the street to notify the sheriff.

"You're stupider than I thought you was." Mad Dog's growl barely cleared his throat. "If'n you think you can walk right up to him…shit, man, he'll come right out on the street here and shoot you dead."

Let him try, Caleb thought.

As they approached the town jail, Zeke was coming across the snow-packed street to meet them.

"Whaddya got, Marlowe?" he asked, walking alongside.

"Mad Dog McCord."

"Damn it. If you don't beat all! I'd a swore this varmint was down Mexico way by now." Zeke eyed the outlaw and called to his deputy to run for Doc Burnett. "You done real good work…as you always do. And the dirty desperado is still breathing. Let's get the sonovabitch down and lock his carcass up."

"I ain't handing him over yet. So step back, Zeke."

Caleb turned his gaze to the second floor of the judge's building. Just as he'd hoped, the commotion on the street had brought the great man to the window. And Elijah Starr was staring out from a second window.

Caleb locked eyes with his father and then swung down from his saddle. Going back to the bay pinto, he dragged Mad Dog off the horse.

The killer howled in pain as he landed on his shoulder at Caleb's feet. He didn't try to get up.

"Let me have him, Marlowe," the sheriff implored, sounding worried. "You'll get the reward for this cuss. Don't you fret none about that."

Caleb towered over the sheriff, and he spoke directly to him in a low voice. "Trust me, Zeke. Now, there don't need to be no shooting. But if there is, you don't want to get caught in the middle of it. So you just move away. I'll hand the blackguard over to you when I'm done with him."

Zeke's bristly eyebrows arched as he took in the words. He looked up at the window where Starr was standing. Then, to his credit, he did exactly as he was told and hurried back up onto the sidewalk in front of the jail.

Grabbing the prisoner by the scruff of his neck, Caleb hauled him up into a kneeling position, facing the window.

"Say it."

"I can't. You see him there. He'll kill me."

"Say it." He took hold of Mad Dog's wounded shoulder and squeezed it.

"All right!" the killer yelped.

"Loud enough for those up there to hear."

"Got a confession to make," McCord yelled.

The judge slid open the window a crack.

"Now." Caleb held on to the shoulder, feeling fresh blood. "The rest of it."

"I…I killed Frank Stubbs."

"Again."

"I shot him in the back. I killed Stubbs."

A gasp rose from the crowd of onlookers that had gathered. It looked like half the town and three-quarters of the miners in the region were there watching.

The prisoner tried to pull away, but Caleb held him. "You ain't done yet."

"There's more," Mad Dog called up at the window. He cast a panicked look at the window where Starr was standing like a grim statue.

"Tell him," Caleb ordered, shaking him.

"About them double-crossers you got working for you."

The judge abruptly disappeared from the window, as did Elijah Starr. Considering Patterson's suspicion of everyone since the death of his former bodyguard, Caleb hoped the words were enough enticement for the judge to come down to the street.

The letter he'd received from Duke Ortiz wasn't enough to convict Elijah Starr, but Mad Dog's confession after the shoot-out this afternoon had supplied a few more nails for his coffin. He'd been correct about Starr recruiting John Rivers while they shared a cell in Elkhorn's jail. Deals had been made. Plans had been set.

After escaping from their escort on the way to Denver, John Rivers and Mad Dog McCord had gathered up a new gang. Once Starr had been freed by the judge to work for him, they'd met him in Denver and traveled south to Pueblo.

That was when the fear of Starr had been driven into McCord. He said the one-eyed man had gutted one of the gang members in front of the others, just for mouthing off about how things should be done. Mad Dog was a killer himself, but that day he learned he was working for the devil himself.

After hiring some no-account cowpunchers, they'd stolen the herd of longhorns coming from Texas. A bunch of Texans died, but that's what they were paid to do.

Mad Dog told him Starr knew everything about Caleb and Henry and their plans.

The punchers had driven the cattle up to a railroad siding north of Pueblo, where the longhorns were loaded onto waiting cattle cars. From there, Starr traveled by train to Denver, while Mad Dog and John Rivers and what remained of his new gang went back to Elkhorn.

Starr had more jobs waiting for them back in Elkhorn. The money was good. They'd had to shoot a miserable mine owner and torch Caleb's ranch. Other than that, as long as Rivers stayed clear of the sheriff and his deputies, cards and drinking were the order of the day.

The confession was no good unless the right man heard it all. Mad Dog was doing the job the judge had tried to hire Caleb to do—work for Starr. The question was: How much of all this was Patterson aware of?

The door in front of them opened. A half dozen of Patterson's armed guards came out. Four of them were carrying rifles. The two buffalos Caleb met before were standing at the end of the line, smirking and displaying the pistols under their coats.

"I'm putting my money on one of them big fellas eye-balling you there on the right," Mad Dog said.

Caleb let go of him and unfastened the thongs over the hammers of his twin Colts. He'd take at least half of them down before they got him. More people were gathering on the street by the minute. Behind him, he heard folks scattering to get out of the line of fire.

Doc Burnett, with his surgical bag in hand, pushed through the crowd near the sidewalk.

"Stay right there, Doc," Caleb called out. His friend stopped. Beside him, Sheila and Red Annie appeared. He recalled they were all supposed to have dinner tonight. Red pushed her coat back. She was ready to fight, should the need arise.

Behind the line of bodyguards, Elijah Starr came out of the building, and behind him, the judge himself.

The two men pushed past the guards. Starr stood next to the judge.

Patterson shot a quick glance around at the crowd. "Marlowe, you surely know how to make an entrance. What's this all about?"

Caleb's eyes remained on his father. The older man's pistols were loose in the holsters. Starr's face might have been carved from granite. His expression was one of absolute contempt.

Elijah Starr had good reason for his barely contained rage. He'd dug a hole for Caleb, but he hadn't buried him in it quickly enough. Mad Dog was supposed to be his gunslinging right-hand man. But right now, with McCord in custody and singing like a meadowlark, the one-eyed man standing beside the judge had to know he was going down. Not even Patterson could save him. This change of fortune had to come as a hard blow.

Caleb hoped so. But he also knew there was one person Elijah Starr would be sure to take with him once the shooting started.

"What is it, Marlowe?" the judge's voice rang out. "You say this man has some information for me?"

Mad Dog, still on his knees, tried to edge away from Marlowe.

"You chopped the head off one snake…and then hired another."

The day Starr had been released from jail, Caleb had gone to the Silver Elk Hotel to confront him, to face his father. After all the years and the miles, their day had come.

But Caleb wouldn't draw first.

"You're saying my men are disloyal?" Patterson asked.

"Don't know nothing about these other fellas. But I've brought you enough proof today about one man, the devil standing beside you."

Elijah Starr's right hand inched toward his Colt.

Caleb looked into his father's face, and years melted away. They were back in Indiana. Back in the silent, gloomy rooms of the house where he kept Caleb's mother prisoner. No one allowed to come into the house. No one allowed to visit her when she showed the cuts and bruises she'd received at her husband's hand.

Caleb recalled all the times he'd wanted to hide when he saw that look come into his father's face. For Caleb knew his old man would start on him just to provoke her anguished and protective maternal response. Elijah Starr used the son to get to the mother. He was the devil.

Caleb's heart raced, but he felt the familiar coolness take over his head. He was at peace with who he was and what he had to do. His hands were still and ready.

Like pages of a book, pushed by a breeze, the years flipped by. He was sixteen. The horror of his mother's bloody body on the floor. He'd arrived at the house, only to find her beaten to death and Elijah Starr standing over her, the stout cane in his fists.

The memory of hammering away at his father's face—again and again and again until he couldn't strike him even one more time—was right there in his mind, as vivid as if it happened yesterday. Elijah fell. And Caleb left his father lifeless on the kitchen floor, or so he thought.

But Elijah Starr lived. He lived. And now, he stood glaring at Caleb, his hand a whisper away from his shooting iron.

"What's Starr done?" Patterson asked, his voice carrying over the crowd that was silent as the dead.

"He's still working for Eric Goulden. He's gonna take you down, Judge."

Starr went for his gun, clearing leather in the blink of an owl's eye.

Caleb realized at that second that his whole life had led him to this day, to this moment. All the innocent people he'd stepped up to protect over the years had only been replacements for the mother he hadn't been able to save.

All the lives of killers that he'd cut short had only been replacements for the man he hadn't killed soon enough.

But, in the end, it all came back to this man…and to the mother who had given her life to keep him safe. To the mother who, in her unhappy time on earth, had never rested easy while this man lived.

To the untrained ear, it sounded as if the shots had been fired as one. But he knew better.

While his father's shot went wide, Caleb's bullet tore through the eye patch, entering Starr's seething, twisted brain through the same eyeless socket that, as a child, Caleb was sure was a window to hell.

Elijah's Starr's head snapped back as a pink cloud painted the building behind him. His other eye, now as sightless, stared into a dark oblivion. He sank to his knees, the pistol dropped from his lifeless hand, and he fell forward.

No one else moved. No one drew their guns. No one even breathed.

Caleb's eyes shifted, moving along the line of people until he found the faces of the ones he called his friends. Doc. Red Annie.

Sheila.

And there, beside Sheila, he saw his mother. She was standing and watching him, her face smiling gently as it did in their quietest moments so long ago.

As he returned her gaze, soft snow began to fall. And then, she was gone.

"Rest now, Mama. You can rest now."

CHAPTER THIRTY-FIVE

Six weeks later

CALEB AND HENRY SPENT THE NEXT SIX WEEKS rebuilding the barn and Henry's cabin. The weather had helped, what with the cold easing a little during the day and only an occasional dusting of snow at night. Henry forecasted that January would be hellacious.

Money was going to be tight till spring. Caleb had gotten paid bounties for John Rivers and for Mad Dog McCord. That had helped, some. And they'd cut the numbers in the herd, selling the meat in town and shipping the rest to Denver by sledge. Mr. Lewis at the hardware store and Mr. Wilson at the general store had grubstaked them for building supplies and feed and such in exchange for a percentage of their beef profits over the next two years. That worried Caleb a little, but he was reconciled to it.

Duke Ortiz and Bass Dart returned to Elkhorn, having decided to winter here until they thought Tex Washington was ready to travel. The three of them came over often. The more hands, the faster the buildings went up. As Christmas drew nearer, they were starting to make some noise about heading home. Bass said, as a Louisiana native, he'd never get used to this cold. And Caleb knew Duke wanted to get started on rounding up a herd for next year's drive.

The thousand longhorns were gone. What Elijah Starr had done couldn't be undone. The cattle had become the possession of Eric Goulden, and there'd be no getting them back. A person would have better luck prying a rabbit out of the talons of a turkey buzzard.

Caleb and Henry had made a deal with Ortiz regarding the herd he was bringing them next year, and it was a good one. Duke kept saying his family honor and the honor of the vaqueros was at stake, and Caleb finally stopped arguing about it. At least Ortiz had agreed to take some of the bounty money to put toward the purchase, but getting him to take even that had been a battle.

Caleb and Henry were keeping the ranch. Judge Patterson had given up on the idea of finding a reason to run them off. For now.

The work they'd been doing over the past six weeks had been hard and honest, and Caleb's ribs and bruises from falling off the side of the mountain had healed up completely. In general, he felt that things were shaping up. For the first time in his life, he was feeling truly settled.

The occasional itch to get away into the mountains, to the sounds of the birds and animals, and to the clean air that had none of the acrid taint of towns or mine works was just that. An itch. He was a different man now, and he knew it.

His discussion with Sheila out by the smoldering barn

had helped him more than she knew. She'd convinced him to stay and fight. She'd forced his eyes open to see and recognize who he was. Caleb Marlowe was a gunslinger, a fighter, and a killer when the need arose. And that was fine. This was the frontier. This was the life that he'd chosen and that Sheila was trying to find a place in. They were not as different as he'd thought. They were survivors.

There were other things that helped Caleb feel settled too.

Mad Dog McCord's public confession had been enough for the judge. He'd ordered Zeke to set Henry free that same night. McCord's debt to society had been paid soon enough and had drawn a good crowd. On the gallows, the blowhard had made some long, rambling speech about his hanging drawing a bigger crowd than any other hanging in the history of hangings. Caleb wasn't there, but Zeke had told the story with gusto.

More important than anything else, Elijah Starr was gone for good.

Day after day, they made progress on the barn. But the fly in that pudding was that, with all the work they'd been doing, Caleb had no time to go to Doc's house for chess and dinner. He missed the games and the company, but more so, he missed Sheila. From all he was hearing, though, she'd been damn busy herself with her Ladies' Event Planning Committee and their preparations for the Christmas gala.

He didn't know anything about the arrangements for

the upcoming shindy. The fire had put an end to talk of the event being held out here. Where exactly it was to be held and what was going on, he hadn't been told, and he hadn't asked. He figured it would come clear soon enough, tomorrow being Christmas Eve. He and Henry were expected to be in Elkhorn around suppertime.

Henry had been making regular trips to Wilson's General Store, buying gifts for all his women. Caleb was starting to wonder if he had a soft spot for Mrs. Wilson, but Henry denied it hotly. In any event, he'd made his final trip to town this morning while they were supposed to be hanging the barn doors.

When Henry finally got back and they settled down to work, the chucklehead had started in on him again. "You told me you wasn't buying gifts for nobody."

Before this year, Caleb never thought about the tradition of gift giving at Christmas. When his mother died, that tradition had died with it.

"Wilson asked me this morning if you was happy with all the packages you picked up."

"I'm happy."

"Where are you hiding them? How come you never said nothing?"

With Henry's cabin finished last week, it was good not having his friend in his hair every minute. "None of your business."

"Who did you buy for?"

"Quiet down, and wedge that side. I don't want it moving while I auger out these last holes. Let's finish this."

Henry worked diligently and in silence for roughly two seconds.

"So, did you take any of my very helpful suggestions about what to buy and what not to buy the lovely Miss Sheila?"

"Did you see the damn door move when you started flapping your gums? It's gonna be spring, and we still won't have this last door hung. Pick it up and wedge it. Use your tongue for a wedge while you're at it."

Henry hefted his side and shoved the wedges back in, trying to look offended.

"Good. Keep it there." Caleb cranked the auger.

"Hope you didn't do nothing boring like buying her a book or nothing. Do you know she has subscriptions to three magazines?"

"How do you know that?" Caleb slid the bolt through. One more hole and they were finished. He moved and put the auger bit through the hinge, then started cranking.

"Mrs. Lewis let it slip one day when I was in the hardware store. She believes Sheila Burnett must be the smartest person in Elkhorn with all the reading she does."

Caleb didn't need Mrs. Lewis to say so. He already knew.

"She's too old for you to get her hair ribbons."

"Did those wedges move?"

"Gloves are usually a good gift. She ain't fond of wearing them, though, I noticed."

Caleb frowned at his friend. "Oh, you noticed, did you?"

"You didn't get her one of them new, bright-painted

fans Wilson got in his front window, did you?" Henry's face soured as if that were a terrible idea. "Every one of them saloon girls over at the Belle got one. You gotta be careful about offending a woman, Marlowe. It can be tricky. I remember this one gal I knew up in Denver—"

"Henry!" Caleb barked.

"All right. Just trying to help."

The auger went through, and Caleb pushed in the bolt.

Henry was paying no attention to the business of the door whatsoever. "I do believe Miss Sheila is the only woman in Elkhorn that's got everything. Her and Belle Constant."

Caleb popped the wedges and carefully swung the door out.

"You go in there, and put these nuts on them bolts," he ordered. "When I get the door wedged again, tighten 'em good. And maybe I'll let you out by New Year's."

Henry went inside, and Caleb could hear the nuts going on

He never stopped talking, and his muffled voice was still coming through the door. "She's another one that's tough to buy for. That Belle, I mean."

"I think you should give that present for Belle particular attention."

As surprising as it was that Henry was buying a present for the saloon owner, it was a relief to have him paying attention to someone other than Sheila. Maybe Caleb would finally be able to put aside the occasional urge to knock his friend's teeth out.

"Done," his partner declared, coming out and sounding like he'd done the whole damn thing himself.

The two of them stood back and inspected their finished work. The barn was finally finished. Again.

Bear got up from where he'd been working hard supervising over by the wall and plunked his butt down between them.

Henry patted the dog's head. "You get a gift too. I saved you an elk bone."

Bear looked up, his tongue hanging out the side of his mouth.

"All those packages you picked up at Wilson's. Did you get me something for Christmas?" Henry asked.

"You're standing here, ain't you? You didn't hang. That's your gift."

"Good. I didn't get you nothing, either."

━━━━━━━

The town of Elkhorn was divided into two distinct parties on Christmas Eve.

Toward the center of town, the management of the Silver Elk Hotel had moved the shiny statue in the lobby and replaced it with a large Christmas tree. The branches were weighed down and decorated with an abundant quantity of colorful, hand-painted ornaments. All imported from Germany, folks were saying. Inside their dining room, the Christmas Eve reception spread rivaled dishes being served in New York and Philadelphia on this very same night.

The guest list had been carefully reviewed and approved by Judge Patterson.

Sometime during the past couple of months, the Ladies' Event Planning Committee's vision for the celebration on Christmas Eve had parted ways with what the judge had in mind. Some members of the committee— one in particular—had taken exception to the idea of leaving folks out.

So, toward the eastern end of town, a huge tent—the kind usually seen over the heads of elephants and tumblers and flashy ladies standing on equally flashy horses— had been erected in Main Street, more or less under the nose of the great man. Just a few doors up from the judge's building, the tent started outside the door of the Belle Saloon and covered quite a bit of ground.

Inside the canvas hall, a temporary wood floor had been put down for dancing. There was a platform set up for the saloon's piano, a fiddler, an accordion player, and a banjo man. Tables and chairs had been carried out from the Belle and several other saloons and set up with white cotton cloth coverings for folks to sit at while enjoying the festivities.

At the far end of the dance floor, a tall tree had been set up and adorned with colored ribbons, brightly painted pinecones, and an assortment of silver and gold ornaments.

Outside the other end of the tent, an ice palace had been built using thousands of blocks of ice. With two bonfires burning at a safe distance on either side of the pavilion, the palace glistened as if it had walls of polished gold. As the evening drew near, every child in town had decided that the grown-ups could have the tent; the ice palace belonged to them. Operating on that belief, children were swarming happily through the arched gate, over the walls, and battling noisily for possession of the two squat towers.

Beyond the ice palace, a prayer service would be held at midnight. A new traveling preacher had been hoping that both factions in the town would come together on Main Street to celebrate the Christ child's birth.

Most of the Christmas festivities had been paid for through the generosity of Belle Constant.

Inside her saloon, the bar was gorgeously trimmed with red calico and a long, white cloth. Sprays of evergreen bound with red, white, and green plaid ribbon—the contribution of the Scotsman behind the bar—had been hung between the looking-glass panels. Formerly broken lampshades had been replaced with new ones. And for first time in the history of that celebrated building, the floor had been scrubbed, sanded, and scrubbed again. No other saloon in Elkhorn could boast such elegance. Indeed, the Belle had a glow to it that hadn't been seen for years.

The owner herself was resplendent in finery newly imported from St. Louis, watchfully overseeing the final preparations, both inside the saloon and in the canvas hall as well. All afternoon, she and her girls—also arrayed in their most demure yet colorful dresses—had been cordially welcoming ladies from town who had appeared, sometimes timidly, bearing food and baked goods for the evening's festivities. Most of the women had never even peeked in the door of the Belle, never mind stepped foot inside.

By the time the pale sun gave up its battle and descended behind the wintry clouds at the horizon, all was in readiness.

Kegs of brandy and baskets of cognac, champagne, and other wines were appropriately positioned and staffed by the Belle's capable employees.

The musicians struck up their tunes at six, and the celebration began with toasts, songs, dancing, speeches, and eventually a champagne supper. Fat hens, quails, steaks, hares, pound cakes, and pies were consumed and washed down with prodigious amounts of alcohol.

Around eight o'clock, Caleb found Doc Burnett on the sidewalk in front of the Belle, talking with Bass Dart, Duke Ortiz, and Tex Washington. The wounded cowboy was standing and using crutches, but Caleb had to take a second look at the young man. Tex was sporting a new extension to his leg, from the knee down.

"What do you think, Marlowe?" Doc asked as he joined the group. "Tex's new leg arrived two days ago."

Having served as a surgeon during the war, Doc was well informed about the latest improvements to designs of artificial limbs. Caleb had heard Henry say Duke Ortiz was paying for it.

"How does it feel?" Caleb asked.

The young man took couple of steps up and down the sidewalk and held it out for inspection. "I'm standing. Won't be doing much dancing, but I'm getting around."

Duke slapped his cowpuncher on the back. "We'll save that for next Christmas. Now, let's go get some more of that pie before these miners eat it all."

As the three Texas cattlemen went for the dessert tables, Doc and Caleb looked around them at the crowds.

"How come you ain't over at Patterson's party at the Silver Elk?" Caleb asked.

"I was invited." Doc grinned at his friend. "But I had a strong feeling that Sheila didn't want me to go."

"No?"

"To be clear, I believe she said something about shooting me in the leg if I so much as took a step into that lobby."

"She got a beef with the judge? What about?"

Doc looked steadily into Caleb's face. "You, my friend. She wasn't at all pleased with the way he tried to run you out of Elkhorn. And that daughter of mine has a gift for holding grudges."

He'd come to know that about Sheila. She spoke her mind and had no trouble calling a spade a spade.

Caleb pulled a wrapped parcel bound with twine from inside of his coat. "I got you a gift. Hope that's all right."

Doc smiled and pulled a wrapped parcel out of his pocket as well. "And I have something for you."

Good thing Henry wasn't around. For sure, he'd take exception to Caleb having a gift for Doc and not for him. He waited, watching the older man open his first.

"Thought maybe you could use a few pointers."

"That's too funny." Doc stared at the copy of Phillip Stamma's *The Noble Game of Chess*. "Open yours, wiseacre."

Caleb opened the gift and let out a snort. The two of them had bought the same thing for each other.

Doc tucked his copy into his coat pocket. "I guess that means neither one of us will have an unfair advantage over the other."

"Nope. But you might want to keep that hid from Sheila. She's bound to be beating us both regular by summer as it is."

Caleb saw Gabe and Paddy over by the ice palace, so he took his leave of Doc and strode into the street to talk to them.

They were both wearing the gifts he'd given them earlier—the same black, wide-brimmed hats that he wore.

"Gabe, your folks here?" he asked, glancing around.

"They're coming over a little later," Gabe replied. "Pa wanted to make sure the livery was locked up for the night."

Speaking to Malachi, Caleb had learned that the cousins were due to arrive any day.

"I'll be looking for 'em." Caleb gestured toward Paddy. "Mind if I have a private word with this bandit?"

"Sure enough." Gabe pointed to one of the palace towers. "I'll be storming that one when you're done."

"Everything all right?" Paddy asked, worry in his voice.

"Yep, I got something I want to ask you." Caleb placed a hand on the boy's shoulder.

He knew what he wanted to say, but the words were having a hard time forming. This was going to be a big step for all of them.

"I'd like you to pack your things over at the Rogers's place and move out to the ranch with me and Henry next week."

Paddy stared, looking like a statue for a few seconds. His eyes finally blinked, and a couple of tears fell on his cheeks. "You mean it?"

Caleb nodded. "We both want you out there. I want you out there. Hell, Bear wants you out there."

"You mean, for a little while?"

"I mean for good."

"For good," Paddy repeated. The back of the sleeve went to his face as he wiped away tears. "I was hoping, you know. But I…I didn't think after the fire and all…"

Caleb pulled Paddy into his arms. He wasn't too used to displays of affection, but he figured he could get used to it. "Seems like Christmas is a fine time for finding family."

The boy stayed there for a few moments. When he finally pulled away, he nodded to Caleb. "You won't be sorry. I promise. I'll make you proud of me."

"I know you will."

Paddy ran off toward the palace, calling out to his friend.

"Gabe!" The boy's words came back to Caleb over the voices of the other children. "Gabe, I got a family!"

The boy's reaction caused something to squeeze inside Caleb's chest. He moved away to breathe in some cold air and fight down a burning sensation that had formed in his throat.

For so many years, he'd run away from situations that made him feel too much. Anger he understood. That was an emotion he could do something about. But family, affection, commitment... He ran a hand down his face as the reality of the man he was becoming hit him hard.

Caleb Marlowe, the lone frontiersman, was making way for a new Caleb Marlowe. He was hesitant as to whether he was truly up to the task, but he was committed to doing his best for the young boy. Hell, the die was cast.

Involuntarily, his hand slid inside his coat pocket, and his fingers wrapped around a small box. He had to find Sheila.

Inside the tent, the musicians had the crowd in high glee with a reel that filled the dance floor. The huge canvas hall was crowded, and more people were coming in all the time. The tables at the end were all taken.

Twenty people or two hundred people... it made no difference. Caleb's eyes immediately found her.

Sheila was wearing a hooded velvet coat the color of burgundy wine that was edged with white fur. Beneath it, a matching dress. The hood was pushed back, and she'd worn her golden hair in braids piled on top of her head. As always, she was the prettiest thing he'd ever seen anywhere.

She stood just away from the dancers, speaking to a tall woman standing beside her. Her face was animated.

The two of them were completely unaware of all the men's eyes directed their way.

He started toward them but was arrested by someone grabbing his arm. Henry, drink in hand.

"Who in blazes is that redhead with Sheila?"

Caleb took a second look at the two women and then smiled to himself. "You ain't met her?"

Henry shook his head, obviously unable to tear his eyes away. "No, I ain't. But she's a killer, for sure."

At least he had that right.

"Want me to introduce you?"

"You know her?"

"'Course. She's a friend of Sheila's." Caleb slapped his friend on the back. "But first, put the drink down. Straighten your collar. Wipe that food off your face."

Henry put his drink down and went through motions of straightening his clothes, but quickly realized Caleb was joshing him. "Let's go."

They started toward the women, pushing their way through the merrymakers.

"I always loved tall women."

"That right?" Caleb asked. "And short ones too, if I ain't mistaken."

Henry ignored him. "But redheads are something else."

"And blonds. And brunettes. And—"

"Shut up." His eyes were locked on the new paragon of feminine beauty. "A damn goddess, here in Elkhorn. How did I ever miss this one?"

"Some men are just blind." Caleb stepped in front of

Henry as they pushed their way through the last line of people.

Sheila saw them approaching. She immediately faced him and smiled.

"Marlowe."

"Sheila."

The tall woman ignored them, keeping her attention on the dance floor. Henry tapped Caleb on the shoulder, indicating with a jerk of his eyebrows that he was waiting.

"Sheila, could you introduce—"

"I can talk for myself, Marlowe," Henry cut in, stepping up next to him. "Miss Sheila, would you be kind enough to introduce me to your lovely friend."

Annie O'Neal took that moment to turn around.

"Red, you sure clean up nice," Caleb said.

"Blame this one." She elbowed Sheila, drawing a smile from the other woman. "She says to me there's a first time for everything. Mind you, it ain't the first time I been roped into wearing a getup like this. I just don't believe in us women needing this horseshit of being uncomfortable all the time. You ever wore a damn corset, Marlowe?"

"Just saying, you look real fine tonight, Miss O'Neal," Caleb said.

"Don't get used to it. I'll be back to being Red Annie before you can blink twice."

Henry stood there, silent as a rock. His tongue was obviously tied in a knot.

Red finally cast a look his way. "Henry, you clean up good too."

"Thank you, Annie."

That was all he could get out, and Caleb was ready to kick Henry for not returning the compliment. An awkward silence hung in the air. Even the musicians had stopped between numbers.

Zeke came up in that moment and joined their circle. The burly little sheriff looked up at Annie, and Caleb thought he was licking his chops under all those whiskers.

"Why, Miss Red, would you do me the honor of a dance?"

"Hell no, Zeke," Henry said, cutting in. "She's dancing with me."

Taking Red Annie by the hand, he pulled her toward the dance floor as the music started again.

She looked back over her shoulder. "Should I kick his ass for not asking proper-like?"

"Let him have this dance," Caleb called out to her. "You done overwhelmed the boy."

They watched the two disappear into the crowd of dancers. Zeke, undaunted, turned his eye on Sheila. "Would you…"

Caleb cleared his throat and shook his head. The sheriff shrugged and set off in search of less dangerous prey.

A smile broke across Sheila's lips. "You and Henry."

"Zeke deserved it."

"Why, because he put Henry in jail?"

"Because when four humans are having a conversation, he shouldn't interrupt."

"And we all know what a sparkling conversationalist

you are." With a laugh that was as pleasing to his ear as a rippling creek in spring, she linked her arm with his. "Come back here with me. I have a gift for you."

She steered him toward a table close to the canvas wall. Disengaging her arm, she picked up a long, scarlet satin parcel, bound with green ribbon.

"Sheila, you didn't have to do nothing for me."

"Open it," she said, her eyes shining.

The cloth wrapping fell away, and Caleb was left holding a leather rifle scabbard, decorated with beaded designs that he knew were Arapaho.

"I did the whole thing. Imala gave me the elk skin and showed me how to make and stitch it and how to do the bead work and…" She took a breath. "Do you like it?"

Caleb had to swallow twice to get the words out. It was getting to be a tough night in that respect. And he didn't reckon it was going to get much easier.

"It's a beauty, Sheila. I ain't never seen anything so fine. Thank you."

She beamed happily for a moment and then grew serious. "I asked Imala if she wanted to join us tonight, but she said no."

"I ain't surprised."

Caleb understood completely. Talking to her, he knew that Imala would never replace her people's spiritual beliefs with what was expected by white people and the Bible. Celebrations like this weren't for her.

"The rifle scabbard you have now is so worn, and I thought you could use a new one."

"You're right. And you done beautiful work on it. Thank you."

Her face glowed. She was obviously happy with his reaction. "Should we go back? I'm going to force you to dance with me, you know."

"Before we go..." He reached inside his pocket and took out the small box. "I got something for you too."

Hesitantly, Sheila took it from him. "What is it?"

"Open it and see."

She shook the box and held it to her ear.

"It ain't gonna talk to you. Open it."

Caleb loved the fact that she savored every moment. Her bright smile said she was already pleased that he'd bought her a gift.

"There's something inside the box," he reminded her.

"There is?" she teased, finally lifting the lid.

Inside, nestled into a bed of satin material, a large, gold locket and chain gleamed in the lamplight. She picked it up and held it in her hand like it was a newborn chick.

"This is beautiful, Caleb." She turned it over. "It has my initials carved on the back!" She raised the locket to him. "Can you help me put it around my neck?"

"Not yet. Got something inside too."

The clasp was delicate. Her fingers hurried to open it. Caleb tried to help her, and their hands became entangled. She didn't hurry to pull away.

Finally, she pried it open. Inside, she found a gold nugget he'd been saving since his days in Montana.

"I've never seen one of these." She held it up to the

lamplight. "Amazing. Is this what gold looks like when they find it?"

He didn't answer her right away. He had to line his words up right. There was so much he wanted to say.

"Here it is. Everyone keeps telling me I don't talk much, so hear me out."

Her blue eyes were unwavering as they looked into his.

"Henry and I are staying. Tonight, I told Paddy he'd be moving his things to the ranch. But there's a lot that we've lost, and a lot of rebuilding we need to do. I don't know when everything will get squared away and the place will get set up enough for me to do any asking."

The lights shone like stars in Sheila's eyes. Caleb took her free hand in his, feeling the softness of her skin in his rough palm.

"So, I'm thinking…maybe, when things get settled in my life, we can get that nugget melted down and made into a ring."

She blushed. Her mouth opened to say something, and she paused before the words came out. "What are you doing, Marlowe? Are you proposing?"

"Maybe. I'm thinking ahead." He lifted her chin, and his head dipped until there was only a breath of air between them. "If that was the question I was asking, what would you say?"

She leaned forward and kissed him. Caleb kissed her back in a way he'd never allowed himself to do. Someone going by whistled, and the two separated.

"What's your answer?" he asked.

"I'll have to talk this over with Bear. But...maybe," Sheila said with a mischievous glint in her eye. "Now, let's go dancing."

Discover more action-packed historical westerns from Sourcebooks in *Dead Man's Hand* by David Nix

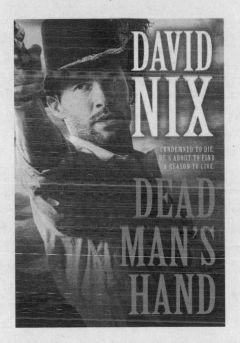

CHAPTER ONE

October 1867, Unorganized Territory, Western U.S.

NO BURDEN PROVES MORE TERRIBLE TO A LONER THAN the holding of a life in his hands. Jake Paynter held two hundred while staring down the barrel of his captain's revolver.

"Lieutenant," growled Captain Sherrod, "you will obey my order or receive a bullet."

Jake flicked his eyes aside to find the buffalo soldiers of K-Troop and the lone Shoshone scout watching the unfolding tragedy with frozen alarm in the broken hills above the Green River basin. The light snow that had been falling for an hour obscured the distance, creating a bubble of horses and men crowned with a dusting of white atop hats, blue coats, and manes. He met the riveting gaze of Sergeant Gus Rivers, who'd fought alongside him since '62 after escaping the cotton fields of Alabama. Gus slowly shook his head while sliding a hand toward the trigger of his carbine. Jake returned his attention to the captain.

"No, sir. I will *not* lead the men into that draw."

Sherrod's scowl deepened as he thumbed back the hammer. "Damn you, Paynter. This is your last chance."

Seconds passed in the silence of the deadening snowfall, marred only by the stamping and huffing of impatient horses. The gun's barrel began to quiver, and the captain lowered his weapon. "You contemptible coward. You shame a nation." He whipped his head aside. "First Sergeant!"

"Sir!" A chiseled man with a peppered moustache and manic eyes stepped toward them.

"Shoot this man."

"With pleasure."

A rifle butt met the side of Jake's skull, dumping him to his knees in the snow-covered sage. He looked up to find the sergeant looming over him. Ambrose Blackburn had seemed like the second coming of God Almighty when Paynter had first laid eyes on him as a seventeen-year-old looking to join the fight in Texas. He had quickly learned otherwise. When Jake had finally fled Blackburn's command, he'd never imagined encountering the man again. But when the Plains Army began accepting former Confederate officers to fill noncommissioned officer roles, Blackburn had joined up. The mocking hand of fate had placed him under Jake's command, where Blackburn had resumed his mission of corruption and violence. In service to those twin devils, his former commander pressed the barrel into Jake's throbbing temple and leaned over the stock toward his ear.

"Been waitin' five years for this, Paynter," he whispered. "Shoulda never turned coat."

A vision of violence erupted from Jake's memory. Of

Blackburn reveling in the blood and frenzy of wanton death, framed by a wall of fire consuming innocent souls. Jake's anger surged, and he ripped the carbine away from Blackburn's grasping hands even as a shot roaring past his head robbed sound from his left ear. He rolled to his feet just in time to catch his would-be executioner in the chin with the rifle butt. Blackburn crumpled into a heap. Another shot whistled past Jake, raising a burning line alongside his neck. He flipped the rifle in his hands and put a bullet between Sherrod's eyes before the captain could arrange a second shot. His commanding officer rocked back from the blow and stared in disbelief while a line of blood leaked down his forehead to the bridge of his nose. He toppled to the ground, spreading a red halo in the snow around his head, a dark angel of war gone still. Jake ejected the spent cartridge while stumbling to his feet and swung the rifle toward the man nearest him, ready for a fight. Corporal Stubbs raised his eyebrows while holding his carbine loosely in one hand. He stretched out an open palm.

"I don't never poke my nose into the quarrels of white officers. Like to get a man killed."

Jake spun in a half circle to find similar restraint from the rest of the troop. He lowered the rifle and put a hand to his stinging neck while Sergeant Rivers pushed through the startled ranks.

"Lemme look." Gus probed the wound until Jake winced. His old fighting mate grunted. "Missed the artery. Luckier'n a goose the day after Christmas."

Jake's eyes drifted to his dead captain and the bleeding first sergeant. "Not for long."

Gus nodded and pointed to Jake's unattended horse. "You know you gotta run now, right?"

"Where?"

"Anywhere." Gus gripped Jake's shoulder and steered him toward his mount. "Penalty for killing a superior officer is death. Don't matter the reason."

"Go north." Jake looked aside to find the Shoshone scout, Darwin Follows the Wind, addressing him. "North to the Wind River country. Find Beah Nooki, my grandfather. He will give shelter."

"Beah Nooki," Jake mumbled. He paused to spare the unconscious Blackburn a parting glance and entertained the whispering urge to put a lead ball in the man's brain. He was already in neck- deep, and nobody deserved it more than Blackburn. The whispers passed, and he rocked back into motion without satisfying his bloodlust. He was a killer, not a murderer. He turned over the first sergeant's rifle to Gus and mounted his horse. Corporal Stubbs handed up a cloth sack.

"Hard tack and jerky. For the journey."

Jake let the offer hang before reluctantly taking another man's ration. "Many thanks."

"G'luck, sir."

Jake surveyed his troop a final time. Good men. Strong men. Determined men who served the Tenth Cavalry, one of two all-black mounted regiments in the U.S. Plains Army. The plains tribes had taken to calling them buffalo soldiers, a designation of respect. Jake felt the same. He nodded before addressing Gus. "You're in charge. Lead the troop back to the fort. The white officers will look to place blame on you for not tryin' to stop me. Tell 'em whatever you must to spare yourself and the men."

"I will tell the truth."

"Please, Gus. You know what'll happen."

"Right." Gus cast a gaze into the draw. "Way I see it, you fled into the basin and we lost you in the snowfall."

Jake dipped his chin. "See ya, Gus."

"Only if the devil don't see ya first."

Jake wheeled his mount and rode north through the parting soldiers. Across the treeless expanse of rolling hills lay the Wind River country and the coming teeth of winter. He hoped the Shoshone would show him more mercy than Sherrod and Blackburn had, but lamented the fact that he deserved none for all the terrible things he'd done.

CHAPTER TWO

Seven Months Later, St. Joseph, Missouri

"Seems a good day to die."

Jake tore his gaze from the crystal-clear sky beyond his cell window to find Corporal McQuaid grinning through the bars, clearly pleased with his observation. Jake locked an unwavering gaze on the young soldier until the smile became a memory.

"Ain't no such animal, kid. Death has the gall to ruin even the best of days."

McQuaid launched a study of his beaten cavalry boots. "I reckon so. Hadn't given it much thought."

"Youth never does."

McQuaid lifted narrowed eyes at him. "But you ain't more'n, what, twenty-five?"

"Twenty-four."

The soldier rocked his head back and forth in apparent consideration. "Don't matter anyhow. We've come to take you."

Jake nodded. He'd waited three days for this moment. Oddly, the end of waiting brought him relief, an extra expanse of lung that seemed to have closed before. "They gonna give me a trial before they hang me?"

McQuaid's boyish smile returned. "You ain't heard? They ain't said nothin'?"

"No." He drew the word out slowly to mask his annoyance. "But if you are so inclined, might you share with me what I've not heard?"

"Telegraph arrived from Fort Bridger not one hour ago. Seems they want you shipped back to the territories for trial and hanging. General's considering it now. Although I wouldn't get yer hopes up. He seems itchy for a public spectacle."

The corporal's advice proved pointless. Jake had long ago decided that hope was for the delusional and children. Everyone else should know better. "Let's go, then."

The corporal motioned to the jailer, and within a minute, Jake found his wrists and ankles clapped in irons. As he shuffled from the cell block, a pair of soldiers clad in cavalry blue fell in behind him. His rank-and-file escorts seemed less enthused than he was. McQuaid motioned to the men.

"Privates Evans and Muñoz, in case you were wonderin'."

"I wasn't."

Once outside, he scouted the area with a grimace. Still a hellhole. Peeling-paint buildings crowded a street turned marsh from three days of rain. He turned aside to find a familiar face waiting for him, now clad in civilian clothing rather than cavalry blue.

"Gus. You still here?"

"Clearly." Sergeant Rivers offered an apologetic grin.

Paynter recalled the first time he'd met him, just before the skirmish at Island Mound in '62. The man's relentless optimism had rallied the men against the enemy and earned him a promotion. That, and his angular frame turned steel in the cotton fields of Alabama before his escape to freedom. Too bad he'd gotten caught up in Jake's quagmire.

"Thought you'd be long gone by now."

Gus shook his head and flashed his recurring wry smile, like he knew about a really good surprise and was just waiting for everyone else to catch up. "Nope. Army cut me loose and told me to bring you back. I don't get back pay lest I do. Now that I'm mustered out, I need the coin. Sorry I was the one to track you down. It was either me or someone who'd just as soon put a lead plum in ya."

"You did what you had to. I'm just glad if someone's making a dollar on this fiasco, it's you."

"Here, I brought somethin' for ya. You left it at Fort Bridger with all your stuff." Gus extended a familiar slouch hat, faded from six years of wear during war and peace. The emblazoned "1" of First Kansas Colored stood in the center of the crown, uneven from blood, sweat, and sun. He recalled the day the regimental tailor had stitched the emblem into the crown after the battle at Honey Springs to cover a near-miss bullet hole, and how that simple kindness had transformed the hat into more than just headwear. Jake accepted the hat and placed it on his head, where it settled comfortably in a joyful reunion with his skull. He rubbed his fingers along the brim to meet at the tassels.

"Thanks, Gus. Thought this was tossed on the rubbish heap long ago."

McQuaid stepped between them. "Got to move on, Paynter."

Gus fell in behind the soldiers as the procession moved along. The run of boardwalk ended, forcing the parade onto the road. Paynter's manacled slide-step passage along the rutted street would have raised a cloud of dust if not for six inches of mud and manure. By the time they arrived at the office of the military liaison, his boots had disappeared beneath a sheath of Missouri crud.

"Wait here," said McQuaid before he stepped inside. Jake decided to pass the time by memorizing the smell of biscuits wafting from the restaurant across the street. He'd miss biscuits. And sausage gravy.

The door flinging open recaptured his attention. General Bartlett, the Butcher of Blacksburg, strode toward him before halting the distance of a dead body away. Why did all generals walk like that? As if each step eternally possessed the soil beneath it. Was the attitude a product of the rank? Or was the rank a result of the attitude?

"You're a lucky dog, Paynter." The general's upper lip curled left as if drawn by a fisherman's hook. "As much as I'd like to stretch your neck myself, the War Office wants you returned to the scene of your disgrace as a lesson to the soldiers. Don't want those boys in the Tenth contemplating the prospect of killing an officer without dire consequences. You know what they're like."

Jake returned the general's disdain with an unflinching

gaze. "I do know what they're like. You, on the other hand, seem to know nothin' but how to return men to their families in pieces."

The general's palm lashed Jake's cheekbone, rocking his head to one side. He returned his glare to the man, tasting blood. Red feelers crawled into the general's cheeks to rise above his well-manicured beard.

"Rot in hell, Paynter." He spun on his heel and strode away. "Take him to Blue."

Jake was in motion again as a nervous McQuaid prodded him along the road.

"Why'd you do that?" The corporal seemed distraught at the display of disrespect to a commanding officer. Jake smiled for the first time in weeks.

"It's what I do. Or so I'm told."

He plodded along, accruing more mud than he thought possible, while pondering what "Blue" meant. Was it a grim moniker for the gallows or some other torture device? He almost hoped so. Dying in Missouri seemed preferable to an eight-hundred-mile journey for the purpose of hanging at a remote outpost. He groaned when they approached a line of prairie schooners stretched along the border of town, outlined against the setting sun. No such luck. He continued shuffling until McQuaid halted before a man whose face seemed constructed of discarded saddle leather. A spectacular moustache covered all but the point of his chin, and blue eyes pierced Jake like a dagger in a tavern brawl.

"You the killer?"

ACKNOWLEDGMENTS

We'd like to thank our peerless editor and friend Christa Désir, for starting us down this trail and serving as an unflagging source of encouragement and flawless guidance. We are truly blessed to have you in our lives.

Many thanks to our publisher Sourcebooks for their support and energy and for working endlessly to get everything right. Jessica, Rachel, Katie, Stef, Heather, Dawn, Kelly, and everyone else on our fabulous team.

We'd also like to give special thanks to our friends and readers and fellow writers who have provided us with tremendous warmth when the cold winds began to blow. You all know who you are, but to name a few: Susan King, Carol Palermo, Sherry Brown, Chris Uljua, Deirdre McGoldrick, Nancy Hummel, Lisa and Don Shaia, Kathy and John Bryant, Farzaneh Bordbar, Kristie and Daryl Lowry, Laura and Brian Donorfrio, Heather and Ray Turri, Joann Morris, Janet Marlow and Alan Brennan, Nhu Tran and Will Sayre, Betsy and Matt Hoagland, Mary and John Fracchia, Wendy and Casey Sayre, Cynthia Johnson/Evelyn Richardson, Lorraine Heath, Katherine Weidel and Zach Brazo, Jean and Jim Cotton, Deb Cooke, Dorisanne Soyka, Sandra Zubik, and to the scores of others who have filled our mail with cards and messages of love and support.

We'd be sadly remiss if we failed to mention our loving family. And of course, a huge thank you to our sons and their spouses and our grandchildren, for whom we dedicate every word and every breath.

And finally, to our readers...thank you. We hope you continue to enjoy our novels, including the special adventure you'll find on the pages of *The Winter Road*, in which you'll see Henry Jordan and an orphaned girl fighting hard to survive the dangers of the mountain trail.

Until next time...

ABOUT THE AUTHOR

Nik James is a pseudonym for award-winning, *USA Today* bestselling authors Nikoo and Jim McGoldrick. They are the writing team behind over four dozen conflict-filled historical and contemporary novels and two works of nonfiction under various pseudonyms. They make their home in California.